Leaving Rock Harbor

A Novel

REBECCA CHACE

Scribner

New York   London   Toronto   Sydney

SCRIBNER
A Division of Simon & Schuster, Inc.
1230 Avenue of the Americas
New York, NY 10020

First Scribner hardcover edition June 2010

SCRIBNER and design are registered trademarks of The Gale Group, Inc., used under license by Simon & Schuster, Inc., the publisher of this work.

For information about special discounts for bulk purchases, please contact Simon & Schuster Special Sales at 1-866-506-1949 or business@simonandschuster.com.

The Simon & Schuster Speakers Bureau can bring authors to your live event. For more information or to book an event contact the Simon & Schuster Speakers Bureau at 1-866-248-3049 or visit our website at www.simonspeakers.com.

Designed by Carla Jayne Jones

Manufactured in the United States of America

10 9 8 7 6 5 4 3 2 1

Library of Congress Contol Number: 2009049526

ISBN 978-1-4391-4131-1
ISBN 978-1-4391-5008-5 (ebook)

For my father, James Clarke Chace, in memory (1931–2004)
And for Pesha and Rebecca

"The birds of passage are in flight already . . . swans or geese . . . happy things."

—Masha, *The Three Sisters*, Anton Chekov

Leaving
Rock Harbor

1916

❧

"A MAN CAN CHOOSE WHAT HE DOES WITH HIS OWN life," Papa said to me just after it happened, when I was the only person he would speak to in the upstairs room of the Poughkeepsie house, where the shades remained drawn day after day, his wrists wrapped in bandages that were never removed in front of me. His engraving tools had been taken away from him, we all thought, for good.

"What should I tell him?" I had asked Mother when I came downstairs. She looked up at me dry-eyed and fierce. "No, he can't. You tell him that he can't choose anymore."

I stood there, dazed, and looked past her at the pale yellow cross stuck on a nail above the door. I had made it in church the year before, folding the long reeds into crucifixes for Palm Sunday; they started out green and dried to yellow.

1

"Go on," Mother said.

I couldn't imagine saying such a thing to my father. He told me what to do, I couldn't tell him.

Papa wouldn't talk to her. The doctor said to let him have his way if it kept him quiet. Rest was the most important thing for nerves, he said. Mother had found Papa in the bathtub of the third-floor bathroom four days earlier, and she had been punished for it ever since. Strange how people tell you that you're lucky when what they mean is that both of your parents could be dead, instead of one recovering from the unspoken and the other from her husband. Skin of the wrists wide open, but still his fist to her face and her stumble and smack against the porcelain sink and the cool floor. The tiny hexagonal tiles had been wiped clean, but there was a permanent pinkish color in the grout. I checked every day. It could have been worse, my mother's two older sisters kept saying to us over endless cups of tea, as if they were gloating over the possibility. We hadn't left the house since it happened, and I thought we might never leave again. The rest of my life would be the aunts coming and going, bringing food and talking late in the kitchen with Mother, while I sat upstairs alone with Papa. It was early January, and the Hudson was frozen across to the other shore; the snow had been on the ground forever, and I already couldn't remember Christmas. I was fourteen years old.

I kept imagining the warm red water of that bath, but I stopped short of picturing his nudity, which disturbed me more than I wanted to admit. If it had gone the way he wanted, coroners and other strangers would have seen him naked. Mother and I hadn't slept much and were mostly past tears; her face was still discolored and swollen. Maybe he couldn't speak to her because of her face. She changed his bandages and dosed him with laudanum, but he turned to the wall when she entered the room. Papa, who was always pulling her onto his lap and embarrassing her by reaching for her hand in public.

"Go on upstairs and tell him," she said again.

"*You* tell him," I said, surprised that I didn't care anymore. I was usually the one who cared too much. I could never let things go, and Mother said that I worried everything to death, but I didn't understand how everybody was supposed to stop asking questions all the time. It was hard to tell if it was early morning or late night; the only sound was the occasional crack of frozen branches from the trees outside the house. That was when Papa most wanted me there, to talk and talk and talk. I was supposed to report everything he said to Mother, and I tried hard to remember, but he talked so much and I got so sleepy.

Mother pushed herself up from the table hard, and I thought she was going to tell me off. But she nodded her head sharply at me instead and went straight upstairs. They were still talking when I finally fell asleep, and from then on Mother ignored the doctor's orders.

"He needs to work," she said to her sisters when they tried to talk her out of moving away. "He needs to work as an engraver." He had been given a chance as a cotton broker working for my grandfather, but after Grandpa died, Papa ended as he had arrived from Manchester, England—an engraver for the patterns on print cloth, a mill hand. Papa always started strong, but now I was old enough to see that it didn't sustain, to wonder if maybe it wasn't everyone else that made bad things happen to Papa. Mother saw the notice for skilled workers needed in Rock Harbor, and two months later the three of us were standing at the railing of a boat carrying us up the Sakonnet River from Rhode Island Sound. We had taken the Fall River Line from New York, and then changed for a smaller ferry to Rock Harbor. There were so many mills along the waterfront that it looked as if we were entering a cloudbank, a horizon of smoke below a blue April sky.

The move had happened quickly, and the only thing Mother insisted upon was transplanting her roses at the very last minute, so that they would have the best chance of survival. The four squares of raw dirt in our yard mapped our departure that morning. She cradled those roses wrapped in rags and newspaper all the way to Rock Harbor, looking to me like a stricken immigrant with a stained bundle in her arms. When we got off the boat, I was embarrassed to walk down the gangplank with her and held Papa's arm instead. Even after everything that had happened with Papa, it was Mother who embarrassed me, not him. Mother had always been elegant, tall enough to carry the weight she put on over the years; she had a square figure and a worried face. The heavy auburn hair that she brushed and pinned up every morning was the luxury she allowed herself, but nobody ever saw her with that rope released down her back except for me and Papa. I still had almost no figure at all, and when I squeezed lemon juice into my hair over the summer, trying for that red-gold color of hers, it dried to a stiff, pale brown. Still, the day we arrived in Rock Harbor was the first time I looked at my mother and wished she were a stranger.

She was thirty-four, the same age I am today. Now I can see how terrified she must have been, and how much she must have loved him. I'm a long way from Rock Harbor, so that's a story I can tell, sitting out this humid afternoon with its unfamiliar light, writing letters and tearing them up. Miles from home. I want to say that I don't know how any of it happened, but maybe that's not true. It's easy to see your life coming when every choice you make comes out of only two things: too much fear and too much luck.

I thought that Rock Harbor was the place to be in 1916, and I wasn't the only one. Everyone was making money in the war years.

"This whole city is built on granite," Papa told me when I walked him to his very first shift at the Flint Mill, on the way to my first day of school. He touched the gateposts gently. "It's good stone. New England stone." Papa had made his crossing in 1884, wearing all the clothes he owned and carrying the long metal box that held his engraving tools. He was ten years older than Mother, and it showed in his face and ropy arms. He had the dense build of a Welshman, and he was looking spick-and-span with a new haircut. He was making a good start of things, though he must have hated having his wife and daughter watching him every minute.

We were both so afraid we might lose him.

I walked home alone every day from Borden High School. I pretended not to care, but I felt ugly and untouchable. I had arrived in the middle of the year, and to make things worse, they had placed me in the tenth grade, a year ahead, since the schools were better in Poughkeepsie. I had turned fifteen in February, but I still looked younger than the rest. The Portuguese girls would never have thought of walking with me, and the Irish and French Canadians stuck together. I couldn't make conversation with any of the girls.

In Poughkeepsie, I had so many cousins in school that I never needed to make new friends. I hadn't cared that the girls in my class didn't like me because I was a tomboy; my bad habits were protected by the boy cousins when the girl cousins disapproved. In Rock Harbor, kids came and went as quickly as their parents' jobs lasted at the mill. You had to make a fast impression at Borden, and I couldn't bear that I was so ordinary. I didn't want to hide my new breasts under the smocking of my dress like I had back in Poughkeepsie, but these girls knew I was an impostor, and I felt erased by all of them into sudden silence. I learned to think of them as Corkies and Canucks, just like their neighborhoods, and realized that, despite the new houses built by the mill for recent arrivals like Papa, our neighborhood was the worst one. I never got the accent right, but I learned to say that I lived "up the Flint." It was the Portuguese neighborhood, but everyone in Rock Harbor said "Pawtugee," syllables strung together as clean as a whip.

I met Papa at the mill every day when his shift let out and brought him lunch on Saturday. Mama and I didn't have to talk about it; we both liked making sure that he came right home. The shift didn't end until five o'clock, so for two empty hours I walked around the Highlands, where the owners and cotton brokers lived, straight up the hill from Corky Row. I memorized the houses with graveled drives that looped semicircles before closed front doors. There were smooth lawns and rhododendron bushes bordered by dark blue vinca, but I never saw anyone gardening. There was a row of mansions along Highland Avenue, and I had a favorite, painted pale yellow with four white columns facing the avenue. A porch swing hung expectantly on one side of the wide plank stairs that led to the front door. That house looked exactly the way it was supposed to look, not like some of those other ones that were imitation gingerbread cottages or red-brick châteaus.

I was pretending to be someone who belonged on Highland Avenue when Joe Barros came spinning out from the side yard of "my house" on a bright red bicycle. It was the week after Easter, and the blossoms were already falling in drifts. Joe didn't see me standing there as he shoved some bills into his front pocket with one hand and steered with the other.

He skidded when he saw me, one hand still in his pocket.

"Hello." He looked nervous, not the way he did at school. I knew who he was. Joe Barros was captain of the basketball team and Winslow Curtis's best friend, even though he was Portuguese. It was why he had that black hair, and skin almost the same color as his startling brown eyes, which were lighter than I expected them to be, though I was too shy to hold his gaze for long.

"Hello." I didn't know whether to pretend that I hadn't seen the money.

"Frances, right? Frances Ross." I didn't think he would know my name and decided that I hadn't seen anything after all.

"Frankie," I said. Frances was for strangers or trouble.

He looked up and down the block. "What are you doing here?" Joe pulled his hand carefully out of his pocket.

"Just walking."

"This is Winslow's house," Joe said, as if I had asked him. "He gave me his bicycle because he has a Model T now."

"Winslow Curtis?" I was wondering where Winslow was at the moment, and about that money. I wasn't surprised that my favorite house belonged to Winslow Curtis. Winslow's father was president of the Massachusetts state senate. People in my neighborhood said that Winslow was going to Borden instead of Tabor Academy because his father wanted the Portuguese vote. They said his father had bought Winslow his own sailboat to make up for it.

I wondered if Joe was lying. People said a lot of things about Portuguese boys.

"Do you want a ride up the Flint?"

"With you?"

"Have you ever ridden on the back of a bicycle before?"

"No," I said. "And I'm not starting today."

He laughed and steered closer, showing off. "Girls aren't supposed to. But you're from Poughkeepsie, aren't you?"

"How come you know that?"

He was rocking back and forth in front of the leather seat, the balls of his feet balancing him on the cobblestones.

8

"My sister rides on the seat and I pedal, like this. I'll bet Poughkeepsie girls do it all the time."

I tried not to smile at the idea of Poughkeepsie girls being tough.

"How about if we go somewhere else, just for you to learn?"

"I don't need to learn." I started walking again, hoping he would follow, and he did.

"I won't let you fall, I promise."

Something in his voice made me stop. He wasn't teasing anymore, and the way he was staring made me look away.

"What was that money you put in your pocket?" I asked.

He stopped rocking on the seat, and everything became very still.

"I saw it, so I'm wondering," I said.

"It's Winslow's money. We have an arrangement."

"Why would he give you money?"

"Why do you want to know so much?"

"It looked funny, that's all."

"He gave it to me."

He pushed off, and I expected him to bike away just like that, but he circled around again. I stayed right where I was. Why shouldn't I know so much? Why should he look so nervous?

"I'm not a liar," Joe said quietly. "Nobody knows about the money but Winslow and you, now."

I wanted him to be telling the truth. "I won't tell anyone," I said. "There's nobody I talk to."

We looked past each other, and I hoped he would

believe me. Joe slid his shoes back and forth against the sidewalk and looked back at Winslow's house.

"If I can't give you a ride, I can give your books a ride, can't I? They won't get hurt."

He took my satchel so carefully that it made me want to trust him with everything, and for the first time since we moved to Rock Harbor I stopped worrying about Papa every ten minutes. Joe rode next to me all the way to the mill, turning the bike back around in big circles if he got too far ahead. He was telling me about working in the weave room.

"I've only got a Saturday shift right now. I need my education," he said. "I'm not going to be a mill hand forever. I've got other plans."

"What else can you do?"

"I can play basketball, I can swim, I can sail a boat and ride this bike and talk you into letting me carry your books."

"Papa says mill jobs are the best work there is."

"Your father's an engraver, right? From England? My papi was a picker from São Miguel, Azores. He worked in the carding room. The air in that carding room is thick all day long."

"I'd like to see it." I kicked at the sidewalk. "My mother says I have to finish school so I can get a job in accounting. She says Papa's going to work it so that I stay out of the big rooms."

"She's right."

I gave him a look. He had no idea who I was. Nobody was going to treat me like a baby.

"You said yourself you've never been in there," he said.

"Why don't you take me?" I stopped walking. "I'll go with you any Saturday."

We were at the gates of the Flint Mill now, and Joe swung off the bike and handed me my books. The leather strap around them was warm from being tucked against his waist as he rode. Papa was waiting outside the dye shed, and he hurried toward us. I didn't want Joe to meet him, to see him, to ask anything about him. Joe saw my face and looked over at Papa.

"I can't take you into the mill," Joe said, turning his bicycle around quickly. "Your father wouldn't like it, and then I couldn't see you anymore."

After that, Joe started showing up to walk me to school after I had turned the corner from our house in the morning. I never saw him after school, and I avoided the yellow house in the Highlands now that I knew it was the Curtises'. I wondered why someone like Joe would even want to talk to me. Maybe it was because I was from somewhere else, or maybe because I was so new to boys paying attention to me that I still told them what I was thinking. Even so, Joe Barros shouldn't have been paying attention to me. He was the boy everybody loved. He was so good at basketball that even though he was Portuguese they had made him captain. The team had won State two weeks before we moved to town, and people crossed the street to talk to him. But basketball was only part of it. He was with Winslow all the time, and they both acted as if it didn't matter that Joe was Portuguese. But it mattered to everyone else, even me. The way he walked me to school but never asked me to meet him after; the way he looked at me but never tried to kiss me. I knew the way we talked every morning was a secret. When we got in sight of Borden, he always pulled ahead, as if we hadn't spent the last twelve blocks together. Maybe that was how Portuguese people were, I thought. Maybe I liked him more because he was Portuguese. I still didn't know how pretty I was.

It was the last Sunday in June, about an hour after we had gotten home from mass, when Winslow Curtis and his older sister, Alice, with Joe riding in back, pulled up in front of our apartment in the new Model T. If Joe hadn't been there, I would have thought they were at the wrong house. I never saw Joe on the weekends, though I always thought about him working his Saturday shift just a few blocks away. Alice Curtis was older and hadn't ever attended Borden, but I could tell she was a Curtis from her jaw cut like a triangle, her black hair and pale skin. The Curtis siblings looked like a race of gods to me. Joe had introduced me to Winslow only once. I saw him in the hallways and the school yard, but I was sure he didn't remember me. Mother pulled me into the front parlor, and Papa went out to the porch.

"It's Joe Barros," I told her. "He's at school with me, and Winslow Curtis, he's at school too. I don't know her, but I think she's Winslow's sister."

"Why are they here?"

"I don't know."

At school, Joe acted as if he hardly knew me, and I didn't blame him. He was a year ahead of me and I was

invisible. Our morning walks had ended when school let
out, a week and a half ago.

"What have you done?"

"Nothing. I never do anything!"

"May I help you?" I could tell from Papa's voice that
he wanted to get rid of them, and Mother and I looked
at each other. Papa didn't do well with the unexpected.
I pressed my nose against the window until Mother
yanked me back to sit properly next to her. She had been
gardening, and she undid her long, dirty apron, folded it
hastily, and tucked it under the cushion of the horsehair-
stuffed love seat without shaking off the dirt. I stared at
her.

"They will come in to us," she said, daring me to say
anything.

Winslow walked right up the steps and shook Papa's
hand, as if there was nothing unusual about this visit. I
kept my eyes on the window facing the street. Papa's lips
stretched into something that wasn't quite a smile. Winslow tipped his straw hat, ran back down to the Model T,
opened the hood, and waved at Papa to join him. I knew
that Papa wanted an escape, but now the men from the
neighborhood had gathered around to look at the car.
Papa looked anywhere else, panicked. Winslow took a
few steps away and said something I couldn't hear as the
other men drew back expectantly. Papa looked at Winslow, with his smooth, lucky face, took a breath, and
walked down the porch steps. Winslow gave him all the
room he needed.

"Thank God," Mother said quietly. She was staring
even harder out the window than I was. Papa leaned in,

and Winslow stepped next to him, pointing down at the engine.

"Thank God," she said again.

Joe and Alice used the knocker instead of just rapping on the door, staring straight into its frosted glass as if they couldn't see us sitting just to their right, inside the bay window. This was the sort of thing that pleased my girl cousins but always made me want to laugh. I worked at being grown up, and when Mother went to open the door, I remained seated with my hands folded in my lap. Joe introduced himself and Alice, and I said again that Joe, Winslow, and I went to Borden together. The more formal Joe was, the harder it was for me not to laugh. But I could endure anything to be able to ride in the Model T with those two boys.

Joe told Mother that Alice was going to be with us, and could they have the pleasure of my company for a drive to the shore?

"You are Winslow's . . . ?" Mother asked. "You are . . . ?"

"Joe Barros," he said again, quietly. She assumed that Joe worked for Winslow's family, and he didn't correct her.

"Joe is the captain of the basketball team," I said to Mother. "He—"

"You look too old for high school," Mother said.

"I'm going to be a senior next year." He smiled right at her. "I run six looms at the mill, summers and weekends." Mother didn't have any idea how to respond to that smile, and she turned to Alice.

Alice didn't bother to hide her boredom or disapproval, but Mother didn't seem offended. Mother knew who Alice was the minute Joe introduced her. Alice wasn't beautiful, but she had glamour. She was tall, with a face like the kind of doll most girls linger over but can never afford. She looked just how I imagined Rose Red to look, from the old Grimms' fairy tale; she had painted her lips into a perfect cupid's bow, and her dark hair balanced above her face with just the right amount of disarray. I didn't know how she could manage to make it look simultaneously careless and perfect. She walked around the parlor examining everything, playing a single, ironic note on the piano, and ignoring my mother's invitation for her to have a seat. I had the uncomfortable feeling that she might not want her clothing to touch the love seat, where I was still stranded over Mother's hidden apron, hardly breathing.

Mother introduced herself to Alice by her first name: Abigail, which she never did with young people. She ignored Joe and dropped hints to Alice that we were a family who really should have been living in the Highlands, like the Curtises; we were only staying up the Flint by some inexplicable circumstance. Our apartment was the first floor of a triple-decker, three apartments built on top of each other, which were rented out by the mill. We had electricity instead of the old gas fixtures, three bedrooms, a formal parlor, and a back garden. Mother had to have a garden, she explained to Alice, and we were planning on building a gazebo in the back, but rooms on the ground floor were dark.

"I miss our house in Poughkeepsie," Mother said. "It was filled with light."

That was a lie. She used to complain that the sky was always gray in Poughkeepsie and nothing had enough sun to grow.

"I prefer it here," I said. Mother gave me a look, and we all ached into silence again.

I had managed to raise the hem of my skirt and caught Joe glancing at my ankles, then away. I was ashamed of Mother for acting as if he were invisible, and ashamed of myself for thinking that flirting with him could make it all better.

"We have a membership at a small beach club," Alice said to Mother in her unhurried voice. "Down by the Point."

Mother nodded, though I knew she had no more idea than I did where the Point was in relation to Rock Harbor.

"Just an afternoon swim," Joe said.

Through the window we could see Winslow and Papa walking around the Model T for the hundredth time. "Is the automobile safe?" Mother asked Alice.

"It was a gift to Winslow from our father," and to interrogate Alice any further was out of the question. Say yes. Yes. Yes, I chanted silently.

"Very well," Mother said finally, and I couldn't help jumping to my feet as if sprung from a box. Joe tried not to laugh, and Alice looked even more irritated. I wondered how much older Alice was than Winslow; she looked young but acted old.

"But I will not allow you to go in the ocean," Mother said. "I'd rather you didn't sit in the open air in a bathing costume. You could get chilled."

I stared at her for a beat. She knew I didn't own a bath-

ing costume. She lowered her eyes and took me gently by
the arm into the pantry, out of sight of the others.

"Mother, you know I can't swim," I whispered.

"And glad of it," she whispered back. "Or they might
realize you don't have a bathing costume." She smiled, and
I saw that she was excited too. "Be seen and not heard," she
whispered fiercely as she jerked my skirt down and pinned
last year's hat to my head. I pulled a curl free on each side,
wanting them to cling to my neck like the Gibson girls';
Mother wet her fingers in her mouth and pushed them
back against my scalp. I was disgusted by her spit but said
nothing. Then she laughed and let the smallest curl go free.

"You're very pretty," she said, putting her hands on my
shoulders. "Have a good time, and take Alice Curtis as
your model."

"I will. Thank you!" I put my arms around her and
kissed her cheek. I was the same height as she was, and
she laughed again, looking young herself, with the smell
of earth lingering on her hands. I pulled her around in a
circle that was almost a dance until she pushed me away,
but I could see that she was happy. I suddenly knew why
she talked about going back to Poughkeepsie for a visit
so often. I had been convinced it was because she hadn't
adjusted to Rock Harbor yet, but it wasn't only that. I was
the closest thing she had to her sisters, and I was always
walking away from her. She glanced into the mirror above
the sink, and I saw her cheeks were flushing the same as
mine. She doesn't have anyone to talk to either, I realized
all at once.

But I completely forgot my mother as soon as we
rounded the corner, with Winslow at the wheel in his

straw boater and Alice beside him, adjusting her hat and complaining about having to put on such a charade. The Model T was so loud that everyone had to shout to be heard, and I don't think Mother would really have wanted me to imitate Alice if she had seen her in the car. Alice stuck a cigarette into a tortoiseshell holder and told Winslow to drop her off at the office of one of the biggest textile brokers in Rock Harbor. Even a newcomer like me had heard of this man and his wife. The assembly hall at Borden was named after their family. Winslow and Joe seemed familiar with the routine and pulled up in front of a downtown office building without turning off the car, which didn't idle so much as sputter and bang.

"Back before dark!" Winslow called after her. Alice nodded without turning around, opening the side door with her own key.

"She's not coming to the beach?" As much as Alice had intimidated me, she was a girl, and I had never been alone with a boy who wasn't a relative, much less two boys. Fifteen-year-old girls did not spend time with boys without a chaperone, as Joe and Winslow knew well enough.

"You don't mind, do you?" Winslow looked confidently into the backseat and caught my eye. "Alice is a good kid, but she hates the beach." I knew a dare when I saw one. He and Joe would be seniors next year, when I would be a junior. I wondered if they knew that I was the youngest in my class.

"Of course I don't mind." My throat tightened. "May I sit up front now?"

"I told you she was game," Joe said as he hurried to open both doors for me so that I could move from the

backseat to the front. I settled into Alice's spot and tied my
scarf over the top of my hat and under my chin, as I had
seen her do. If she could do whatever she wanted and still
have a good reputation, so could I. Winslow started driving out of town, and Joe sat in the center of the backseat,
leaning forward so that his head and arms rested between
us. I was trying to be proper, and I wanted to be brave, but
it was a relief that the car made so much noise that it was
hardly possible to talk.

We rode past the older mills, their walls streaked by rain
and soot, and as soon as we left the cobblestones behind,
the road turned to hard packed dirt and Winslow stepped
on the gas pedal. The countryside looked different seen
from an automobile. The grass at the side of the road went
by in patterns of pale yellow and green, with tall brown
cattails shooting up unexpectedly.

"Ever been in an auto before?" Winslow asked, cupping
his mouth with one hand to be heard. I looked to see if he
was making fun of me, but he wasn't. "You feel all right?
Some girls—"

"Ladies," interrupted Joe.

"Some *ladies* don't feel so well the first time."

"I feel fine, thank you."

I felt like shouting and laughing—this was like flying,
like sledding, like nothing I had ever done before, and I
didn't want it to stop. Now we were passing houses that
people used as their summer homes, cottages with gray
fences covered by wisteria and long green lawns that led
down to the Sakonnet River. White hydrangeas bloomed
along the stone walls that bordered the road, and I glimpsed
the water between the trees. I pretended not to notice that

Joe and Winslow were taking turns glancing over at me. I wondered if Winslow thought I was Joe's girl, and since I could never quite tell what Joe thought about me, maybe Winslow knew more than I did.

"Have you had many ladies in your auto?" I asked loudly. "Ladies who haven't felt well?"

Winslow looked surprised, then burst into that distinctive Curtis laughter that went up and down his register in one breath. Winslow still laughs like he's the luckiest man in the world.

"You're the first girl we've had in the devil wagon!" he said. "I hope you're not too careful about your reputation."

"Don't worry." Joe leaned his head on his arms, closing his eyes. I looked at those long black lashes, thicker than any girl's. "He's just trying to scare you. I told you, Curtis, she's from Poughkeepsie. They don't scare easy."

"Where is Poughkeepsie?" Winslow asked. "And how come all the girls are so brave over there?"

"Poughkeepsie is on the Hudson River," I said, unable to answer the second part of his question.

"Have you ever seen the ocean?" Winslow asked.

"We took a boat here. We went to New York and changed to the Fall River Line. I've seen New York Harbor."

"I want to go to New York someday." Joe said. "I'll take the Fall River Line and try my luck in the city."

"New York is swell," Winslow said, and we all knew that he must have been there lots of times. "But New York Harbor isn't exactly the beach. Have you ever been to the beach?"

"No. I can't swim."

"Can't swim? Didn't you ever swim in the Hudson?"

"It's a big river."

"It's a big ocean," said Winslow. "But don't worry, you stay in Rock Harbor and you'll learn."

I stared at him. I couldn't imagine swimming in the ocean.

"You will," said Joe, smiling at me. "Winslow can teach you. He taught me."

I was wearing a corset and gloves at Mother's insistence. I didn't own a bathing costume, and I wasn't supposed to be unchaperoned with a boy. But that afternoon it became easier and easier not to care. We passed fields of corn that were beginning to shoot their green stalks high, and black and white dairy cows that looked up, unaccustomed to the sound of an engine. Winslow honked his ridiculous horn and started the cows loping in a circle, banging themselves against the hayricks. Winslow honked again, and he and Joe laughed, but he stopped when I said no.

"Poor things," I said. "They're only cows."

"And you're a peach," Winslow declared, taking his hand off the horn. "She's a real peach, Joe."

"Look at this, Frankie," Joe said with a slight frown, and I wondered if he didn't like Winslow calling me that. "Now it gets pretty."

We came around a bend at the bottom of the hill, and Winslow swung us out onto a small bridge over a pond filled with white water lilies. There was a gristmill and a general store at a second bend. It all looked as if it had been painted into place.

"Slow down, Winslow," Joe said. I could hear an edge in his voice, but Winslow seemed oblivious.

"I'm going slow already, Mr. Landscape." Winslow grinned. "He'd be a poet if he wasn't so good on the court. He does write poetry, don't you, Barros?"

"Cut it out," Joe said, and he pushed himself back into his seat, staring out at the scene. I couldn't see his face because of the size of my hat, and I was afraid to tip my head too much one way or the other. Winslow glanced back at Joe and seemed about to say something; then the river opened up before us and I was glad nobody was talking anymore.

The trees gave way to a dark blue river that ran next to the road. It was a wide river with green marsh grass and small wooded islands down the middle. A white egret high-stepped along the edge of a mudflat, dipping its long beak delicately into the water. Swans were visible farther off, white wings carved like stone onto their backs; black-beaked and slow-moving, they swam together until the very last moment, when the automobile got so close they had to fly. They even took flight without hurrying, rising up with a lumbering grace. I was relieved that Winslow didn't honk again. Big elm trees hung over the road, there were no farmhouses or summer cottages in sight, and I felt as if we were the only human beings for miles. Joe told Winslow to pull over, and Winslow smiled as if he knew Joe was going to ask, and he steered across the road to an opening in the shoreline. The engine quivered into silence.

"We're nearly there," he said. "Can you smell it?"

"What?"

"The ocean."

Winslow walked to the edge of the river, squatting on his heels and pushing his hat back on his head. The quiet settled over us, and Joe stayed in the car, sitting right behind me, staring out at the river. His stillness made me nervous. I didn't know what was expected of me. I tried not to fidget, and eventually I started to hear the splash as a fish hawk hit the water on the far side of the river and the clumsy landing of Canada geese on a sandbar. Wild irises leaned near the edge of the water, their delicate purple blossoms the shape of an open mouth, tethered by tough green stalks. I felt Joe's gaze heating up my neck and face. Then another auto came into sight from the other direction, honking and weaving all over the road.

Winslow jumped up, shouting, "It's Taffy! Taffy Kent!"

He waved energetically at the car as it passed. I caught sight of white sleeves rippling over pale arms and girls hiding behind hats, screaming at the driver to slow down. The driver waved at Winslow as he went by us; his car swerved sharply, and the women squealed again. A straw boater exactly like Winslow's came flying out of the car as the driver regained control and went past with a couple more honks. Winslow ran after the hat and picked it up, walking back to us and laughing as he brushed it off.

He looked at Joe and me, then back out at our patch of river—all the birds had fled. Joe was staring straight ahead without smiling, anger flaring up from him as quick as air, and I wondered what had gone wrong, but Winslow shrugged. "Taffy's hat," he said. "I'll hold on to it for him."

Nobody explained why that other car had made Joe so angry. Maybe those people didn't like having Joe around, or maybe he was like me, wanting to pretend that we were the only ones in the world. I was nervous as we drove the last mile to Winslow's beach club. I knew it would be packed with Taffy Kents and Alice Curtises, and arriving alone with two boys, one of them Portuguese, could brand me forever. Then we came up over a hill and I saw the ocean. It was just beyond the top of a low stone wall overgrown with thorny beach plum, the curled green leaves covered with pink blossoms. The road ended in sand. When I first saw the water, I gasped, and Winslow turned to me. He smiled, then drove straight into the sand and turned off the car.

The beach was empty, and I had never seen so much horizon, the spread of dark water ridged with disappearing white. It's like looking at the sky, I thought; you've been told that it goes on and on forever, but most of the time you just can't think that way. A long beach with high dunes was across an inlet to our left, and I could see the waves breaking twice: once far out along an unseen ledge, and then again and again onto a wide patch of sand marked with striped umbrellas. A row of rocks led into the sea, and a small green boat made its way between them. A man in a red sweater leaned over the side, pulling crab pots, and I remember how vivid the colors looked that day. A day of impossible brightness.

I tried to say something and blushed instead. Joe and Winslow looked at each other and laughed.

"It's not New York Harbor," said Winslow. "But it's what we've got to live for up here, besides the mills."

"It's better than New York Harbor," said Joe.

"How would you know—" Winslow began, but I interrupted.

"No, he's right. It is!" I turned in my seat so that I could see both of them at once.

Winslow took a cigarette out of a silver case, passed one to Joe, and they both lit up. "This is the Atlantic Ocean," Winslow said. "Nothing between us and the war in Europe."

"Except the Atlantic Ocean," I said, and they both surprised me by laughing.

"Let's go," Joe said to Winslow, his eyes going gold in the sun. "The waves look good today."

They began to clamber over the low dunes toward the water, but I hesitated.

"What is it, Peaches?" Winslow called back, and I saw Joe suppress another frown.

"I was wondering about— Isn't there a beach club?"

"Sure there is, on the other side of that cove." Winslow looked quickly at Joe, who was staring at the horizon as if he wanted to pin something against it. "Once we get settled I'll go get us some cold drinks and sandwiches. It's—"

"What Winslow doesn't want to tell you," Joe said, looking straight at me, "is that they don't allow people like me at the club."

I stared back at him. "No Portuguese?"

Joe laughed. "See, Winslow, she really isn't from around here. She doesn't even know how to pronounce 'Pawtugees.'" Winslow looked at the ocean. Joe took a few steps toward me. "No. There's no Pawtugees at the club. Not as guests. They rake up the seaweed in the morning and make sure there's no Pawtugee men o' war washed up that people might step on."

"What's a Paw-tug-ee man o' war?" I asked, awkwardly copying his pronunciation.

"It's a jellyfish with a bad sting," Winslow said. "So, yes,

25

that's true, and it's an unfortunate thing. A stupid, unfortunate thing. But that's why we come over to this spot, right, Joe?" He sounded as hopeful as a little boy. "The beach is better here, actually; there aren't as many rocks, and it's not so crowded. Same waves, better view."

"I've been here before, Winslow. Don't bother."

"And since you've been here before, there's nothing to be surprised about, is there?"

He and Joe looked so hard at each other I thought the only way out might be a fistfight. I didn't say a word or pull my eyes away. I knew what was different; I was here this time. It was my fault. Ten seconds might have been forever. Then Joe broke it, shoving his hands in his pockets.

"You bet," he said. "Nothing's different. Don't know why the beach club doesn't claim this cove too."

"Oh, they own it." Winslow was offhand, relieved. "The members just don't like to walk down here because it's too far from the cabanas."

I held out my hand to Joe. "Can you help me over the dunes?" I asked, and his shoulders dropped as he came hurrying back to take my arm. I held on tighter than I needed to, as if that could say something like sorry.

Winslow ran back to the car and brought out a driving blanket that he spread on the sand. Once we were over the dune, there was no road, nothing in sight but the sea, and I wondered at myself, all alone with these boys, but I wasn't scared anymore. Nobody would see me here, nobody had to know anything.

"I'll be right back with some drinks," Winslow said as he kicked off his shoes and rolled up his trousers. "Sorry there's no umbrella," he said quickly, watching me tuck my skirt under my legs and adjust my hat to block the sun. "I'll see what I can do."

Joe sat down, using less than a corner of the blanket, and we watched Winslow hurrying down the beach. I couldn't see any sign of umbrellas or cabanas in that direction; the club must have been blocked by the high rocks that surrounded the cove.

"I hope you don't mind," Joe said quietly. "We've never brought anyone here before, and I wasn't thinking about umbrellas and such."

"I don't need an umbrella." I pushed my hat back so that I could see the whole horizon. "I hate parasols, I'm always losing them. That's why I didn't bring one myself. I've lost every one I ever owned."

"Still—"

"Tell me the names of those islands out there."

There were two islands stuck on the edge of the horizon. Joe moved in a little closer and pointed, shading his eyes with his other hand.

"That one, the closest one, is Cuttyhunk. It's an Indian name. Still some Indians living on the island, I heard. Indians and old whalers. They don't have electric light out there yet, but there's talk of building a windmill."

"What about that one?"

"That's Martha's Vineyard. You see the white bit?"

"Where?" I leaned in a little closer, careful not to brush his arm, which was still holding steady, his finger pointing east.

"There. See that smudge? Looks like a fog bank. Those are the cliffs at Gay Head. Big clay cliffs, higher than those dunes over across the inlet."

27

"How far away is that?"

"About a day's sail. I've never been, but I heard about it. There's a leper colony out there too, on one of those little islands, Penikese, but you can't see it from here."

"Lepers?"

"Sure. The state puts them out there."

We sat without speaking for a long time, and I was glad it didn't matter.

Eventually we heard someone calling and turned to see Winslow clambering over the rocks toward us. He was carrying more things than he could handle, and as he got closer we could hear him singing. It was as if a marching band had suddenly appeared on the beach.

"He's bringing us a party," Joe said.

Winslow was grinning and waving bottles of ginger beer as if he had struck oil. He had a beach chair over each shoulder, another one slung around his neck, and he was carrying a huge yellow umbrella popped open above it all. Joe ran to take the umbrella from Winslow and held it over both of them as they arrived, spinning it up and around in a circle as Winslow continued to bellow some kind of marching tune. Then he dropped all three chairs at once.

They set up the chairs and umbrella, and insisted that I sit down; then Joe and Winslow disappeared into the dunes to change into their bathing costumes. I took my hat off and let the breeze whip sand against my cheeks like dry rain. Winslow and Joe ran past into the water, showing off for me as they dove under the first wave and came up with their dark heads wet and smooth. Their bodies matched like a pair of young seals, arms thrown out stiffly when they rode the waves, then fluid as they floated up and over the top of the curling water before it had time to break, scatter, and disappear. I couldn't stop smiling as I watched the two of them. I knew how lucky I was that day; I was watching it become a memory as fast as it was happening.

But it was hot and salty, even under the umbrella, and eventually the boys convinced me to take off my shoes and stockings so that I could wade ankle deep. The waves rushed around my feet like green ice that turned clear as soon as I looked down, my toes magnified by the unexpected freedom. In the tide pools the water was warm, and hundreds of periwinkles nubbled the rocks, their tiny antlers extended and withdrawn with the washing tide. Mussel beds formed dense clutches of indigo over and under the sand, with fine shreds of yellow seaweed weaving them together.

Eventually, we went back under the umbrella for sandwiches and ginger beer, and Winslow insisted that I bring my bathing costume next weekend and promised, between long swallows, that he would teach me to swim. Acting as if our day was part of a long-standing tradition was one of the ways Winslow had of making you feel like you had known each other forever. I pretended right back. The ocean was narcotic, and the boys seemed so at ease in their matching black-and-white-striped bathing costumes. Winslow was taller, and his shoulders were perfect, with his hair blowing straight back off his forehead and a creased grin. Joe was lithe and had that skin which pushed me away and pulled me back in, his curls like wet paint. I had to remember to act as if I were looking out at the water.

As Winslow got ready to take the first bite of his sandwich, Joe put up a hand and stopped him.

"Hey, get off!" Winslow pulled away, laughing.

Joe picked up Winslow's gold pocket watch, which lay on top of the driving blanket. He stared down at the watch and ordered: "Now chew."

Winslow looked at me, then chewed as hard as he could.

"No, no." Joe grabbed Winslow's arm and held back the hand with the sandwich. "Let's see if you can't do it better next time."

Winslow looked uncertain. "What are you doing, buddy?"

"I'm pulling a Taylor on you."

Winslow tried to shake loose. "What the heck, Joe? What's a Taylor?"

"It's at the mill," I said. "It's a scientific method. My father told me about it."

Joe nodded, let go of Winslow, and looked at me. "What does your father think? What do the other engravers say?"

"He hates it. He says it won't last."

Joe leaned into Winslow. "There are these men at the mill with stopwatches, timing everything as you work. They watch you do everything, simple stuff like replacing the bobbins." Joe stared at the face of Winslow's watch, which he was still holding in his hand. "Those Taylor men would tell you to hold your sandwich between your thumb and forefinger so you can do the job a half second faster. But the only reason you might have done it slow at all is because they were watching." Joe flipped the watch in the air and caught it over and over, never missing. I thought he was crazy to play like that, but neither boy seemed concerned.

Joe kept talking. "And the speedups they've been pulling make it even worse. The foremen just keep turning up the speed without telling us. You should see these old men who have been doing the same job forever. Now they have to please this Taylor fella, but the machines are also going faster because of the speedup, so they're all confused."

"Like this?" Winslow started bringing his sandwich up to his face faster and faster, slamming it into his mouth mechanically. Bacon and bread went flying. I started to laugh. "I think I saw something in the funnies about that," Winslow said finally, wiping his chin. "A boy was spooning with a girl, and this man with a watch was telling the boy he should be more efficient."

I got quiet, surprised that Winslow would talk about kissing in front of me. I kept my face carefully neutral when I felt him glance over at me.

"I wish it was only spooning," Joe said. "You've got to do more than read the funnies, Winslow. I mean, they're no good, the speedups."

"So, I'll read the front page sometimes, but what can *I* do about it?" Winslow was halfway through the remains of his sandwich.

"Aren't you the owners?" Joe was still speaking quietly, but his voice hardened. "It's your mill."

"No, no, it's not," Winslow said, as if he had heard this before. "It's my father's, if it's anybody's, and *he* says it's run by all the other stockholders. Our business manager, what's his name . . . Jeremiah Parker."

"Bones Parker," Joe said.

"And I hardly ever see Ham, you know that." Winslow

pushed his toes into the sand and wiggled them free. A wave drenched his feet, and he dug them deeper, chasing a hermit crab out of its hole.

I had never heard anyone call his father by his first name before.

"What do *you* do about it?" I asked Joe.

"Huh?" He turned toward me as if he were thinking about something else.

"What do you do when the man tells you how to load the bobbins faster?"

Joe smiled. "Aw, me and my pals, we just pretend to do it until he walks away. Then we go back to our bad old ways."

"See?" Winslow got up and brushed off the sand. "It doesn't matter anyway."

Joe looked up at the sky, and I wondered what he wasn't saying.

"Let's teach Frankie how to swim, Curtis," he broke out suddenly, turning to face us.

"What?" I felt my face going red. "I don't have a bathing costume."

"No, and I bet you won't have one next weekend either." Joe got to his feet and pulled me up with him. He stepped in close and reached a finger to touch the edge of my skirt, which was belling out from my waist in the offshore breeze. I stepped out of reach.

"I can't learn how to swim without one."

"Why not?"

"Sure, why not?" Now Winslow was up and closing in on me from the other side. I took another step back toward Joe.

"Because—because everything will get soaked."

"That's what happens when you swim," said Winslow. "It feels good, and then everything dries off."

"And nobody knows you ever got wet," Joe finished, and they looked at each other and laughed. I laughed too but found myself unable to move, the two of them were now standing so close to me. The boy cousins in Poughkeepsie used to try to bully me, and I was never ladylike with them. I struck out my arms and pushed Winslow and Joe both hard in the chest. They stumbled backward, and I started running down the beach.

It wasn't hard for them to catch up, with my long skirt flopping around me. As soon as they did, I slowed to catch my breath, which was short from even that much running, my ribs straining against the corset. I looked warily from one to the other. They were exactly like my boy cousins and nothing like them at all.

"Come on," said Joe, taking my hand and tugging me toward the edge of the water. "The first swimming lesson is today."

I pulled back. "But my mother will know. My clothes will be wet."

"We won't go above your waist," Winslow promised, his eyes turning darker green as he faced away from the sun. "Your skirt will dry before you get home. Your clothes will be sandy, but they won't be wet. I promise."

Joe reached for my other hand, and I let them pull me down to the water, shaking my head but going.

"Nobody can see us here," said Winslow, stepping into the waves without letting go of me. "This is where I taught Barros, right, Joe?"

"He's a good teacher," Joe said. "Go on, Frankie." He let go of my other hand.

I looked back at him. He couldn't just leave me like this. "No, it's too cold, Joe! I can't swim, I really can't!"

But Joe just stood there as the water got higher, up to my knees, thighs, and farther. Winslow was standing in front of me now, holding both of my hands, letting the waves break carelessly over his back.

"Don't be scared," Winslow said quietly, and I saw that he wasn't teasing anymore. "I'm going to hold you by your waist for just a moment. Is that all right?"

My skirt floated out around me, and the cloth felt heavy as it swirled in the low surf. I had already ruined my skirt; maybe there was no reputation left to guard. I gripped his hands harder.

"Here we go!" Winslow said, and just as a wave came surging into the shore, he lifted me by my waist so that my feet left the bottom. My skirt swung around me and I screamed, pulling myself closer to Winslow. He held me tight, laughing, and my feet found the sand again as the wave let me down.

"Oh!" I gripped him hard, afraid of losing my footing, afraid that my heavy skirt would drag me down so far that I would never come up again. "Is that what swimming is like? So—so—"

Another wave came and he lifted me again. The spray soaked my face, and I shut my eyes as I felt the weight dropping away and the rushing pull of the current.

"This is just what swimming is like," Winslow said into my ear as he held me up high again and again. "Only you don't need anybody to hold you."

I turned back to the shore to look for Joe and saw him standing with his hands on his hips, silhouetted by the afternoon sun so that I couldn't see his face. He raised one hand and waved at me, and I almost let go of Winslow's arm to wave back. Never more frightened. Never happier.

Four days later, Papa brought me to the dye room, where the engravers worked. I was warned about how hot it could get in the mills during the summer, but that day had one of those smooth skies that fills you with hope. Papa had always insisted that I meet him out in the yard, but today was different. Today I was going to meet Mr. Clay, the chief accountant, to talk about my working in the office on Saturdays. As I walked across the main yard, I looked up at the rows of windows. There were five stories, and I wondered which floor Joe was working on. The windows were kept shut tight even on the hottest days so that the loose cotton wouldn't blow into the machines and gum up the gears.

The dye room was nothing more than a large shed built against a back corner of the main building, and when I first walked in from the yard, I couldn't tell which one Papa was. The engravers were all dressed the same, with leather aprons and heads bent close to the metal sheets they were working on. Everything in the dye room was hot to the touch, and there was the potent smell of ink and metal, which I suddenly realized was the scent of my childhood. I hesitated just inside the door, clutching tightly to Papa's dinner pail; then he saw me and waved me over to his workbench. The air was thick with what I thought was dust. Papa told me to put my handkerchief over my mouth so I wouldn't breathe the metal shavings. But none of the engravers covered their mouths. They spoke with an accent like Papa's and kept things neat around their workbenches. The engraving tools I was too familiar with were wiped clean and laid in their proper places. Papa introduced me, and I was on my best behavior so that they would like Papa. I remembered how his friends in Poughkeepsie had acted at the end, as if whatever was wrong with Papa might be contagious.

Papa took off his apron and hurried me back across the yard and straight upstairs to the front office. I knew that this was where he and Mother wanted me to work once I graduated from high school, and maybe summers before that once I had the accounting skills. Mother hadn't wanted me to meet Mr. Clay so soon. She argued with Papa, saying that we should just let things stay as they were and see how Papa felt in a year or so. I was sure that she wanted to wait and see if we could move back to Pough-keepsie and didn't really care about my bookkeeping career as much as she pretended to. But when Papa threatened to invite Mr. Clay over to our house if she wouldn't let me go to the interview, she gave in. She knew that Papa meant what he said, even though Mr. Clay would never accept, and that would get Papa the wrong kind of attention.

Papa arranged everything, and it was his first real contact with management, so by the time the day came, Mother and I were both strung up by his constant talking. Mother had fussed so much about my appearance for this first meeting that I almost rebelled and pretended illness. But I had been lucky that she hadn't complained very much about the sand in my clothes after my trip to the beach. She talked about how there might be another invitation from Alice Curtis soon, and it didn't seem to occur to her that I had gone all the way into the water, once I confessed to wading up to my knees. I left the house on the day of my interview with my scalp throbbing with hairpins and my corset tighter than ever. It wasn't the way I wanted to look my first time inside the mill. I had always thought I would be walking around with Joe, dressed in my regular school clothes. I hated that my parents insisted on doing it this way and hoped that Joe wouldn't see me walk by looking like a pincushion.

"I can't walk," I complained to Mother after Papa had left for his shift. "I feel sick and can't bend."

"You won't have to bend," Mother said.

Luckily, there was no sign of Joe, but I'm not sure how well I managed my meeting with Mr. Clay. I had no real opinion about working in accounting. I liked math well enough and knew that I'd have to go into the mill eventually. The way Papa talked, the office workers had a life of ease: no cotton dust, no danger, and a good paycheck for sitting at a desk doing sums. "It won't be that different from going to school," he told my mother. But the accounting office was much grander than school, and the two women working at desks in the outer reception area looked much older than me. There was a thick Oriental rug on the floor, and lamps shaded by ovals of green glass. Mr. Clay's office was behind a beveled door with his name stenciled on it in gold letters. The centerpiece of the room was a large wooden desk with legs like a lion's paws, each claw curled around a ball that was carved to look like the earth. I could just see the ridged outline of the United States. Behind the desk was a narrow man with papers piled in four stacks, one for each corner of the desk.

"You see that organization, Frances?" Papa was calling me Frances and speaking louder than usual because he was trying so hard to please. I could barely stand the embarrassment, but I was trapped there with a fixed smile that I hoped made me seem oblivious. Papa was behaving the way he did when Mother called him "overexcited," and I was terrified that he wouldn't stop talking.

"Mr. Clay never mixes things up with the pay schedule. No sir, and that's why. Look at that organization."

Mr. Clay was clearly pleased that Papa had noticed. "Each corner is for something different," he said. "Here is this week's payroll." He pointed to a pile of pale yellow slips weighted down with a piece of glass that had a butterfly suspended in the middle. "And over there is next week. Can't give you yours till tomorrow, though, Allen."

Papa laughed obsequiously. All I wanted to do was get out before Papa or I did something wrong. Mr. Clay came from behind his desk to shake my hand, and I noticed that he was too tall for the room. He loomed over Papa and me like a spindly grasshopper in glasses. The interview was over before I had quite caught up with its beginning. I tried to remember how to breathe shallowly inside the corset as I followed Papa back down the main staircase.

"Good job, Frankie girl," he said. "I think he liked you fine."

I could feel the building shudder with a great, rhythmic beat. I touched my hand to the wall of the stairwell, and the brick quivered against my palm.

"We're next to the weave room," Papa said. I looked around quickly, as if Joe would suddenly appear, but Papa didn't even open the door off the stairwell. "Each floor is for a different job. The ground floor is where the looms are set up because they're so heavy, and the top floor is where it ends up as finished cloth, all wound in bolts, printed and dyed. This is some building, isn't it, Frankie? The cotton comes straight from the fields down south, just a bundle of dirty white garbage packed with seeds." He frowned. "It's easy to forget that's how it all starts when you're just doing your part all day long."

"Can I see it, please?" I asked. "Can I see how it looks when it first arrives?"

"No, Frankie." He laughed, but I knew he was serious. His nervous manner had dropped away the minute we left Mr. Clay's office, and I was glad to have my father back, though the switch was so fast it threw me a little. He started down the stairs ahead of me. "Down in the carding room is no place for you. Your mother would have fits."

"She doesn't have to know." I stopped and put my hands on my hips. Under the material, the corset was hard as wood. I had done my job for him, now it was my turn. The carding room was where Joe's father had worked. "I'd rather see the carding room than the office. I don't even want to work in an office with that skinny old man."

"You'll be lucky to work in the office." Papa took me by the arm and started yanking me down the stairs. I stumbled slightly but knew better than to resist him. Another switch, why hadn't I seen it coming? I knew his temper as well as I knew my own.

"You want to swallow so much cotton that you can't

even get across the courtyard without stopping to breathe? Is that what you want?" He was shouting now, and his grasp made my eyes fill up.

"No." I would not allow myself to cry. This was all my fault. I had ruined everything just when he was feeling good.

He stopped pulling me down the stairs long enough to make room for a girl to pass. She was wearing her hair up under a cap; her bare arms and legs had the color and texture of cracked leather. She was wearing boy's shoes, and I guess I must have stared, because she glared at me, then dropped her eyes quickly, afraid to let herself look at me like that. Papa hardly noticed her. I had gone numb below the elbow. We went down one more floor and across the yard to the dye room without speaking. He stopped in front of the open doors, let go of my arm, and quickly ran his hands through his hair. I felt the spiked tingle of blood rushing back from my shoulder and stood absolutely still. The whistle blew for his shift to start again after lunch, and we both looked up at the Flint Mill clock tower; its gothic hands were pointing straight up at the sky, where three gulls wheeled against the blue. Papa just barely brushed my arm with his fingertips in the same spot he had been gripping so hard; I willed myself not to flinch.

"Beautiful, isn't it?" He was looking up at the sky. I nodded. It was.

"I only want you to be in a good place. You know that."

"I know."

"What else do you know?"

This was an old game from when I was little. I didn't want to say it.

"What else do you know?"

"That my papa loves me." I was wooden.

"That's right, he does." He patted my arm longer than he needed to and quickly walked me to the gate, giving me a kiss on the forehead before turning back to the dye room.

"What about your dinner?"

"If the machines are good, I'll kip into it later."

I walked home sorry and furious. Yes, he loved me, but if there was a bruise, I would have to hide my arm from Mother. He loved me but always spoke about the machines as if *they* were his children: "If the machines are good, if they behave." On the days when they didn't behave, his dinner pail came home untouched. "The machines were bad today, I couldn't leave them." When there was trouble, the second hand in charge of the dye room would have to get a machinist to come, and that made a hard day for everyone. If the engravers got behind, the second hand would catch it from the overseer and the pay could be cut that week, or someone might lose his job. I knew as well as anyone that Papa couldn't lose this job.

That night I dreamt I was walking through deep snow near our old house in Poughkeepsie, but when I tried to make a snowball, the snow was made of cotton, and the flecks of dirt were cotton seeds. I woke up wanting to see more of the mill than the stairwell and the office. I wanted to see where Joe worked.

There was a long mural drawn on a roll of butcher paper across the back wall of the lobby at Borden High, mapping the mills and telling us how many were running now and how many were still being built. The city council had proposed a nickname for Rock Harbor: "Cotton Cornucopia," but there was another contingent that wanted "Bobbin Town," and the student body was holding a vote of its own. The Wampanoag River was represented on the mural by a long blue ribbon glued along the length of the wall. The Wampanoag was half as wide as the Hudson, and permanently shaded by the mills as it flowed through the center of the city and out into Mount Hope Bay. The biggest mill was the Standard Linen and Printworks, with its great square clock tower ringing the bells the whole city lived by. At school, they would change the clocks to match the hours from Standard Linen; everyone did. We always got the bells from church and the bells from Standard Linen mixed up, and that sometimes made us late for mass.

Mother insisted that we go to church every week, but I just moved the words of grace and salvation through my mouth. I had my Holy Communion when I was seven, and I had a fine communion dress to wear down the aisle, not a hand-me-down but made from bolts of store-bought cloth and fitted just for me. White on white on white, and whenever I looked up Mother was looking at me with her lit-up smile. There was such grandeur in our row of girls that the little Poughkeepsie church seemed to have grown vaulted ceilings in the night. But when I finally tasted the wafer and the wine, I realized they were nothing at all like flesh and blood. I had believed in the body and blood of Christ, but despite my disappointment, I danced and twirled all day; then my dress was wrapped in tissue paper, and Mother went back to her sisters to discuss everything about everything, and I wished that I felt more changed.

I was expected to stay out of the way of my mother and her sisters. Mother was the youngest, and I would listen to her laugh when they were cooking together, or waiting in the summerhouse for the day to cool off. I always wanted to be right there with her. But Mother would twist my hair absently around her finger and ask too quickly what it was I needed. The three of them would pause as I shifted, once, twice, and went away blushing to the thicket at the bottom of the garden. I would lie curled tensely on my side in a hollow spot between the raspberry canes, and hear their voices start up again as I crammed half-ripe berries into my mouth, listening hard for their secrets. It was never long before one of the boy cousins would pull me back into the games that were all one long game we played for years. We pretended to be animals on the flattened grass paths between our houses. We played Hunt and Gather, Victim and Prey. Nobody else seemed to pay as much attention to their mother as I did.

It was hot. So hot that the sheets stuck to the backs of my legs when I woke up in the morning. So hot that nobody slept well the night before. Papa had walked the airless hallway, pacing by my door in his undershirt and shorts. I wished I could join him when he sat on the front porch in the middle of the night, but Mother would never let me sit out front in my nightdress. The whole house had the taut feeling of insomnia. I drifted in and out of sleep all night while the sky went slowly from black to blue, and then it was the Fourth of July. Joe and Winslow had promised to take me to the annual parade; Winslow's father was sponsoring a big clambake at Quincy Park to solidify his reinstatement as president of the Massachusetts state senate.

Even though it was a national holiday, Tuesday was ironing day at our house. The clothes had been boiled, washed, and hung out to dry on Monday. Now I had to heat the irons after breakfast and clean the table for ironing. Papa must have been the only engraver at the Flint Mill with shirts starched so hard they didn't need their hangers. I did his best shirt, linen collar and cuffs, so he could wear them to the parade. Then there were the dresses, fourteen total for Mother and me, and the petticoats and underwear, with each ruffle starched as well, though nobody was allowed to see them. Mother opened the window and worked as hard as I did, but I didn't want to be sweating like that before going to the clambake, my hair all tied up in a rag and losing its curl in the heat.

Papa had tried to make our house festive by tacking up four small American flags on the front porch. Most people in the neighborhood had done the same, since the flags were going for a penny each down at the store, but there was no breeze to help them flutter. Papa made our favorite breakfast of kippers and eggs while we worked, but for once I couldn't eat them. The smell was too much for me, and even plain eggs smelled like fish. I pretended to have an unsettled stomach and drank three bottles of ginger beer before noon.

"It'll give you gas," Mother said. "We won't be able to do up your corset."

"I'm not wearing a corset today, it's too hot."

"You will wear a corset or you won't go at all."

" 'You'll wear a corset or you won't go at all!' " I mimicked.

That started it. It ended with me sweeping all of the ironed clothes off the kitchen table onto the floor and her calling for Papa, which she almost never did.

"Now what's this? What is this?" Papa looked sleepless.

"She threw them onto this dirty floor," Mother said, kneeling and starting to pick up the clothes, which had been starched so hard that they didn't change shape in their flight. The back of her dress showed sweat between her shoulder blades.

"No, you let me, Abigail. Let me." Papa took her under both elbows and lifted her to her feet.

"I can manage." Mother was breathing fast, and her face was mottled red and white, the tall spin of hair coming unpinned.

"Frankie will clean this up," Papa said. I stood still, convinced that I would say something terrible to her if I opened my mouth. "Come. Sit." Papa got Mother a glass of water from the sink. "Sit in the garden, where it's cool."

"But there's no air." Mother's voice was tight in her throat.

"Oh, yes there is. You've just been working too long in this heat. Go out back, in the garden."

He led her to the garden, and she sat down heavily in the old wicker chair he had found buried under the weeds when we moved in. He had put in a new seat and painted it white to look like the chairs on the big porches of the

Brayton Hotel down at the harbor. Everything was sad and sorry now. I was terrible to make him take care of her. But when I heard her drinking the glass of water, I couldn't stand the sound of her swallowing, her very breathing. I wanted to run out the front door, but I couldn't move. Waiting for my punishment, ankle deep in clean laundry.

My father came back in, closing the door carefully so that it wouldn't slam behind him.

"Papa—"

He stepped in front of me to the sink. "Don't, Frankie."

He pumped another glass of water. "Drink," he said. "You go sit on the front porch and cool down. It's too hot is all. Too hot." He wiped his forehead and smiled his determined smile.

I swung my legs defiantly over the rail of the front porch, where I found an old paper fan decorated with a view of Rock Harbor. "Cotton City U.S.A.," it said in sweeping, bold letters, as smoke poured proudly out of a reproduction of the city's skyline. I fanned my rage into a breeze on my face and neck. Through the glass panels on either side of the front door, I saw Papa on his hands and knees picking up the laundry. He moved slowly, pushing himself up with the help of a kitchen chair and stacking the clothes back onto the table. I couldn't stand it.

"It's all right, Papa. You sit. I can finish."

He looked at me. "I don't mind." He meant it.

"No, I don't either." I meant it too.

He nodded and went out to join Mother while I hung the dresses along the high pole that ran under the eaves of the back porch and put the dry linens in the sideboard. Tomorrow I would be rubbing that very sideboard with furniture oil. The same tasks repeated on the same days, for nobody but us. In Poughkeepsie we had rotated hosting Sunday dinner with the aunts, but here it seemed pointless. When all the laundry was put away, I went to my room, filled the washstand with cool water, and cleaned myself carefully. I knew it wasn't likely that I would be allowed to go to the parade now, but I had to get the smell of sweat and starch off my body. My parents' voices came up through my window from the backyard, no surprises:

"Two boys, and I don't know where his sister will be."

"They'll probably be at the rally, don't you think?" I could imagine Papa rubbing his eyes. They were weak from engraving in the dim light of the dye room, but he refused to wear glasses when he worked. "They seem like good boys."

"Not the Portuguese one. They get ideas." Mother's voice was calmer, but I knew she would have the final say.

"The Curtis lad is always with him."

"She can't go without a chaperone."

"They went to the beach together."

"The Curtis girl was there."

I squeezed the washcloth against the back of my neck and let the water run down between my shoulder blades. Taking the towel from around my head, I leaned over the china basin, which had a pattern of red and yellow flowers in the center. I let my hair fall loose, making a curtain around the edge of the bowl. I remembered the first day I could reach it without my little step stool, what an arrival that had been. My washbasin was the prettiest thing in my room, set in its high wooden stand with rods for hand towels on both sides. Once a week the metal washtub was set in the middle of the kitchen, with the doors closed off to Papa for privacy but never to my mother. She poured water from the kettle next to my knees, which I kept curled tight to my chest, and warned me not to waste time. Someday I wanted to be allowed to waste time, naked and alone in the water. I dipped my finger into the washbasin and spun it around until the water swirled over the china flowers, promising myself a new life someday, when I was grown and gone.

When Joe and Winslow came by to pick me up in the Model T, Papa told them that I would be down to the picnic later, after I had finished my housework.

"Tell her we'll be at the clambake at five o'clock for my father's speech."

"Yes, I'll do that, Winslow."

The car started up again and drove away. I cried for a while, slept for a while. I woke to the sound of a marching band playing in the distance, knew that I had missed the parade, and when Papa knocked on my door, I went downstairs to apologize to my mother. It must have been good enough, for I was allowed to go to the clambake with my parents by trolley, wearing my corset.

Hamilton Curtis was a big man with a voice that reached at least halfway up the hillside in Quincy Park. I had never seen him before, and he didn't disappoint me. A crowd was gathered in front of a wooden platform at the foot of the hill. Families had spread picnic blankets, and though it was still hot, the men and children ferried plates of steamed corn on the cob and clam fritters back to the women waiting under umbrellas and sunhats. After an enthusiastic introduction by the mayor, who was as thin and nervous as Ham Curtis was solid and unhurried, the senator walked forward and took a long moment with his hands outstretched as if to embrace the whole city. He was wearing a pressed white linen suit, and he looked from side to side, nodding to the top of the hill in acknowledgment as the clapping increased rather than subsided, and the men and boys began whistling.

"Rock Harbor!" he began, and then repeated himself several times, pretending embarrassment that he couldn't quiet the crowd. "Rock Harbor! I have only one thing to say about the war in Europe: Let's keep our boys *over here,* and send our cotton *over there!*"

Everyone cheered, and some boys set off fireworks down by the clambake. Ham Curtis smiled indulgently. He never stopped pacing the small platform as he spoke. His gray hair looked windblown, as if he had just gotten off the train from Washington and run over to Quincy Park (though the state senate met in Boston). He spoke about expanding business in Rock Harbor, building even more mills to keep up with the demand for cotton in Europe. We needed more streetlights, and an expanded rail system that would take us up to Fall River and beyond that to Providence. When you listened to Ham, you felt as if he were bringing the rest of the world to us, but not because we were a small city; the senator made us feel that Rock Harbor was the center of the world, and maybe we weren't so small after all, with someone like him taking our concerns to the Massachusetts state senate.

He mentioned President Wilson in a confidential way, as if they had recently lunched together to discuss the problems facing Rock Harbor. It was a smooth reminder that Ham Curtis had actually played host to William Howard Taft when he came to Rock Harbor for the Cotton Centennial, back in 1911. Joe told me that Senator Curtis had brought the president home to stay as his guest. Winslow had spent the night in the same house as President Taft, though he would never have told me himself. Winslow almost never talked about his family.

I watched him standing to the right of the platform with his older brother, Tom, and Alice. Joe had told me that their mother died just after Winslow was born, and Alice had acted as the senator's hostess ever since her coming-out party three years ago, when she turned sixteen. The Curtis siblings were dressed perfectly, and their attention was turned correctly to the senator. Then Winslow's dog, Roxie, a black mutt who sometimes rode in the front seat of his Model T, ran up the steps to the platform and jumped right up on Winslow, throwing him off balance. Winslow squatted down to pat her and said something over his shoulder to Alice, who kept her eyes on the senator and pushed at Roxie with her heel to keep the dog from jumping up again. Winslow grinned and whispered into Roxie's ear as she wagged happily in front of him. Not only was Winslow the baby of the family but he was acting younger than his age, and I wasn't sure I liked it.

Ham Curtis spoke for about half an hour. He would have to stand in an election in November, as the members of the state senate were decided by popular vote. However, unless someone really wanted to take him on, Ham could plan to lead the state senate for quite a while. But he had ambition and influence beyond the state, of course, and when he spoke you understood why people called him the "Massachusetts William Jennings Bryan." He was certainly the most important person I had ever seen. Ham talked mostly about prosperity and growth, and never mentioned the war in Europe again. He ended by inviting everyone to be sure and eat plenty at the clambake, and after sunset the fireworks display, also sponsored by his campaign, would begin.

Papa brought us plates of food, and I had my first taste of the early white-kernel corn I had seen growing in the fields on the way to the beach. The corn seemed to have absorbed the salt air as it grew, and it popped sweet and hot inside my mouth. Mother leaned back against the pillows Papa had brought and looked contented. Her hair was back in its concentric circle, and she reassured herself by pushing the hairpins in unnecessarily. I tried my best to eat without letting hot butter drip down my chin but licked my fingers surreptitiously after each littleneck clam. The sun was still hours from setting, but the quality of the light had changed. The humidity had eased, and Papa filled his pipe and watched the smoke drift into the sky as if that were the most important thing he had to think about. There was a fragile calm on our picnic blanket.

Joe caught me with my fingers in my mouth. A shadow fell across the blanket, and I turned away from him, embarrassed. He was dressed in his best clothes, his hair was slicked back, and I could see that he was nervous with my parents right there.

"Evening, Mr. and Mrs. Ross, Frankie."

I found a handkerchief and wiped my fingers. My face was hot, and I felt like a child. In his good clothes, Joe looked older.

"Evening, Joe." Papa smiled briefly at him without getting up. Mother opened her eyes and nodded, then closed them again, pretending to sleep, I guess. Joe looked past me into the trail of pipe smoke.

"What do you think of Senator Curtis?" Papa asked.

"I think he'll get reinstated, if that's what you mean." Joe narrowed his eyes at the platform where Ham Curtis and his entourage were finishing up the glad-handing and moving toward the food line. "He's not going to change anything around here. Everybody I know is talking about the speedups and stretch-outs. That's what more growth means for us. He doesn't talk about that."

"No, he wouldn't." Papa's voice was mild. "But it's good for us to have a Rock Harbor man in the state senate."

"I guess," said Joe shortly, then he seemed to catch himself. "I've been in the mills since I was seven."

Papa looked at him and nodded, respect flickering for a moment. Maybe that was enough of an explanation. Maybe Papa didn't care so much that he was Portuguese; maybe Mother wouldn't care so much if Papa didn't care. Maybe I wouldn't care either.

"Here comes the Curtis boy." Papa nodded at Winslow, who was walking toward us with a plate of corn and steamers. His linen suit was still crisp, but his tie was pulled loose at the neck, and his black hair had blown away from the clean middle part. Mother's eyes popped open as Winslow bounded the last few steps to us and started talking nonstop.

Could he take me to the fireworks tonight? The family

would be on the Curtises' private boat, which was going to anchor in the harbor to watch the display. This year the fireworks were supposed to be the best yet, according to his father, and being on the water gave you the best seat in the house. Joe was coming, and couldn't they have me along as well? Alice would be there, he added quickly, seeing Mother's frown at the mention of Joe, and Winslow would bring me home safely. Word of honor, Mrs. Ross.

How he managed all that while sitting familiarly on our blanket and eating his meal was beyond comprehension. But Mother sat up, made room, and laughed at every joke. Joe watched with a detached smile, and by the time Winslow had finished his first ear of corn, I had permission to go.

It was my first real introduction to the Curtis family, and I think I got the whole picture that night, even though I didn't know it then. When we arrived at the town dock, Winslow began ferrying guests from the dock to the boat, rowing the tender with his shirtsleeves rolled up, and it was easy to picture him on the crew at a university someday. I hung back at the landing near Joe, wanting to avoid the other guests. Everyone was beautifully dressed, with the younger women wearing the shirtwaists and jackets that had become acceptable now that corsets were being dropped. We were the last to leave the landing, and once we got into the tender with Winslow, Joe whipped out his mill apron, which he had kept under his arm in a tightly wrapped bundle.

"Can I leave this under the transom, Winslow?" he

asked. "I have to work the night shift at ten. I figure I'll head over there right after the fireworks."

"I can row you back whenever you want," Winslow said. "Ham is looking forward to seeing you, Joe. He saw you play last season."

Joe asked again if his apron would really be safe in the dinghy.

"Sure, sure." Winslow pulled us up next to a wooden ladder that was hooked over the stern. The boat was grand by any standard. The gunwales were bound with wide, polished wooden railings, and it was impossible to find the mark of a brushstroke in the white paint. The brass fixtures reflected everything back in a way that made the boat look bigger. ACES HIGH read her name in gold letters. Joe raised his eyebrows.

"Isn't this Jimmy Spencer's boat?" he asked.

"Jimmy's lending it out to Ham for the campaign. It looks good on the Fourth."

Joe frowned before scrambling up the ladder and reaching a hand to help me. I had been climbing trees and rocks in long skirts my whole life, but the bouncing of the tender against the big boat made it harder, and the bottom of the ladder moved unexpectedly as I stepped onto it. I had to accept Winslow helping me from behind and Joe practically hauling me in from above. When I got up on deck, there was Ham Curtis, holding a drink and watching me pant for breath.

"Welcome aboard," he said in that very public voice. "You are?"

"A friend of Winslow's, sir. Frances Ross."

"How are you, Senator Curtis? Great speech," Joe said,

his teeth flashing as he held out his hand. Joe started to run up front to help Winslow fend off, but Ham caught him by the arm.

"Here's our basketball star!" he announced to the other guests. "This is Joe Barros, who led the Borden team to the state title this year." There was an obligatory murmur as every head turned to stare at Joe. Joe nodded at Senator Curtis and tried to pull away. "Going to get us the title again next year, Joe?" Ham asked, still holding tight.

"I'm certainly going to try, sir. Winslow and I will both do our best."

"Oh, Winslow." The senator laughed. "He does well enough on the court, but you're the one who brought the title home, Joe. You put the rest of those boys to shame." He leaned over as if to whisper, but he knew how to whisper in a voice that carried. "It's in the blood."

Joe said nothing, and Ham continued, a little quieter now. "And from what I hear, the Curtises were able to help make that title possible with a little extra allowance, eh?" He laughed, waiting for Joe to join him in the joke, but Joe kept staring straight ahead. "Don't worry, boy," Ham said, releasing Joe's arm and clapping him on the back. "Winslow's not in any trouble with me over it. Glad to hear he was ready to help out. Anything for the team."

Alice came up to us. "Let him go play with his friend, Daddy," she said. "You know that Winslow can't do anything without him."

Joe nodded quickly at both of them and hurried forward to the bow. The senator turned to me, and I wasn't sure whether to hold out my hand or curtsy, so I did neither. I must have seemed very rude, but Ham held out both of his hands and clasped one of mine between them. The senator's hands were big and warm; they felt like hands you could trust, a politician's gift.

"Frances Ross," he said. "You go to school with Winslow? At Borden?"

"Yes, sir."

"What does your father do?"

"He's an engraver, sir. At the Flint Mill."

"What's his name?"

"Allen Ross."

"Huh . . ." Ham Curtis seemed to be considering. "No. Don't know him."

I was impressed that he might, though. I assumed he must go walking through the factory whenever he was in town, calling hundreds of laborers by name. Ham was still holding my hand tightly, and I didn't know how to disengage. The senator seemed utterly at ease, and he looked into my eyes for what felt like a very long time. I tried not to blink. "Sweetheart," he said over his shoulder to Alice, "meet Winslow's friend, Frances Ross."

"We've met," Alice said to her father. "Refreshment?" I took the glass of champagne she plucked from a nearby tray. "Now, Daddy, Tom sent me over here. He said to tell you that he really needs your opinion on something." She took her father's elbow and steered him away while the senator gave me a parting look of helplessness that was surprisingly boyish. I thought I saw Winslow's brother, Tom, in the group of men on the foredeck, but I couldn't be sure. I'd never seen him before the rally. Joe and Winslow had disappeared. The women were sitting in deck chairs at the stern, staring out at the harbor as the men's conversation scattered into the air, half lost in the rocking of the boat and general hum from the shore, where people were gathering to watch the fireworks.

"He's not going to give us any trouble."

"It's sewn up in Providence."

"If he does . . ."

I was afraid to take an empty deck chair and afraid to sip the champagne until Winslow and Joe came back, their shirts soaking wet.

"We just had to wash off the muck from the painter, it's so hot!" Winslow said, shaking his hair like a dog.

"The rope was only getting our *hands* dirty." Joe caught a towel Winslow threw to him. "But Winslow . . ." They looked at each other and laughed, so maybe everything was all right after all.

"Come on," Winslow said, including me in his laughter as if I already knew what they were talking about. "How about something to eat?"

"No, no, I'm not hungry." I didn't dare eat anything in front of these people. I was hoping I wouldn't spill the drink I had been handed.

Winslow pulled three deck chairs together for us around a plate of raw oysters on ice. He slung the towel across his shoulders. "You can't drink champagne without oysters. The senator wouldn't like it," he said gently as he held one out to me. "Neither would I."

I obeyed, hating the taste of the first one and laughing with the boys when I couldn't help but make a face. Joe loved oysters and taught me that they tasted better with a little lemon squeezed on top. Winslow drank two glasses of champagne quite quickly, but when I finished mine, Joe asked if there was any lemonade and switched us both over to that.

I felt much less worried after my first glass of champagne. The boat was beautiful, and Rock Harbor looked impressive from the water. The brick smokestacks rose up in neat rows along the river and spread out in both directions to the newest mills, which lined Water Street. Everything seemed brighter: the small boats bobbing near shore, and the Brayton Hotel with its red, white, and blue bunting spread over the porch rail. I didn't care so much about my outmoded dress, and I liked having these two young men sitting on either side treating me almost as their equal, only better. It was with the Curtises that Fourth of July that I discovered I shared the family's taste for alcohol.

The whole group gathered for sunset on the afterdeck, and all the windows in the mills turned copper at the same moment. The senator shouted out, "Look at the moon!"

We turned, and he was pointing at the white crescent just over Chapham's Rise, the lowest of the seven hills. Someone began to clap, and soon we were all clapping. We applauded the moon, the setting sun, and Ham Curtis for making it all happen at once. It got dark very quickly, and we crowded to the bow, which had swung with the tide toward the shore, to watch the fireworks being set off on the beach. I was drinking another glass of champagne; Joe had nodded when I glanced at him for permission. Everyone except Joe and me had been drinking steadily, and Winslow climbed up to the crosstrees of the small mast. He sat above us all with his bare feet dangling over our heads. Nobody seemed to mind what Winslow did.

I was separated from Joe as the display began. He must

have found a place to watch where he was out of the way, but I was wedged in closely between people I didn't know. It seemed that more and more people kept arriving by private boat the closer it got to showtime, and another yacht had rafted up right alongside us. People were going back and forth between the two boats, and Joe could have been anywhere.

The first fireworks went off, and our cheers were echoed by the people onshore. They were hanging out of windows, on top of roofs, or sitting right in the middle of the steepest streets down to the waterfront. There were some loud bangs, and a shower of white sparks that surprised us all with their height. I tried to peer around the shoulders of a man in front of me, and as I did I felt a hand pressing tightly against the small of my back. Before I could turn my head, I heard Ham Curtis's voice saying quietly, "There. That's better. You can see now."

I was afraid to move, and really, I couldn't have. Everyone was turned to the display including him, and when I twisted my head back, I could only see his face in profile. He wasn't looking at me. He was watching the fireworks and exclaiming with everyone else, but his hand kept moving. He edged his large fingers around my waist in a manner that could have been protective but wasn't. When I tried to move away, his hand gripped tighter, and I froze. Once he had reached around me, he didn't move his hand anywhere else, just kept it tight about my corseted waist, pulling my backside close against him. I could feel him through his trousers, and I wasn't seeing anything anymore as he pressed rhythmically into me; somehow it felt in time with the fireworks. He pulled me back last and hardest against him with a moaning breath that only I could hear. Roman candles lit up the beach, and our tightly packed group separated. Ham didn't glance my way as he released me and turned to the others, ready with a remark that made everyone laugh on cue.

The men separated from the women for cigars, and out of nowhere violins began to play. I wasn't sure if I could remain standing. I touched the small of my back where Ham had rubbed himself, but it was dry. Had anything really happened? This music: had they found room for a chamber orchestra on the boat? Why couldn't I see the musicians when the music sounded both close and far away? There was the sound of applause as the first song came to an end, and I heard Alice insisting on playing "her music." The chamber orchestra changed into a ragtime band, and I stared uncomprehendingly as Alice leaned over a long-legged box with a metal horn attached to the top. The heavily beaded tassels on her dress were swinging like another set of breasts below the ones nobody was supposed to touch. The pieces fit together for me at last: I had seen pictures of a Victrola in the Sears catalog but never actually heard one. The back deck began to tremble with dancing. I lurched over to the back rail and leaned against it for balance, looking away from the city.

The water was flat and black, and the champagne seemed to have lost its effect. I wanted more. I wanted to feel the way I had before the fireworks display, but that would never quite happen, no matter how much champagne I helped myself to that night or any night.

I don't know how long Joe was standing at the rail before I noticed him. The sounds of the party rose around us, conversations competing with the phonograph music, which sounded otherworldly and out of tune. All the voices blended into an atonal march that I couldn't keep up with.

"I've got to clock in pretty soon." Joe leaned his back against the rail.

"How late do you have to work?"

"It's the graveyard shift—ten to six."

"So late."

"I wanted to see the fireworks tonight. Pretty good, huh?"

"Better than Poughkeepsie."

"Ham Curtis didn't really pay for them, you know." Joe moved closer to me. "It's the campaign money they raised from other people. Though I've got a feeling it's all mingled together, whether it's paying for the fireworks or the coal bill."

"Is that unusual?"

He smiled at me. "No, not exactly unusual. You know much about politics, Frankie?"

"Don't make me out to be dumb, Joe." I turned to face him. "I just never got that interested in politics. . . . Who's Jimmy Spencer?"

Joe laughed.

"You said he owned the boat. Is he here tonight?"

"No."

"What about him?"

"What do you mean?"

"I told you not to treat me like I'm stupid, Joe."

"I don't think you're stupid. Jimmy Spencer is Providence mob, all right?" Joe looked around, and I guess he was afraid his voice might have carried more than usual over the water. "I'll tell you more later, smart girl. But this is not a smart place to talk about it."

"What about you?" I asked. "How do you know about politics?"

"I'm interested. I don't like much about it, but it's fun to watch the fireworks from the Curtis boat." He grinned at me. "Did you have fun tonight?"

"Wonderful."

I checked the back of my dress again, self-consciously; bone dry.

"Winslow was giving me the money I should've been making at the mill," Joe said suddenly. "That's what you saw that day. It was so I could go to practice instead of working my usual shift. Coach understood about me quitting the team; he knew that we needed the money I made doing afternoon shifts. It was Winslow's idea to replace that money so I could keep going to practice. I didn't want to do it."

"But you won," I said. "You went to State."

He looked out at the water. "And Winslow didn't care at all about the money. For him, you know, money's just . . . there."

"Do you think he told the senator?"

Joe shook his head. "I'd bet not. I'm not going to say anything to Winslow. He just did what he thought was the simplest thing. But he doesn't talk to Ham, and it doesn't matter, 'cause that man finds out everything in this town. That's the way it works. You see how the senator acted tonight when he first saw me? Like I'm one of his polo ponies."

"But you did win, Joe."

"I know." He turned his back to the water and smiled at me. "That was good."

He moved closer and put his hand over mine on the railing. I knew he was going to kiss me, and I closed my eyes, but when he came so close that I could smell his salty skin, I pulled away sharply—not wanting anyone to touch me again that night. Joe let go of my hand and turned back toward the railing as if nothing had happened. I was hardly breathing. I wanted so much to put my hand back on top of his, but we froze next to each other in the summer air, more formal than ever before.

I don't know how long we stood there, but that's how Winslow found us. He was loud and barefoot, dancing himself down the side of the deck. Joe seemed relieved to see him, and I didn't know what I thought. I couldn't make sense to myself anymore. Joe told Winslow that it was time to bring the tender around and take him back for his shift at the mill.

"I'd better take you home too, Peaches, or your folks will never let you go out with the Curtises again," Winslow said drunkenly, and I wondered if he really believed that any parents would forbid their daughter to go out with him. He took Joe's arm, and they walked together toward the bow. "I'll drop you at the mill and drive her home." Winslow untied the rope and towed the small boat toward the stern. "Let's say good night to the pater."

The "pater" barely noticed we were leaving. Alice had her music on, and the stern of the boat was low in the water from all the dancing. Ham Curtis waved a hand at Winslow from the bow as he pushed us off and took the oars.

"Ham liked you," Winslow said to me. "He told me so. 'Sweet as plum jam.'"

I wanted to push Winslow overboard with his movie idol looks and dense good humor. What did he know about his father? How many other girls had he brought around? Down to the fishes, I thought, thinking of some poem I had memorized for school.

"What did you say?"

"What?" I didn't realize I had spoken aloud. Joe and Winslow were both looking at me.

"Something about fish," Joe said. "Keep rowing, Curtis. I don't want to be late."

"Oh. 'Down to the fishes.' Is that it? I don't know." I was embarrassed. "Just a poem I had to learn for the poetry contest. Some dumb poem."

"Let's hear it," said Winslow. "Come on, Frankie. We all had to do tenth-grade poetry. Declaim for us!" he said, leaning forward on the oars and grinning. I sat up straight and began:

> *Down to the fishes,*
> *Is where I will be,*
> *If my love is wandering, looking for me.*
> *Down where the eels and the octopus linger . . .*
> *I'll never . . . no more . . .*

"Oh, I don't know, I can't remember the rest. I can't even remember who it's by," I said.

"Actually, you're right, Frankie. That is the dumbest poem I've ever heard," Winslow said. "I don't even want to know who wrote it."

I hadn't liked the poem myself, just that first line. Down to the fishes, I thought again, rolling the words around my head. Maybe I was drunk too. Maybe this was what it felt like to be drunk. Down to the fishes. Winslow tied up and jumped onto the dock, but instead of reaching down a hand to help me out, he stood and put his hands on his hips.

Last night, the moon had a golden ring,
And tonight no moon we see!

"Don't!" said Joe, pulling out his apron from under the seat and jumping onto the dock, then turning to take my elbow as I clambered out of the boat. I hated that he was careful with me now.

"Cut it out," he said, shoving Winslow gently. "*That's* the dumbest poem ever, and you don't even have the first line right."

"No, no! I know the whole thing," Winslow said. "Come on, it gets better."

"You drive better than you recite poetry, Curtis. Let's go."

But Winslow repeated his tenth-grade poem to us all the way to the car, with Joe trying to make him stop. They kept it up until we got to the big iron gate of the Flint Mill. Winslow shut off the car, and we could hear the rhythmic slamming of the looms on the other side of the brick, like surf.

"Why don't they take a day off for the Fourth?" Winslow said.

"Wouldn't be patriotic. There's a war on," Joe said. He didn't move to get out of the car.

"Not our war," I said.

"Not yet." Joe looked up at the building. "But they want the cotton."

"Ham says we won't get into this war. It's their business," Winslow said, half-yawning.

"Papa says we might," I said.

"Nah," Winslow said.

"You'll see France anyway," said Joe. "Didn't Tom go to Europe after he graduated?"

"And Alice went." Winslow nodded. "But that was before the *Lusitania*."

Just then the shift whistle blew, and I jumped in my seat. Joe and Winslow laughed at me. People were filing out of the mill, gray clumps walking together as far as the gate, then splitting apart. The only way to tell the men from the women was by their caps or head scarves.

"Going to be a light shift," Joe said, looking at the people leaving. "Always is, the late one. But especially 'cause it's the Fourth." He got out and slammed the door, leaning against the open car window so that he was right next to me, looking out at the nearly silent crowd going home. "You want to know a funny thing? It's the greenhorns that wanted the day off more than the rest of us. They want to celebrate Independence Day and they aren't even Americans yet. Funny, huh?"

"Makes sense to me," I said.

"Well, you're a little funny yourself," Joe said. He was so close that I could have reached out to touch his arm. Instead, I put my arm along the top of the car door, so that the hairs of my forearm mingled with his; nobody would notice but me.

"Joe, can't we come into the mill with you? Just to see where you work?"

"Why would you want to do that?"

"Because I've never seen the big looms. You never tell me anything about it."

"Nothing interesting about the weave room."

"It is to me, come on . . ." I reached farther, put my hand over his, and felt him go still.

"What about your folks?" He couldn't look at me.

"I'll just tell them I stayed late on the boat. Winslow can still bring me home."

"It's a great idea," Winslow said. "I've never seen you running those looms either. Six of them, eight? Heck, Joe, that's a lot of looms."

"Not like some guys."

"Me and Winslow can go in separately, so you don't have to know anything about it," I said.

Winslow grinned. "I can sure go into that mill if I want to, wouldn't you say, Joe?"

"Sure." Joe looked worried, but then the shift whistle blew two short blasts and he pulled his hand away, grabbed his leather apron from under his arm, and slipped it over his head as he ran in. And he was gone into that crowd of gray just as if he were anybody.

Winslow parked the car and led me to a side door of the mill. I had entered through the big gate when I came with Papa, but Winslow clearly knew his way around. The streets were quiet now that the shift change was over, and I looked around to make sure nobody was watching. Winslow saw me hesitate as he held the door for me.

"We're just going to have a little tour and then go home. Maybe half an hour."

He pulled the door shut behind us. They had electrified the mills a few years earlier, and dim bulbs were mounted in the old gas fixtures at each landing. The stairwell was painted white, but the stairs themselves were dark, and as we stepped up I could feel indentations that had been worn into the wood by hundreds of shoes. I held tightly to the railing as Winslow led the way. There was the rushing noise of the mill all around us, and I smiled to myself in the dark.

We climbed the stairs to the third floor. Winslow opened a door, but instead of seeing a room filled with looms, I saw a smaller room partitioned off from the rest of the floor, with machines turning out flat sections of raw, dirty cotton. The air was filled with small bits of white fluff; we had walked into a humid snowstorm. None of the windows were open, and we stepped through delicate whirlpools of cotton dust on the floor.

"The picker room," Winslow shouted into my ear. "They keep this place a little separate in case there's a fire." He led me closer to a couple of men who were systematically cutting the wire hoops off bales of cotton before tossing them into the square mouth of a big machine. The machine split apart the bales, spitting out fist-size chunks onto a conveyor belt. Everyone working in this room was dark-skinned, darker than Joe, which meant they were either Negroes or Cape Verde Islanders. Or maybe they just looked darker than Joe because the skin around their eyes and collars contrasted so strongly with the white film of cotton that covered their faces, hair, and arms.

They saw us come in but didn't respond. I felt beyond foolish in my summer hat and beige shoes. I wanted to leave and I wanted to stay. All that iron machinery pounding around us made me feel like I was finally at the center of something that mattered: the hard industrial heart of Rock Harbor. I kept staring at the men who were keeping it going. I had been taught not to stare into the face of any man except for my relatives and the priest. But when I looked down, I couldn't help seeing their feet. Nobody was wearing shoes. At first it was hard to tell that their feet were bare because they were so covered with white dust, skin floured like my mother's hands on baking day.

"That's the bale breaker," Winslow said, and he led me past the first machine to where the men were taking chunks of cotton off the conveyor belt and breaking them up even more before throwing them into bins to be wheeled to another part of the floor. I felt as if I were standing inside a walled-up city block.

"My father used to bring me here every week till I memorized it," Winslow shouted. I winced at his voice right in my ear but nodded. "He thinks it'll make a difference when I'm maybe running the place. Tom's set for politics, and I'm for the mill." Winslow's face was expressionless, and I wondered what he really thought of it all.

He led me over to a line of three machines, which pulled the cotton onto metal rollers with little spikes set into them. They reminded me of the player piano rolls that belonged to my aunt in Poughkeepsie, only bigger. Much bigger.

"The breaker, intermediate, and finisher," Winslow yelled, pointing at the three huge rollers. "They're all pickers." The cotton was being pounded and stretched, but it still looked dirty and was filled with brown bits. I saw something moving quickly underneath the machines and pulled my dress close to me. I was afraid it was a rat, but it was a child. A girl crawling on her hands and knees under the machines with a wad of cotton stuffed into her mouth. It was hard to tell how old she was because she was coated in cotton lint and dirt. I only knew she was a girl because she was wearing a kerchief. Her hair and skin had collected enough cotton dust to make her the same color all over. The only visible difference between her skin and her clothing was a change in texture. She was picking at the floor over and over, and she didn't look up at us.

"Winslow." I grabbed his arm. "Look."

Winslow glanced down without changing his expression. "She's cleaning up the dirt and cotton seeds that fall down from the picker. That's how come they call the kids 'mill rats' till they grow up enough to quit that job. Scurrying around like that won't last forever."

"Why has she got that thing in her mouth?" Her lips and cheeks bulged out from her face, and after every pick at the floor she wiped her nose clear with her sleeve.

"It's just cotton," he said, looking more closely. "She must be stopping up her mouth so she doesn't breathe too much dust while she's working under the machine."

He turned away and pointed at the lumpy mass that was coming out of the last of the three pickers. "There's the lap," he said proudly, as if he had made it himself. It came out of the machine in a flat mass that looked like dough which had been rolled out for cookies and dropped on a dirty floor.

"Now it gets carded," Winslow said.

He led me away from the pickers and the gray-dusted children I now saw crawling under each one. Everyone knew there were children working in the mills. I simply hadn't thought about it, and I kept looking back as Winslow led me away. The carding machine looked like two huge combs that took the dirty white dough and for the first time made it look like it might someday be cotton. The lap was pulled through more rows of metal teeth and finally came out as a twisted piece of rope that was looped into tall metal cans.

"Those are the slivers, there in the cans," said Winslow. He was so casual about it. Showing off for me, sure, but it was like he was taking me around his house. I wanted him to repeat everything to me. All these words—"lap," "sliver," "breaker"—they were in a language everyone knew but me.

When the tall cans were full, they were replaced by empty ones, and two men wheeled the cans of slivers on their edges, tilting them at just the right angle to be wheeled diagonally across the floor to another big, slow-turning machine. The slivers emerged from it longer, finer, and cleaner than before. This was the comber.

Winslow showed me the intermediate frame, the fine frame, and the jack frame. They were attended by large, dusty men who fed the stuff in at one thickness, then took it out on the other side, a bit closer to something that could be called thread. The men's hands looked bigger as the fiber got smaller and smaller between their fingers.

The fibers were twisted and pulled, and Winslow said the machine was "roving" the cotton. Finally, it was put onto another conveyor belt, which led up through a hatch in the ceiling to the floor above.

Winslow pulled me out of the room and back onto the stairs. He took my arm as we began to climb another flight, but I hardly noticed. The noise dropped as soon as we left the open floor, and it was darker than ever in the stairwell. I would have stumbled if he hadn't held on to me.

"Roving," I repeated out loud, wanting to memorize everything. "Roving the cotton."

Winslow opened the door off the fourth-floor stairwell, announcing, "The spinning room!"

The spinning room was the hottest yet. The spinners were wide frames of metal set on wheels, and Winslow walked me over to the middle of the floor, where the conveyor belt delivered the roving from the floor we had just left. The roving was hauled to the spinners, which were being pulled across the room over and over, wrapping the roving around wooden bobbins as they went. The machines were pulled across by adults, but as soon as a spinner arrived at one end of the room, a child jumped on top of the frame to take away the full bobbins and replace them with empty wooden spools.

"They're doffing," Winslow said, following my look. "Don't worry so much, the girls are usually with their families this way. They'd rather be here making money than home by themselves."

The doffers ran lightly alongside the spinning frame. The smallest ones would climb up to reach the bobbins with barely a break in stride. They didn't seem to notice

the gears moving below them. Their arms were full of bobbins, and I envied their perfect balance.

Winslow watched the doffers with me, but for once
he didn't smile. "Joe's right about the speedups and the
stretch-outs. Seems like everybody's going faster than the
last time I was in here."

"What's a stretch-out?"

"It's when a worker runs more machines than he used to,
more efficient that way. Speedups are when the machines
simply go faster. All that stuff is up to the overseer and
the second hand. Joe thinks that Ham can do something
about it, but he can't interfere with the overseer."

"Where are the overseers? Nobody seems to be watching. Nobody's even noticed us."

"Yes, they have." Winslow showed me a small room
that had a window overlooking the floor and a man asleep
on a bench just below it. "That's where the second hand
stays. He's in charge of the floor, and the overseer stays in
there too. They see what's going on. They know me, so I
guess they don't mind if I show you around."

"But that man sleeping right outside the office, won't
he get in trouble?"

"No." Winslow laughed. "The person who gets in trouble is the one who wakes him up. He's a fixer. If something
goes wrong with one of the machines, he gets it working
again. The fixers can sleep when they want because they
work so fast when they're awake. Ham warned me not to
wake a fixer unless you really have to. He said they'll throw
a hammer at you no matter whose kid you are."

A girl hurried by with a load of bobbins. She had strong
arms and a moon face. I saw her glance at us as she dumped

the bobbins into a wooden tub that was near another conveyor belt leading to the floor below. There was a constant hum and screech from the spinning frames being pulled on their metal wheels and the wooden bobbins whirling on top. I hadn't noticed the smell so much in the picking and carding rooms; on this floor the air smelled like damp laundry and sweat. My Fourth of July dress was sticking to my back by the time we crossed the floor to the next stairway, and even Winslow seemed depleted as he opened the door for me.

"Let's go find Joe," he said. "The big looms are on the bottom two floors."

"What's on the top floor?"

"Spooling, dressing, warping." He looked at my reddened face. "Let's go down to the weave rooms."

I held my breath without meaning to when Winslow opened the door to the weave room. The slamming of the metal looms was so loud it made my whole body shake in time with the building. I felt knocked back and put my hands over my ears. I wanted to return to the stairwell. I saw Winslow's mouth moving, but all I could hear were the looms. Men and women were standing and walking between the big machines. I didn't know how they could ever have gotten used to the noise. Winslow took my arm, and as we started walking by the first loom, a man looked up curiously. I had long since shoved my hat off, and it hung by wet ribbons, banging against my back in rhythm with the looms.

"Joe is over here!" Winslow shouted. "Are you all right?"

I nodded. I wanted to be game, but only for long enough to see Joe and leave. The looms were big, taller

than the spinning machines, and the banging came from
metal bars slamming down over and over after the shuttles
shot through hundreds of vertical white threads, leaving
streaks of color. Some of the patterns were complicated,
and I wondered vaguely who set the machine to follow a
pattern. Maybe that was Joe's job. Winslow was still shouting at me, and I caught words here and there: "warp,"
"weft," "beam," and "slasher." I didn't even bother to nod.
I just stared at those high, harsh machines with their seem-
ingly casual keepers.

Then Joe was right in front of us, wiping his face with
the back of his sleeve.

"You did it, Curtis!" he shouted. "What took so long?"

"Had to give Peaches the tour!" Winslow yelled back.

Joe looked at me, and I could tell he admired me for
coming. I took my hands away from my ears and straight-
ened up. I got out a handkerchief for my neck and face,
and Joe reached over and handed me a canteen of water
without trying to talk. I gulped it down, not caring who
saw me drink from the bottle like a boy. It helped, and
Winslow found a stool for me. I sat down next to one of
the looms, not knowing what else to do.

"These six are mine!" Joe pointed toward the row of
looms. ". . . thread breaks!"

"What?"

"Stop them if the thread breaks!" He cupped his hands
around his mouth, then gave up. It was pointless to talk.
Joe walked over to another machine and checked the bobbins, refilling them from a basket of scarlet-wound spools
at his feet. He seemed fearless as he reached around the
side gears of the loom, loading the new thread into place,

but I had seen people with missing parts who lived in the neighborhood. Mr. Cordiero, who owned the corner store, had no fingers on his right hand, only a thumb. I couldn't help looking at it every time he measured something out. Still, Papa said that most people would keep working at the mill as long as they could. He said that it was safer than fishing, and a lot safer than whaling used to be.

The looms were all moving so fast I didn't know how Joe could separate one thing from another. Winslow and Joe talked, and I considered this strange slamming room where Joe had grown up. Even though I saw him there in front of me, wearing that long weaver's apron, it was hard to imagine who he was inside the mill. Joe walked down his line of looms, and Winslow stayed right next to him, shouting into his ear while Joe nodded and grinned, never looking away from the machines, so I was alone when it happened.

I remember each move I made, one by one. First I smelled smoke and looked down to see the edge of my dress curling slowly back into nothing. I didn't know how it happened, but the hem was a burning red line. I jumped up and shoved with both hands at the bottom of my dress, but instead of only fabric, there was something hard under there. How could there be anything under my dress that I didn't know about? That scared me more and I shoved harder. Something clawed back against my thighs, my underthings, and at last I began to scream. Then I saw a small girl rolling toward the gears as if she had fallen out from underneath my dress. It was her head I had been shoving away, her hard skull. It was all impossible. I saw black oil spreading out smoothly onto the floor around me. Flames and smoke were coming from a metal pan underneath the loom. I hadn't noticed that pan before. How could all of these things have been under my dress? I had just been sitting. Just sitting there.

The girl reached out a hand for me. Her mouth was open, but I couldn't hear anything over the looms. Her hands made streaks of oil on my dress, which was still burning slowly upward. I noticed that the girl was very pretty, a child with a face like they draw in the magazines. She was a dream girl, and none of this could be happening except that the sharpness of the smoke was hurting my eyes. I knew I couldn't get out of that dress, not with the corset on; everything was attached underneath the fabric like a cage. Then I saw what the girl was trying to do: the side gears had caught her and she was being pulled in; the teeth of the loom kept turning and sucking at her clothes. I saw the edge of her bare foot being twisted into the metal. I saw her wide eyes, the tears that came out of them without stopping, and the way she couldn't close her mouth or take her eyes off mine. I saw but I couldn't move. I was watching myself burn.

Then somebody threw me down and away, onto the floor. Joe grabbed the girl and yelled something to Winslow; there was the smell of burning oil and smoke in my mouth, and I couldn't tell if I was still on fire or not. There was a series of slams, and the loom stopped. Then all the looms on the floor stopped, and out of that silence I heard a crashing in my ears. Winslow was slapping his hands on the front of my dress and saying something, but I couldn't hear him. My ears filled with the sound of the ocean, the sound of a shell held close to your ear. The rush of my own blood.

My dress had stopped burning. The girl was crying, more than crying, and people were huddled around her so I couldn't see what was happening. A big gear fell to the floor; somebody must have unscrewed it to free her. I saw blood dribble down the blackened gears and begin to pool on the wooden floor, touching but not mixing with the slick oval of oil. Lots of people were gathered around, and I could hear questions rising from the back, but here at the front there were few words, just quick commands by the men who were getting her out. The girl had gone limp, but somebody was in charge. A man was telling everyone to clear off so they could get this girl to the hospital.

The crowd moved back, and I realized Winslow was holding me up.

"Can you move?" he asked.

"Yes."

"Walk?"

"I think so."

"We've got to get you out of here."

Joe leaned down. "Is she all right?" he asked Winslow, as if I weren't right there.

"I'm all right." I was shaking, furious at something or someone. So afraid.

Joe looked at me, and at the dress. "What happened?" he asked in a low voice, as the people around us began to talk. Somebody was crying.

"I don't know. My dress caught fire. She was under there. What was she doing under my dress?"

"She wasn't under your dress. She was under the loom

and you were sitting too close. She's an oiler. They fill the oil pan so the gears don't heat up too much. The pan must've been empty and she was trying to get to it, and you were sitting there, so maybe she waited too long. The friction, if it's not oiled . . . It's my fault," he said. "Jesus, it's my fault."

Winslow pulled me up. "Come on," he said. "If you can walk, we have to get out of here."

I could walk. I leaned against him hard, but I could walk. It was very quiet. I smelled of burned hair and cloth, and my feet were numb. I stared down at my boots and stockings, which were exposed by the burned-away bottom of my dress and petticoat. I felt naked being seen all the way up to the knees. The tops of my knickers were showing, and I wondered vaguely if my stockings had any holes. My toes kept turning in toward each other. I couldn't control my steps and couldn't look away from the floor; I kept seeing that smear of oil and blood right in front of me.

"Who is she?" someone murmured.

"Look at that dress."

"Fine stuff. What's she doing here?"

Winslow looked around but spoke only to Joe. "I'm taking her home, and then I'll be back to see what we can do."

Joe nodded, and he held Winslow's gaze. "I'll wait here, then," he said. "The second hand went with her to the hospital."

"Who was it?" Winslow asked.

"Her name is Lizzie DuBois."

"You tell the second I'll be back, Joe," Winslow said. "You tell them all that I'm going to take care of that girl." He spoke louder now, loud enough for everyone to hear. "All the medical bills, everything. You tell them I'm coming back."

There was no hiding it from my parents when we got home. My mother said little, helped me change out of the dress, and heated up water to wash my face and hands. She gave me a small glass of whiskey and water at Papa's insistence, and we both stayed very still in the kitchen, listening to Winslow explain to Papa in the parlor. Papa wanted to go back over to the mill with him, but Winslow told him that nobody knew who I was, and if he fixed it right nobody would ever know it was me that was there.

"It will just be me," Winslow said. "Not Joe, not your daughter. This is my fault, and I'm the best one to blame, with my father and all."

"Will the girl be all right?" Papa asked. So far he sounded calm, like anybody's father might sound in this situation. Mother and I glanced at each other and then away, hardly breathing.

"They took her up to Mount Hope Hospital. I'll go there after I get back to the mill and square things over there. I'll take care of the girl, you know."

"It was her foot?"

"Mostly, I think. Mostly her foot."

"Still don't get it."

"No. No, well, I wasn't looking."

"You shouldn't have let Frankie go in there, Winslow."

"Yes sir, I know. I am so sorry."

"It's a terrible thing that's happened to the girl."

"Yes sir, I know."

"Well."

There was a pause.

"I'd better get back there, Mr. Ross."

"Yes, you do that. Let me know how Miss DuBois is doing."

"I will."

Another brief pause.

"May I say good night to Frankie, sir?"

"She's with her mother now. I think you should get back to the works."

"Right. Good night, sir. I'm so—so—"

"Get back up to the mill, Winslow," Papa said quietly.

I heard the car start up, and Papa came into the kitchen. He looked at me, stripped to my underclothes with a sheet wrapped around me. He looked at Mother, then pulled his chair up to the table.

"Young Curtis is going to try and keep your—our—name out of it," he said. "That's so you don't lose your chances at the mill yourself."

"I'm never working in the mill!" I said. "I will never—" I knew this was bad for Papa. I didn't want to set him off, but I couldn't help it. My voice went higher and higher.

He stood quickly and slapped me hard across the face. Everything stopped. I stared, and so did he. My cheek was hotter than the whole long, humid day. All that accumulated heat bloomed below my eye.

"You will listen, now." I saw him looking at the side of my face. He was trembling, but he kept talking. Mother didn't move. "In Manchester, I saw a man taken out of his mill for something like this. Wouldn't hire any of his

people, and the whole family went under." He looked at
Mother. "Should be all right if the girl lives. No reason
to— If she doesn't . . . Well." He was breathing heavily
now, and sweat showed through his shirt. "There. I'm
sorry, Frankie . . ." He trailed off, rubbing an open hand
over his fist and returning awkwardly to his chair. Mother
said nothing; her eyes were flat. She made sure that he was
finished and then got up to stand in front of me. I stared
straight ahead into the pattern of her skirt as if it were
wallpaper. But she knelt, touched my face gently with her
hand, then put her head into my lap and her arms around
my back. I didn't dare move. He had hit both of us now.
Papa, who had never hit anyone before.

"We were worried," she said into my petticoat, her back
heaving now. "You were so late, and we were worried. Anything can happen on a boat."

A boat? Was it still the Fourth of July? The boat seemed
like years ago. Ham Curtis and the Victrola playing ragtime. Mother held me tighter, and I rocked with her,
unable to think anymore. Papa got up and put his hand on
her shoulder. I felt her tremble.

"She's home now and there's no harm done," Papa said
in a strangely calm voice. "Her dress is a little burned, but
what's a dress?"

I looked up at him, wondering. All I could see was
harm done.

"We're glad you're home, Frankie," he said in that same
detached tone, and I lowered my eyes.

Mother wiped her face with the edge of the sheet she
had wrapped me in. I didn't want her to move away, and I
put my arms on top of hers.

"What about her?" I asked.

"Your mother was worried, that's all," Papa said.

"No. I mean Lizzie DuBois. The girl at the mill."

"I don't know. Oilers do have to be careful, you know. Those gears heat up, and they're dangerous." Matter-of-fact.

"But she's just a kid. She's younger than me."

"She might not be that young. They take the small ones for that job."

"Why? Why the little ones for that?"

"Because they fit. The mill rats—" He stopped himself. "The children don't grow as tall in the mills." He took my mother by the shoulders, brought her slowly up from her knees to sit in a chair, and gave her the rest of my glass of whiskey. She drank it quickly and started breathing more evenly, pressing her eyes with a dish towel. Mother hadn't cried when we left Poughkeepsie.

"It was my fault, not Winslow's," I said suddenly. "I could've helped her."

They looked at me.

"I could've grabbed her."

"Grabbed her? Grabbed what?" Papa got up and started pacing. "You were on fire, weren't you?"

"But she wanted me to help her and I didn't do anything." I repeated the facts as if it had all happened to somebody else. Lizzie DuBois's eyes locked on mine, her foot twisting into the gears. Mother gave me a look that I knew was supposed to stop me, but I had to keep telling them. "I was scared because my dress was on fire. But I should have— I could see her . . ."

Papa came over and took my face between his hands. I realized that he was strong enough to snap my neck, but now that I had told them everything, it seemed so unimportant. Let him punish me now. I loved Papa no matter what, and it was all my fault.

"That's the last time you say that," he said. I twisted away, but he pulled my chin back very gently so that I had to look at him. "You hear? It wasn't your fault. I mean it, Frankie. It's not just a story for the mill owners, now. Those oilers got a bad job, is all. But you weren't supposed to be there, and people like to blame somebody. Ham Curtis runs this town, and he won't want anything his boy was mixed up in to hit the papers. It's politics, Frankie. You were never in that mill."

I was never in the mill. I had to repeat it back to him before he'd let me go.

The sun had begun to whiten the mist between the buildings when I finally went to bed that night. An unbroken blue sky arched above the mill smoke. It was going to be another scorcher. I soaped again and again in my washstand. I spread my hands out over the bottom of the bowl so that the flower pattern was almost completely covered. I hated my hands, hated myself for not pulling Lizzie away from the gears. The way her eyes had looked as I did nothing with these same hands that floated clean in the soapy water. My dress would be thrown away because of the scorched parts below the waist, not the clean area where Ham Curtis had relieved his sex against me.

Now, I see the Fourth of July, 1916, dividing my life into two unequal parts. There are such nights; when everything changes either by accident or intention—doesn't really matter which—and nobody actually chooses how they behave at a time like that.

We were wrong about the war. It wasn't over by the boys' graduation, and it was Joe who went to France, not Winslow. Of course they both wanted to enlist, but the army took only Joe, the athlete, the star. Winslow had weak ankles, which doesn't seem like much of a reason, but it was the only reason they would give him. His older brother, Tom, enlisted right away. When it was time to join up, nobody was thinking about people not coming back.

The three of us didn't talk much about the accident after that night. We still went to the beach occasionally, but the boys didn't come around as much as they had before. There were reasons, I guess. Joe was working full-time, and Winslow was attending the polo matches, dances, and teas required of him. I heard that Lizzie DuBois was permanently crippled, and the Curtises had covered all of her hospital bills.

I took summer classes at secretarial school. I convinced Papa that I would earn more eventually if I got more training now. I didn't like typing, but it was better than the mill. I never brought lunch for Papa anymore, and if he heard rumors that it had been me in the weave room that night, he never told me. When I asked about Lizzie DuBois, Papa would give me terse updates: She will live. She is learning to walk again. She is leaving the hospital. I was certain that Lizzie herself would never forget my face. We had stared at each other too long for that. But Ham Curtis didn't want a scandal, and there were accidents at the mills all the time. There were even some federal labor managers at the mills that summer, doing safety inspections. All of the kids stayed home for a couple of days, and Papa complained about things slowing down without them, but I liked those days. The streets were noisy with games of tag and peggyball. It felt like a holiday because everyone knew it was only a game and they would be back at work in a few days. Most of the Portuguese families got together for meals in their backyards. Then the inspectors left town, and nobody talked about kids in the mills anymore.

I met some girls at secretarial school who were older, and they were nicer to me than the girls at Borden. I felt shy around them, never said much, but I liked listening to their stories; most of them had boyfriends or fiancés. On the weekends, they sometimes invited me to the picture show, but mostly I hung about the house hoping to hear Winslow's car pull up with Joe in the backseat. I was like a fly tapping at the window, unable to get out and unable to stop trying to break through the glass. I knew there was another life, even in Rock Harbor, but I wasn't sure how to be invited without Winslow. The class I was taking was called Typing into the Future, and I liked the sketch of a young lady dressed for work on the cover of our workbook. In high summer, when I couldn't sleep because of the humidity, I propped her up on the windowsill so she would look as if she were nodding her head at me when tree branches broke up the moon through the window. Everything sounded possible when I was talking to the other girls at lunchtime, but I was afraid to go to sleep at night. The moment of dropping off was the worst, nobody ever there to catch me and some voice in my own throat that I didn't recognize. I had hot-weather dreams. Dreams where the mill accident was going to turn out differently, but I always woke up too soon.

School began at last, and Winslow and Joe were seniors. Basketball season came and went, and this time I went to all the games, but they didn't make it to State. The school year crawled by like penance for me, though I wasn't sure what I had done to deserve the eleventh grade. Papa talked nonstop about the war in Europe all winter long, but nobody else seemed too worried until April, when President Wilson declared war, making all the boys happy. It was good for the mills. The machines were spinning faster and faster, and the price of cotton kept going up. Most companies had switched over to the coarse military cloth that was needed for the war, and Papa, along with the other engravers, became a union man. The skilled craftsmen, mostly English and Scottish with some French Canadians, formed the Textile Council and got pay raises during the war without much trouble. The strike up in Lawrence had happened a few years before we got to Rock Harbor, and 1912 seemed like a hundred years ago by the spring of 1917. Papa wasn't too concerned with anyone but the engravers. He hated the Wobblies who stood around the mill gates, trying to get people to come to their meetings.

"They want the Portuguese, let them have the Portuguese," he said.

"But what do the Wobblies want to do?" I asked one night over dinner.

"They don't even know anymore." He stopped eating

and leaned into the table. "The IWW was pretty much finished in 1912. Debs is a good man, but even he doesn't back them anymore."

"Who's Debs?"

"He was the Socialist candidate who ran against Taft and Roosevelt. The one who's always in jail. Didn't do too badly, either. But the Wobblies are anarchists. They don't know what they want and will do anything to get it."

"What does that mean?"

"They'll blow things up if they have to. They say they're planning on planting bombs, anyway. They'll blow things up over here, but they're too yellow to go and fight over there."

I looked at him. "They're against the war?"

"IWW stands for 'I won't work.' Should be IWF for 'I Won't Fight.'"

"Well, President Wilson was against the war until a few months ago."

Papa put down his beer glass hard. "'Too proud to fight,' yes, Mr. President. Well, I didn't vote him back in."

"And neither did anyone else at this table," said Mother.

"No, but maybe you'll have the vote by the next election. There's those that say you will."

"But who will there be to vote for?" she asked. "Eugene Debs?"

Papa was right about the IWW not getting very far in Rock Harbor; the war was too good for everyone. Mills were running twenty-four hours a day, and most people were happy to work longer shifts for wages that had doubled since the war began. After graduation, Joe worked as hard as he could in the weeks leading up to his departure for basic training. He was worried about his mother and sisters losing his income, and although he would get soldier's pay, he had broken into better wages in the weave room. He wasn't the only Portuguese mill hand running looms, but there weren't many of them. He couldn't join the Textile Council because he was Portuguese, but he didn't seem to care. All that mattered to him was making sure his mother and sisters were in a good spot.

The night before Joe shipped out we drove down to Newport in our old constellation: Winslow and me up front with Joe in the backseat, leaning forward on his elbows. I still couldn't figure out if I was the kid sister or the girl they both wanted. Sometimes they flirted, sometimes I thought they just liked having an audience. I was tired of it and I loved it, and now Joe was going off to war. Winslow was driving his own Pierce-Arrow; it was his graduation present. He had become a bit of a star. It wasn't just the car, it was polo. He was the best polo player ever to come out of Rock Harbor society. This meant that he was playing on the Newport teams, and his father was so excited that he imported an Irish trainer for Winslow, along with an Irish pony.

"You're not wearing your uniform," Winslow said to Joe as we turned down the long dirt lane that led to the polo fields.

"They don't give you a uniform till you get to training camp," Joe said. "Last night for me in civvies, I guess."

"Too bad, you could've gotten lots of compliments."

Winslow had driven all the way up to Boston the week before to try to enlist at a different office, but he was turned away again.

Long branches of maples joined hands over us, and at the end of the road was a strip of ocean. The fields on either side were trimmed and well tended, and as we neared the last field I could see other cars and unhitched buggies. I had been to polo matches before, but never to a Newport match. Acushnet, New Bedford, Taunton—they all had fields, but this one had a view. Winslow parked near the stable and pointed us toward the viewing stands.

"I'm late," he said. "See you after the match."

"Try to stay on the horse," I said. Winslow had told me this was what the players said to each other before they went out on the field. He nodded, then suddenly stopped on his way to the barn and ran back to us. He grabbed my hands and pulled me in a quick circle, spinning me so fast that my hat fell off.

"There's our girl!" he shouted, laughing.

"My hat! You're late!"

He let go and ran for the barn, still laughing. Joe walked up, handing me the hat. I set it back on my head and turned to him.

"Is it good or bad, Joe?"

"Looks fine."

"I mean, Winslow calling me 'our girl.' I don't know if I like it."

"Too bad." He grinned at me.

" 'Nobody's girl' is more like it." I didn't mean to say that to Joe, or maybe it was supposed to be a joke, but there it was. Joe and I were hardly ever alone together; Winslow was always there to fill any gaps of silence. Joe looked over at the women dressed in pale colors who were gathered in the stands, parasols snapping closed as the sun went behind the low hill we had driven down to get here. I watched Joe's long shadow disappear on the grass.

"Or maybe you're *the* girl," he said.

"I don't want you to go away," I said quietly.

"No, me neither," he said. He still wasn't looking at me. "But then what the hell will ever happen to me here? If I can get paid to work for Uncle Sam instead of Ham Curtis, it'll be a change, anyway."

"Maybe there won't be that much difference."

Joe laughed, finally looking me in the eye. "Does anybody ever tell you how smart you are?"

"I don't have any friends but you and Winslow, remember? Not so smart."

"Who needs more than two friends?" he said. "Come on, we'd better watch this match, or Winslow is going to be looking for us when he ought to be looking out for that ball."

I was nervous about going to the stands, which were painted such a perfect white that I wondered if they were touched up by the stable boys before each game. I was wearing a dress that had been dyed with tea when it got too many grass stains, and I had liked the way the color turned out until now. There were more men on the field than in the stands, since so many of the men from Newport had enlisted. The women from Newport were more European. The younger ones bared their shoulders and collarbones with perfectly fitting dresses, while the older ones had gloves that held their hands close inside. It was all silk in shades of dark blue to cream, depending on the complexion of the wearer. There were so many beautiful women, with their hair swept up to reveal perfect skin and

91

translucent ears. Pearls were everywhere, nesting warmly along the breastbone or suspended from earlobes, half-reflecting that expensive flesh. I couldn't stop staring.

Winslow was a superb rider. He leaned over the neck of his pony to hit the ball as casually as if he were lighting a cigarette. The mallets and ponies were flying around so close together that I still don't understand how they didn't smash against each other. But Winslow always seemed to pull up out of the pack, smiling and turning his pony with his knees as he switched hands to hit the ball coming from the other side. Every time Winslow made a goal the crowd cheered for him, calling his name as they used to do for Joe on the basketball court. Winslow brought his mallet upright for a moment of salute, then thundered back into position for the next round of play.

"He could be a politician, you know," Joe said. "He's got that way about him."

"You think so?" I squinted at the field. "He's not very serious."

"Serious? You don't have to be serious to be in politics."

"Do they all know who he is?"

"Probably, but this crowd doesn't care about politics. They're just bored."

"I wouldn't be bored."

"No?"

"How could I be bored wearing a dress like that?" I asked, nodding toward a particularly glamorous girl.

Joe leaned in close. "You don't need to worry about her."

I knew when to stop talking.

The game was almost over. The shadows of the ponies

lengthened, and the tumbled edges of the stone walls were outlined in black. I was aware of every sound, the crack of the mallet on the ball and the restless rustle of dresses.

"A perfect day," Joe said without looking at me.

After the game, everyone walked out of the stands and across the field. Some of them stopped to press down the turf with their boots where the ponies had torn it up. I used my heels to kick it down, so clean and springy. There was something satisfying in making the green lawn whole again with one swift kick.

"Don't you wish you could do this to the whole world?" I asked Joe as I kicked a tuft smooth.

"For the Kaiser!" He stomped next to me, three in a row.

I stomped on the same ones myself. "For luck," I said.

"Joe's the one with all the luck." Winslow was standing there with hands on hips, changed out of his jersey and looking as fresh as ever. That Irish groom must have rubbed Winslow down with alcohol before turning his attention to the pony. "Do you know you're the only two left out here?" Winslow asked. "The field boys are afraid to come out and 'disturb the gentleman and lady.' So I promised that I'd disturb you." He looked around at the flattened turf. "Anything else you need to kick, Frankie? Or shall we go to Island Park and have some steamers?"

We drove over a series of small bridges that led to an island opposite the town of Tiverton, Rhode Island. Island Park was hardly more than a strip of sand between the beaches. It was an amusement park in the summer, and there were some rough bars that stayed open after the families had gone home. It was the kind of place my parents would never go to at night, but Winslow knew his way around. He brought us to a restaurant with a tilted porch right on the beach. We got a table outside, and nobody looked twice at a young lady accompanied by two men. I could hear the lines on the fishing boats creaking at their moorings, and a lighthouse near the mouth of the river blinked a steady beat. There was no moon, and more stars than ever.

Winslow wasn't the only one drinking that night. Our walk across the polo field had changed the world, and Joe wasn't leaving tomorrow. He drank more than I had ever seen him do; it made him laugh and tell stories with Winslow. I was on my third champagne cocktail, and everything felt clear and light. The boys lit cigarettes, and all three of us leaned over the water. The shoreline framed a small cove in front of us, and I could just see the dark outline of an island.

"How far is that island?" I asked.

"Not far." Winslow tapped his cigarette against the rail. "I used to sail around it in the boat races. Remember, Joe?"

"You sailed around it to duck out of the races," Joe said. I could hear his smile in the dark.

"Let's go swimming," I said. Before they could stop me, I hiked up my dress and was over the rail, climbing down the rocks to the tiny beach.

"Frankie!" Winslow threw some bills on the table, and they came after me. I was kneeling down, undoing my bootlaces.

"What? Too cold for you? Nobody will see us down

here if we're quiet." I walked to the water with one bare foot and thrust it in. "See, it's not cold."

Winslow stepped past me and put a hand in. "Yes, it is," he said. "You've just had too much champagne to notice."

"Isn't that what champagne is for?" I asked. "I'm going swimming."

The boys stripped first, walking a little way down the beach to give me privacy. I took off my dress and hung it on the branch of a tree, then I approached them, standing in deep shadow wearing only my underthings.

"I can't undo the corset," I said with a quiver that almost broke into a laugh, and I turned my back to them.

"I'll do it," Joe said after a beat. "I've helped my sisters often enough." Winslow said nothing, but I knew he wasn't turning away. His nipples had hardened in the cold air, and dark hair curled from the top of his undershirt. Joe pulled at the lacing, and I felt it loosen around my breasts and belly. Breathing at last, I turned to face them both, holding the corset up with my hands.

"You two go in first," I said.

They walked obediently to the edge of the water, and I felt a kind of triumph. Tonight they would do whatever I wanted. I pulled the corset off and flung it carelessly behind me. They were wearing their undershirts and drawers, which puffed ridiculously with air as they entered the water. Then I saw white arms and black heads as they dove beneath the water and surfaced and looked back, waiting for me. We all wondered what I would do next.

I was so flushed that the air barely cooled me as I walked into the water wearing only my white bloomers and chemise. I went in under an overhanging branch and didn't even make a ripple in the dark. Nothing had ever felt this good before. It was the champagne and it wasn't. Winslow had done a good job of teaching me to swim in the ocean, and the boys swam close. I felt fingertips and toes and didn't know exactly whose they were. My hair started to come undone, and I pulled the hairpins out, dropping them down forever, letting my hair and the rest of it go. My breasts were pale shadows breaking the surface, and I turned round and round, shy and not shy all at once. The water turned my underclothing transparent, and my nudity was a secret that made me even stronger in the water. If I could do this, I could do anything. Joe and Winslow circled me, leading me out toward the island. Brushing against me and looking when they could, hardly speaking, any of us. I got there first and climbed onto a rock. I pulled my knees up, and my hair was long enough to drape over my body. Joe and Winslow stayed in the water, bobbing up and down, all of us looking up and out.

"Don't grow up too much while I'm gone," Joe said, keeping his eyes averted.

"Look at me." They both looked. I pushed my wet hair back from my shoulders and stood up quickly. "I *am* grown up."

I stood there for a long moment in the needle light of the stars, shocking even myself before I dove back in. I was fast as an eel, slipping between their arms and voices until we reached the beach again. I got out and walked slowly up to the tree where I had undressed, allowing them to look as long as they wanted. I found my clothes cold and filled with sand and left the corset undone underneath my dress. I spread my hair out behind me to dry in the car, and

Winslow sang all the way home with the windows open. Joe smiled and smiled, his left arm stretched out to touch my shoulders as I fell asleep with my head resting between the two of them. I had never felt so loved.

July 12, 1917

Dear Frankie,

This is the first letter I've written since I got here. First morning I've had to do whatever I want. Training camp is not so bad, really. Pretty easy compared to the weave room if you want to know the truth, and there's some great guys here from all over. The food is the lousiest thing besides the beds. I miss the corn and quahog chowder we'd be eating if I was home right now. Here I am writing about food when I should be writing something you might be inter- ested in. It was swell of you and Winslow to come down to the station that early to see me off. Wish I could've seen you a little longer. They say we're going overseas in a couple of weeks, but they won't tell us exactly where. Some of the fellows here want to go over and lick the Kaiser pretty bad. I guess I mostly want to do my job and come back home. But crossing the Atlantic Ocean, now that'll be something worth telling you about. I keep thinking about you sitting on the rock that last night, when we went to Island Park. Is that shocking? Not to you I'll bet.

Keep well and give my best to Winslow.

I can get letters here for another couple of weeks.

Joe

I read this letter over and over. I rewrote my reply so many times that I filled the wastebasket with fist-size chunks of writing paper. Now that he was gone, everything came out sounding formal. I didn't feel anything like the girl on the rock when I sat alone at my desk. In the end I just shoved a piece of paper into an envelope, something I still thought was all wrong, but I was afraid the letter would miss him if I didn't let it go. It was August by now; I took another typing class during the week and watched Winslow play polo on the weekends. But I didn't give Winslow Joe's "best" as he had said I should; I didn't tell him that Joe had written to me at all, or that I had written back. I felt guilty though nothing had happened that I needed to keep secret from Joe—and I knew that Winslow felt the same way; as soon as Joe shipped out we couldn't talk about him.

Mother and I planted a War Garden in the backyard for vegetables, with the Poughkeepsie roses marking the four corners of our plot. Mother surprised us with her patriotism and put the household on a strict program of wheatless Wednesdays and meatless Tuesdays. Papa followed the progress of the Allies on the same square of newspaper that had been tacked to the kitchen wall in Poughkeepsie. He moved the colored tacks forward and back, forward and back, until the whole top section looked nothing like a map anymore, just a pattern of holes.

Papa didn't want to enlist like most of the men from the mill, though of course the younger ones had to register whether they wanted to or not. Each time he moved the blue and red tacks back and replaced them with black ones he said it again: "Guess I'm too old." The conscription cutoff was thirty, and Papa was forty-six. "Guess I'm too old . . ." When he said it in front of his friends from the mill, he always sounded regretful, but I knew better.

One day I cut out a new map from the paper and replaced the old one, carefully putting the tacks exactly where Papa had left them the night before. Mother was glad I was showing an interest. We had been gathering clothing and food for the famine in Belgium. Whenever I didn't finish the food on my plate, it was always: "Think of the Belgian famine." There was Belgium, looking clean and defined on the fresh newsprint. How could my dinner plate affect people so far away? I covered Belgium in black tacks for the German line.

"It's so small."

"Rhode Island is smaller," Mother said.

Papa came home, took one look at my work, and ripped it off the wall. Colored tacks scattered onto the floor, the sound strangely amplified in the close air of the kitchen.

"Where's my map?" His voice was hoarse and dry, and his hands worked themselves hard against the kitchen table. "What did you do with my map?"

I ran to my room and lay on the bed, listening to that strange, scraping voice of his while Mother's voice rose and lowered and rose again. Then, after a long while, came a knock on my door. There was no question of obedience. I opened the door and stood aside, but he stayed out in the hallway. He was holding his work cap in his hands, and he twisted it first in one direction, then in the other.

"Frankie. I shouldn't have. I know you meant well. Please, do forgive me, girl, and come back downstairs now."

He had retrieved the old map from the trash box on the back porch. I was lucky the garbage hadn't been burned yet. In summertime, we usually waited to do the burning until the evening. I sat in a chair pushed away from the kitchen table and watched Papa put the old map back on the wall, but it was only tacked in four corners, and our pale blue wallpaper showed through the holes in the paper like pieces of sky.

"Each of these holes," he said, pointing at the tattered upper part, where France met Belgium, "each pin was placed where hundreds died. Can you imagine it, Frankie? More than a whole shift at the mill, gone in a day. And that doesn't count the Germans."

"Who wants to count the Germans? We hate the Germans."

"Yes," he said. "We must hate the Germans, of course." His voice was so slow and sad that I couldn't talk back. Mother walked over to the table and set down the colored tacks she had gathered into a saucer. She began to separate them by color.

"I am so glad you're too old," Mother said, touching his arm.

Papa leaned back, pulled her close to him, and kissed her gently on the mouth. She flushed but didn't look at me or push him away. He was smiling now, a little embarrassed but mostly proud. Then we all sat down together at the table and Papa replaced all the colored tacks, checking the evening paper for the latest troop movements as he always did.

Winslow started bringing me to croquet parties and dances at the club. Even if he was just using me as a buffer to protect him from the debutantes, I didn't care. Winslow and I were both pretending very hard that everything was exactly the same with Joe gone, and croquet was fun and dancing was even better. The country club was only about a mile from the ocean, so it was always cool on that porch, even on the hottest days. I loved the clapboard white building with its freshly painted black shutters and model sailboats perched on the windowsills. The club was fairly small and sat on top of a hill surrounded by a few clay tennis courts, a nine-hole golf course, and a view of the sea.

It was a strangely lighthearted summer in Winslow's set. The mothers threw parties for the young ladies without men. They complained about the lack of escorts but actually seemed more cheerful than ever. My own mother wasn't included, of course, but she was glad that I was in the right crowd, and she never minded how late I came home as long as I was with Winslow. Cotton hit twenty-seven cents a pound, the highest price since the war began. As soon as I left the house with Winslow, I forgot about my parents, and once I sent off my letter, I almost forgot about Joe. Gas was rationed, and it was unpatriotic to use it for pleasure craft, so Winslow taught me to sail. He had me listen for the flapping luff of the mainsail and adjust the tiller until the sail was tight and everything went still again in the gasless quiet of the war. Winslow filled up my weekends, and I liked it when he leaned close to me in the boat, his arm thrown casually behind me along the gunwale as he managed the tiller with his bare foot.

Winslow was always intent on catching the last of the light on a perfect stretch of sand, with a bottle smuggled under his coat. I had both eyes open, and I wanted that mouth and those arms more than I let on. He was one of those boys that strangers had to turn and watch, he was so awash with careless grace. It wasn't anything like being with Joe. With Joe, we talked and talked; once he was gone, Winslow and I mostly kept laughing, as if we dared each other not to get too serious. There was so much we didn't want to think about. We would have a drink, turn, dance, and sneak away from the rest to go down to the water, always somehow getting down to the water by the end of the night. The summer reluctantly became fall, and neither of us knew what to do about our ease or our longing.

It was my last year of high school, and I folded bandages for the Red Cross in the basement of the church with other girls my age, but even the girls from other schools found me odd. Girls don't like girls whose closest friends are boys. School had always been lonely, but once I met Joe and Winslow, everyone else had seemed superfluous. The girls only wanted to talk about boys, but with Winslow and Joe, I could talk about anything.

September 22, 1917

Dear Frankie:

I did get your letter just before we left and I thank you for it. Don't worry about the subs anymore, we got through all right. The crossing was not as picturesque as I had hoped. In fact, we were below the waterline most of the time. When we got up topside I was glad to smell the air. But it was mostly gray, and when you know there's subs out there looking for you, it's not all that peaceful to see noth-

ing. At night we cruised without lights, even cigarettes were off-limits up on deck. But I did get to see the stars really well. I got a letter from Winslow. He said that he's got a job working with his father on the war effort. That sounds good. He said you even have blackouts there at night to save on electricity and that everyone is doing what they can for the war back home. He also said that the price of cotton is up again, but I wonder who that's really good for. I've met some interesting fellows from New York who have got me thinking about politics a lot lately. But now we're here, and there isn't all that much time for anything but sleeping when you can. I can't tell you where I am, but I can tell you that I'd rather be with you. So you're a senior this year. Don't write to me about parties and dances, I never cared much for either one. Write to me what you never thought you'd say to anybody and we'll keep it just between us.

Joe

I couldn't remember what I had written in my first letter—there had been so many versions—and I didn't know what to write to him now. I put his letter in a shoe box so Mother wouldn't find it, and every morning I told myself I would write to Joe that night.

Ham Curtis had been recruited to be one of the government's Four-Minute Men, orators who went around the country giving short patriotic speeches. Winslow was hired to book him into Grange halls, traveling Chautauquas, and as the "entertainment" before the picture shows began. Winslow liked it because he could work for the government even though he had been turned down by the draft board. I liked going along because we would always stay for the picture after the speech was over. Ham Curtis got the speeches sent up from Washington; four minutes of "Why We Are Fighting," telling people to buy Liberty Bonds or save peach pits to grind into charcoal for the gas masks. Ham would read right off the page with no preparation. He was so good that it always seemed as if he were making it up on the spot. He got teary-eyed on a regular basis.

Sometimes I helped Winslow by retyping the speeches for his father if the copy was hard to read. I liked going to Ham's local office downtown; it felt important. Ham was never there, and the few people who worked for him in the Rock Harbor office treated Winslow and me with respect. I could play at being Winslow's girl without ever having been kissed, play at being a dedicated supporter of his father even though I knew what he really was, and still get compliments for being a patriot.

Then I got a different kind of letter from Joe.

November 10, 1917

Dear Frankie,

I want to tell you not to worry about me, and we're licking the old Kaiser pretty good and all that stuff the fellows here tell their mothers and sweethearts. But I have never lied to you, and I don't want what might be my last words to you to be a lie. The truth is that it is pretty much dumb luck that I'm not dead. I had my first battle, and though I'm glad I didn't run in the other direction, I wanted to. I wish I could have trained as a pilot; maybe they can see more of what's going on from up there. From where I am you just go in the direction you're told and wait to get shot. Didn't need four weeks of training camp for that. I know I shouldn't tell you this stuff, but I don't think anybody back home knows what is really happening over here. Now that I'm in it I just want to live through it, that's all. If that sounds yellow, I guess you won't think much of me. But I'm glad they didn't take Winslow because I don't want to have any more good friends over here. When you write, don't tell me who else enlisted from Rock Harbor because I don't want to think about them and I don't want to meet them. I wish I knew more about why we're over here. Ham Curtis's speeches don't make much sense to me anymore, or I wasn't really listening. But like I said, I don't think that brains count for as much as prayers, or luck, if you don't believe in God. I still pray every single day, more than once. Write to me about your "boring" days as you said in your letter. My days are boring too, but mostly I can't believe that I am so likely to die doing something like digging or eating or sleeping. It's as bad as the picker room, but there's gas instead of cotton dust and you never get to the end of the shift. You can throw this letter away if you want to. I know it's not what anyone back home likes to hear.

Joe

I wrote back. Joe was right. I had no idea what it was like. None of the boys from our town had come home yet, and all I knew was the way they looked when they left, broader and better-dressed than they had ever looked in civilian life. The optimistic marching band that played them onto the train had made us feel like everything would turn out right. All the boys *we* knew would return as heroes.

Joe's letters made me feel very grown-up, as if he were

writing to somebody else. I knew that I didn't want to write about school-sponsored food drives or weekend excursions with Winslow. But I began to write back. I wrote about a dream I had, or what I was looking at through the window. I tried to show him the inside instead of the outside, those little paths of thought I had when I wasn't talking to anybody. I figured he would think I was crazy at first, but then he wrote back in the same way, and it got so that I had to be alone when I read his letters. I would go to my room, shove the back of a chair against the door for privacy, and open the letter carefully, sitting in the center of my bed. "I'm waiting for the sky to turn gray," his letter might begin, and then we were away. Everything I experienced became doubled. I would be in the midst of doing something and simultaneously be composing my letter to Joe about what I was doing. Except when I was with Winslow. I wrote nothing about that.

My head was a hothouse.

Papa always asked after Joe. He tried to figure out where he was in France, and when there was a big battle reported, he would tell me if Joe was likely to have been there. Mother saw the letters arrive, but she never spoke his name.

Joe didn't write about the offensives. He wrote about the food. The sweet odor of German gas. But never the actual battles. I wondered, of course. But there was no comment I could make about the war that didn't sound idiotic, like the awkwardness of apologizing when someone dies. All I could do was write about what I saw back here, how one day looked different from the next through my bedroom window. At home the battles were about how to live "sugarless, meatless, lightless, and wheatless." FOOD WILL WIN THE WAR, the newspapers kept reminding us, but how bad could things be when everybody in Rock Harbor had a job?

On the night 1917 became 1918, there was Prohibition in Rock Harbor, and Winslow invited me to a "Lightless Dance" at the yacht club. Prohibition didn't seem to make any difference to the people I knew. The "medicinal" bottle in my parents' bathroom cabinet was just that. Mother thought that grown people ought to have the self-control to limit their own drinking and had no sympathy for those who lacked that ability. She thought the temperance ladies were only encouraging weakness of character by trying to outlaw liquor. Ham Curtis appeared "wet" to the wet voters and "dry" to the dry ones. It had nothing to do with keeping a well-stocked bar. Winslow was a good teacher when it came to cocktails, and it wasn't that we drank so much when we were together but that we drank every time we were together. I've never had a gift for restraint.

So the yacht club was welcoming the new year by having a lightless dance. This meant that all of the shades would be pulled down tight and covered with black cloth. There would be small candles set in colored glass holders, and I hoped for a band. The whole country had been ordered lightless every night but Saturday, and the law was taken seriously, especially on the coast. If you had a lantern or even a candle showing at night down by the water, you could be arrested for being a spy. It was mostly hysteria, the idea that there could be more German spies than ordinary people who forgot to blow the lights out, but no one felt safe since a German submarine had cruised into Newport harbor right before we were "officially" at war. Even though the sub didn't do any damage, Germany suddenly seemed as close as Providence.

I kept thinking that something big had to happen once I finished high school in June. I refused the corset for good after that night in Island Park, and though I couldn't get away with a shorter, looser dress like Alice Curtis and her friends were wearing, I did have a long string of beads that I slipped over my neck after I left the house. That night I was wearing a close-fitting yellow dress with black trim that Mother had made for me to attend Winslow and Joe's graduation. It still fit, though it had grown tighter in the bust, and I hoped Mother wouldn't notice the shadow of cleavage I was so proud of. Winslow and I rode to the Point in a trolley with the headlights covered by black cloth, so the Germans couldn't use the trolley lights to track our coastline. It was one of those rare winter nights that is clear and cold with almost no wind. My winter coat over my bare shoulders didn't do much to keep me warm, but it was a kind of cold that made me want to open my coat to the night instead of wrapping it close around me.

"Winslow!" Alice Curtis gestured us over to her as soon as we walked in. There was a band, and the darkened windows and candlelight seemed to amplify the music. "Frankie, what a wonderful dress." Her kisses brushed the air next to my face. This was unusually affectionate, and I wondered how much she had already had to drink. Alice and her friends defined the rules of the younger generation, and once she realized that Winslow was going to keep bringing me around, she began to treat me like a kid sister, and the other girls followed her lead.

The green of her eyes was intensified by a blurred outline of black kohl, and she used lip liner to make her mouth appear even more lush. She had just returned from a shopping excursion to New York. Alice's dress was beaded all down the front and swung just below her knees as she hooked her arms between Winslow and me, walking us to the bar, which was set up in a back room off the ladies' lounge, a nod to Prohibition.

Taffy Kent, a handsome blond who already tended to fat, was playing bartender. He poured each of us a fizzy drink with a shot of something clear from an unmarked bottle.

"To 1918!" he said as we raised our glasses. "I'm off next month, Winslow," he added. "Hope the war lasts long enough for me to get some of the Huns for myself!"

Winslow laughed and was about to say something when Alice interrupted. "Taffy, don't go." She sidled around the table to him. "There won't be one man left under thirty. Frankie is the only girl here who still has any fun."

I blushed and didn't look at Winslow, but Alice went on. "If the war keeps going, Winslow will be even more of a catch in a few months than he is now." Taffy seemed about to say something, but Alice looked away. She bored quickly.

"There are advantages to being turned down." Winslow touched his glass to Taffy's. I knew how much Winslow hated to be reminded of his repeated failure at the draft board.

"But you do your part stateside," Taffy said with a certain arrogance. "We all have to do our part." He looked at Alice again. "Despite your orders to the contrary, Miss Alice."

"Here's an order." She was suddenly reinvigorated. "Make me another drink, and not as weak as the last one, Taffy. I know you don't think we ladies can handle our liquor, but I wasn't the one pitching over the Addisons' porch railing last weekend."

Taffy reached for the bottle. It was no secret that he had a weak stomach, and it didn't seem to bother him that everyone knew it.

"Frankie." She looked at me with her head cocked to one side. "I want you to come with me." She took my arm and smiled at Winslow in a way I wasn't sure I liked. "Allow me to have her for a half an hour, little brother. I'm sure you can find something else to do."

Alice grabbed me with one hand and her fresh drink with the other. She steered us into the ladies' lounge and closed the door. It was a small powder room with a wicker table and a pink satin stool facing a mirror. The door to the W.C. led just off this room, and she left me sitting in front of the mirror while she relieved herself with the door open.

"I hope you're not shocked," she called out from the toilet. "But we're practically sisters, aren't we?"

I didn't say anything. I always felt slow and self-conscious around Alice. She came back into the powder room and pulled off her gray cloche, facing the mirror, her face level with mine.

"You need to do something about your hair." She fluffed out her own bob with her fingers. Her hair was straight and dark and hung in a perfect wedge along her rather square jawline. "What do you think?"

"Your hair looks wonderful," I said.

"Yes," she drawled, looking sharply at me in the mirror. "And I think . . . you *are* very pretty, but your face is too small for all that hair, don't you see?"

My hair was piled on top of my head in a roll I had worked hard on all afternoon, and the pieces I had carefully tied in rags the night before fell in loose ringlets. "My face is too small?"

"Too delicate. It's not your face, silly. It's the hair."

I looked at myself in the mirror, and everything about me was wrong. I was no expert with makeup and had only applied lipstick. My skin showed every freckle and red spot that I wished had chosen any other place on my body to appear. My round cheeks and sharp chin had no trace of character.

"Let me?" Alice reached for my hairpins, and after a few hard tugs the whole artful mass came tumbling down. "Now look." She held my hair up in both hands, shortening it into big loops on either side of my jaw. "It will curl nicely if you work on it, and if you don't . . ." She shook her head again for me to admire. "A bob always looks good, even after you go swimming."

"A bob?"

"Well, why not?"

"I don't know. I thought, maybe next year, or—"

"You're right." She stood up abruptly, letting my hair fall in a clump to my waist. "It's a little too old for you."

"It's not that."

She lit a cigarette and leaned against the wall. "No, I think you're right. What would everyone say at school? Of course, Winslow would adore it."

"I've wanted a bob for a while," I lied carefully. "It really would suit my face. Maybe I'll do it next week." I reached for the hairpins and began to coil everything up again.

"Why not right now?" She was leaning over the back of my chair. I could feel her breasts brushing the nape of my neck through her dress.

"Now?"

"Wait here," she said, kissing me quickly on the top of my head. "Sally always keeps a pair of scissors in her bag. We all got our first bobs in this powder room. They even took away the wastebasket to try and discourage us from doing it." She gestured, and ash from her cigarette flicked onto the floor.

"This will be fun." She put her face next to mine in the mirror. "Don't move."

She slipped out the door as I watched the stream of smoke she exhaled hit the mirror in front of me and float down, covering the vanity with a thin gray haze that disappeared as soon as I looked away and back again.

So Alice and Sally cut my hair while I drank my cocktail very quickly and tried to ignore the hair that slipped down the back of my dress and covered the carpet in a widening circle. Sally carried a comb and hadn't had quite so much to drink as Alice, so the lines were fairly straight. But my hair, which was wavy when it had weight to it, curled up as soon as it was released, and when it was all over, the best Alice could do was flatten my hair with water and tell me how lucky I was to have natural curls.

"Your hair is so buoyant!" she said, pressing a little too hard against the side of my head. "It looks beautiful."

I looked like a sheep.

Sally put down the scissors and reached for her drink. "I don't think there's anything else I can do for you."

"You're perfect," said Alice. "You look just like Mary Pickford."

"Mary Pickford doesn't have a bob," I said. "Do you have a hat?"

"A hat?" Alice giggled and turned to Sally. "Do you have a hat, dear?"

"An *extra* hat?" Sally looked at her, and they both let loose, laughing so hard they were almost spilling their drinks.

"Don't worry." Alice turned to me confidentially. "I can take you hat shopping on Monday. We'll go up to Boston."

"Here." Sally handed me a tube of lipstick. "Reapply and let's go show the others."

Boston. Lipstick. I hated them both as I put on Sally's lipstick and followed them out of the lounge.

Alice escorted me past the bar, looking very important and talking nonstop without my hearing a word she said. Winslow was standing near the band watching them play. He longed to play music but had no talent for it, so he always lingered as close to actual musicians as he could. Alice saw him at the same moment I did, and she darted across the front of the bandstand, dragging me along. Winslow saw Alice before he recognized me, and for a moment I saw what he was like when he looked at another woman. It was only a second, but I remember it perfectly: the way his eyes roamed quickly over my body after he had dismissed my face for that of a stranger. Then, perhaps noticing the dress, he brought his eyes to mine for the first time, startled to find *me* looking at him.

"Isn't she extraordinary, Winslow?" Alice turned me around so he could see me from all sides. "Brilliant, don't you think?"

I was too light to speak. My head was floating above my body, untethered by the alcohol and clumps of hair I had left behind. Winslow came closer and reached up to touch the tip of a curl, but he didn't say a thing. His fingers smelled of men's cologne mixed with cigarettes.

"Well, say something. Tell her she's beautiful." Alice was impatiently lighting another cigarette.

"She knows she's beautiful," Winslow said. "Go away, Alice."

Alice stopped the cigarette halfway to her mouth.

"Go away? Look what I've done to the girl! I give you this, and all you can say is 'go away'?"

"Alice." Winslow was still looking at me, but I couldn't look back.

"Winslow—"

"No, forget it." Winslow unhooked my arm from Alice's grip. "You stay here. We're leaving."

He took me across the dance floor to the sound of Alice's erupting voice, and led me through a small foyer and up the stairs to the second floor of the club. I don't know why I started shivering. I shouldn't have felt any colder with a bob than with my hair swept up. Somehow he had grabbed our coats, and he wrapped mine around me.

"You don't want to be there," he said as we walked down the narrow hallway and up another set of stairs. "Come on." He jiggled a lock and pulled on a door handle, and we went up again. This time the stairway ended in the dark, and he pulled on a rope that hung from the ceiling where the stairs ended. A trapdoor swung down, and a ladder folded out. Winslow gripped my hand, and we mounted the stairs as if we were stepping from the shore onto a boat.

Winslow moved something heavy aside and led me to a love seat in the attic of the club. There were windows on all sides, and as soon as I sat down Winslow stepped away and pulled the trapdoor up behind us, sealing us off. Cold white light came streaming through the curtainless windows all around us.

"Where are we?"

"The cupola." He sat down next to me. "The widow's walk is just outside. The club used to be a whaling captain's house, you know. Actually, he was an ancestor of mine. Owned one of the largest merchant sailing vessels in New Bedford, until she went down one winter. *The Empress of the Sea.* The Curtis legend is that there's a wreck somewhere off Martha's Vineyard filled with gold bullion. About every ten years there's talk about finding it and getting the gold dredged up from the bottom. But everybody around here has a story like that."

Not quite everyone, I thought.

"You hate it, don't you?" I pulled at the side curls as if I could actually do something about them.

"I don't like Alice pushing you around, that's all."

"I let her."

"Yes, well, she's awfully good at it. Let's see . . ." He moved some boxes off the top of a low vanity that was facing us. There was a big round mirror sitting upright, and he wiped the dust away with his sleeve. I saw my face and understood why Winslow hadn't known me.

"I look older," I said. In fact, I didn't hate it so much now that I was away from Alice. "I look so different."

"You do." Winslow turned my face toward him. "If Alice wanted to make a fool of you she couldn't, you know."

115

"So you like it?"

"I like you."

"But tell me about my hair. Tell me the truth, Winslow."

"I'm crazy about it."

He pushed the coat down from my shoulders and began to kiss my neck, reaching his hand behind my head to tilt my face away. He licked my ear, his tongue finding the smallest paths and furrows, and sending me shaking.

"I'm crazy about you, Frankie." He was so close that it sounded like he was speaking inside my head. He turned me toward the mirror before kissing me on the mouth, and when I opened my eyes I saw a stranger being held by a stranger. All of the waiting rushed away. His hands moved from the outside to the inside of my silk dress, and I never thought about anything but how much more of him I wanted.

His breath and mine made dense clouds as they hit the air together. He pulled my dress half up, and when he raised himself and pulled me onto him, there was a sharp pain that made me gasp, and he held there unmoving inside me for what couldn't have been forever. Then in two swift moves, he was widening and deepening the way into my body.

His head dropped heavily, and I felt the sweat of his cheek against my neck, like a seal or a brand. Our hips stayed where they were, with his chest rising and falling hard against mine and the deeper pulse of his heart going from fast to slow.

So this is love, I remember thinking. This is Love.

1918

AFTER THAT NIGHT, THINGS WERE CLEAR FOR A LITTLE while. We had to be in love if we were going to keep doing what we were doing. I was sure my mother would smell it on me. She would see it in my face and in the way I lifted my arms as I undressed for bed. I had done the most terrible thing an unmarried girl could do.

Nothing happened.

My parents looked older to me; they were upset about my bobbed hair, but I could never really be punished like a child again. I waited for the fight over my hair to die down and began to imagine not living with them anymore. Winslow gave me that. He was nineteen, and it was his first time too, but he took care of me in bed. He was in charge of making sure we wouldn't have a baby, and most of all he listened to my skin. The more sex we had the more unstoppable I felt.

Alice and her set still scared me. Alice could take me

down for the fun of making something happen. She was
the one I was most afraid would find out what had happened that night in the cupola. What kept happening
when we took the trolley to "see the ponies" at the stables
outside of Newport. I turned seventeen in February, and if
a man said he loved me, I believed him. It was the oddest
bit of luck that Winslow *did* love me and wanted to marry
me. He kept telling me that he wanted me to be his wife,
and I kept telling him he didn't.

"I'm not rich enough."

"I'm rich enough."

"And besides, I'm from Poughkeepsie."

"I'll move to Poughkeepsie."

"No, no. Please, no."

"Are you sure? We can buy your parents a new house
there." He knew I hated Poughkeepsie.

"This is all after we get married?"

I would be laughing by now, maybe leaning away from
his arm as he tightened it around me. Winslow had a key
to the tack room at the polo stables. We learned about sex
on a wooden floor covered by horse blankets, pushing our
bare feet against the leather tack he had moved aside, and
always smelling the dense odor of horse sweat and manure.

"Before."

Kiss.

"After."

Kiss.

"Whatever you want."

That's what it seemed like. Whatever I wanted.

When Winslow was kissing me, I believed everything
would come out perfectly; it was only later, back in my

own room, that I got scared. I thought about Joe, the letters from him that kept coming even though I couldn't answer them anymore. I thought about this hunger Winslow and I had for each other, and how it unlocked us. We mapped our lives for each other up until this point of overlap that now seemed inevitable. I told him about what had happened with Papa in Poughkeepsie, and he listened; then I was quiet while he talked for long stretches, and he wasn't always joking anymore. He told me to keep my eyes open when we were making love, and he did the same. I watched as his pupils widened in pleasure, and once, when I put my hand on his chest, just after, he began to cry. We didn't have to talk about why, because by then I knew the complicated heft of his life and I loved him and he knew it. He was nineteen and I was seventeen and we held each other so completely. All this and still, when I wasn't in his presence nothing was enough to keep me from feeling afraid.

Winslow was the one who gave me the news.

I heard the sound of his Pierce-Arrow coming down our block long before he got there. The evening shift at the mill wouldn't let out for another two hours, so the streets were quiet, and the sound of a car engine was odd because of gas rationing, and late spring rain and melting snow had turned the streets to mud; nobody was driving when they could take the trolley. I heard the car stop right in front of the house, and Winslow slammed through our front door with one of Joe's sisters right behind him. The girl was

119

talking, and Winslow was talking, and in the middle of it all Winslow handed Papa a telegram that he read aloud in his official British manner, which always got people to pay attention. It was April 25, 1918.

PRIVATE BARROS WOUNDED. STOP. PERMANENT LOSS OF VISION LEFT EYE. STOP. SHIPPING HOME. STOP.

As if someone had been holding up the needle of a Victrola and then dropped it down, the noise all started again. The sister began crying, and I realized I didn't even know her name. She had gone to find Winslow after they got the telegram, and Winslow had come to find me.

"Somebody has to be able to do something for my brother," she said, looking from Papa to Winslow.

My father and Winslow were talking loudly, interrupting each other. Papa dragged them both into the kitchen to look at the map and find where Joe had been wounded; it could have been in a place called Seicheprey, Papa said, where there had been a big battle. Did anyone know where Joe was stationed?

Mother put dishes of food out, then carried them back into the pantry and put the kettle on. She kept trying to get everyone out of the kitchen—the only room where everyone wanted to be. I took the telegram from Papa and read it over and over again. Joe had to be all right. But your eyes were in your head. Had he lost an eye? How could you be shot in the head and be all right?

"Frankie, you have his letters. Find out where he was most recently. Then we can know if he was in Seicheprey."

I looked up at Papa. "What?"

"The boy's letters, Frankie. Run and get them. He writes you all the time. You can help us find out where he is."

"If we know where he was wounded," Winslow said, "then maybe we can see if he's on his way home yet."

Where he was. Something to do. I got the box of letters from my room and ran back to the kitchen. It was only as everyone gathered close that I realized what I was doing. I tried to cover the box with my hands.

"So many letters," said Joe's sister in a low voice. I looked at Winslow; he kept his eyes on the box of letters.

"When was the most recent one?" Papa was ignoring all this. He held out his hand for the box, but I waited for Winslow. Nobody could read those letters aloud, even if Joe was dead.

"Just the postmark, it may be helpful," Winslow said quietly. I handed him the box. He took it, and I saw that his hand was shaking; he steadied himself with his other hand, as if to ground his trembling against the wide wooden planks of the kitchen table, and took out an envelope.

"March second, March twenty-fourth." Winslow looked at the postmarks of the topmost letters on the pile. I could have done that, I thought, stupid, stupid.

"But these letters," the sister said. "They're not opened." She reached in as quickly as a fish and turned over four more letters. "You don't open his letters?"

"I do," I said. "I do, I just haven't—" I dug down into the pile and pulled up the open ones. "See, I do read them, I just . . ." I stopped talking. It was clear enough that no matter what *I* had done, Joe had kept writing.

"That's a lot of letters." Winslow handed me the most recent letter. "Read it if you want to."

"Of course I want to."

121

"Of course she does." Papa leaned over my shoulder. "Joe's sister can't help him if we don't know where he is."

The unsealing of that envelope sounded like I was ripping the whole room open. I tried to read, but there was no real possibility of speaking. I held the paper between my face and the rest of them, trying to hide the obvious fact of my tears.

"Just the name at the top," Winslow said. It was exactly the same pitch his voice had when we were making love. "All we need is the place he's writing to you from." I wanted so much to stop crying as I looked at him.

"All it says is: 'Somewhere in France,'" I whispered.

"What?" Papa reached for the letter, but I stepped back. "Somewhere in France?"

"That's for the censor. They have to do that. I forgot, it's the same with my brother, they do it with all the letters." Winslow adjusted himself so that his back blocked me from my father, protecting me.

"Well, that's no good."

"She doesn't open his letters?" Joe's sister looked at Mother, who handed her a cup of tea but said nothing. My head was pounding, and I couldn't find a handkerchief for my eyes and nose.

"Won't the army know?" Winslow turned to Papa again.

"The army told you what they know. It's all in the telegram."

"Why don't you open his letters, Frances? My brother never writes me so much."

"Can he survive that kind of a head wound?"

"The telegram says he's wounded. That means he's alive."

"But you said they don't know."

"You've got to go to your father, Winslow. They bloody well know where Teddy Roosevelt's boys are, don't they?"

"My father might be able to—"

"Call from the hallway if you'd like."

"I'm coming with you." The sister stood up from the table.

"No, I'll take you back."

"He's my brother, I'm going with you."

"If you really think—"

Papa interrupted. "What I think is that getting Joe on the soonest shipment home could make a difference. Your father can probably make that happen."

"Yes, sir. You're right, sir. You're sure you want to come?" Joe's sister nodded.

The door slammed. Cold wind in and out and they were gone. I had not been able to look at Winslow again. I was suddenly jealous of him and my father. They were so sure of themselves, and Winslow could put off thinking because he had something to do.

I went to my room.

I read the letters that had been coming since New Year's Eve.

They were too much like my conversations with Winslow, and they were nothing like them at all. I saw that Joe was still there. He drew sketches in the margins of small, knobbly trees that lined the roads in France. He never asked why I wasn't writing back. He wrote about the reflected light he saw from the trenches and how watching the artillery fire could almost warm you up at night. He told me about food and card games; they all bet money

123

they didn't have, using stones for coins. He asked what the weather was like in Rock Harbor, if the water was warm enough for swimming yet, and I knew I was a piece of his longing for home. How he missed me even though I was not writing back and had wished those letters away. I told myself I had never made any promises and he had never asked me to; he hadn't even kissed me. He never asked me to wait for him. He should have, and then I would have, I told myself. But none of that made me feel any better as I smoothed out the dirty, thin paper, creased in ways that showed how long each letter had ridden in his pocket. The longer he was gone the more spelling mistakes he made. I had stopped writing because I was afraid that Joe would know everything had changed from the first word. I was sure the way I formed the letters would reflect the places my hands had been. After New Year's Eve, it had no longer been possible to write a world without Winslow.

I read every letter from Joe like penance, and it didn't do me any good at all.

I wrote one letter back, telling him I knew he was wounded and how much we all wanted him to come home. I mentioned Winslow as if I had always talked about him in my letters. Then Joe stopped writing to me, so I knew that he had gotten that letter, and everything I heard about him started to come from his letters to Winslow.

That was in the spring. It felt like twenty years passed between April and October.

Fall 1918

❧

I HAD GRADUATED FROM BORDEN IN JUNE.
I had smiled at my parents and they had smiled at me.
I had helped organize benefits for the Red Cross.
I had stopped writing to Joe.
I had learned how it felt to be envied.
And I had stopped writing.
I had learned how to please Winslow in and out of bed.
And I stopped writing.
I had fallen in love.
And I stopped writing to Joe.

Then August came searing in, and Tom Curtis was killed in combat. I finally saw all of the yellow stars in the windows that showed a family had lost a son. Two sons. Three sons. Winslow stopped laughing so easily, put in more hours working for his father, and stayed home most nights. He told me he would have cried more if he had known Tom better, and then he did start to cry.

On the first of September, my mother slapped me across the face for singing the ditty on everyone's lips:

I had a little bird. Its name was Enza.
I opened the window. And in-flu-Enza.

After, she stared at her own hand, and then her cough came back, bringing tears that she wiped away impatiently. She said she was sorry, she never should have touched me, and quickly folded her handkerchief, hoping I hadn't seen the blood. I saw how narrow her shoulders were, how her wrists were much smaller than they used to be, and I didn't remember when her long hair had begun to go gray.

Winslow and Alice had moved into their aunt Beverly's summerhouse in Tiverton, where the air was healthier. Winslow wrote to me from there that Alice hardly left her room since the news had come about Tom, and for himself, Winslow seemed bewildered. I hated being away from him, hated that I couldn't hold him, even though we were living only ten miles apart. All these deaths were making me selfish. I wanted to do everything for Winslow just when I could do nothing, not even touch the back of his hand or grip his shoulder blades when he held himself close above me. Winslow felt like all the good I had in the world. Ham Curtis, who stayed up in Boston, made a speech about the "Corpse Crisis." There was no keeping up with the bodies. We all wore gauze masks and avoided going past the cemeteries where the bodies were piled up, waiting to be buried.

Then there was an early frost, and the ground hardened up so quickly that the corpses stayed right where they were. Some said the cold weather was a blessing, even if it meant the bodies couldn't go into the ground. The newspapers said that the flu was transmitted more easily in warm weather, but most people blamed the Germans. All the houses in our neighborhood had the yellow star in the window or a wreath on the door. We kept up with the cause of death because the army sent the star and the union sent the wreath. There was plenty of work at the mill, but For Rent signs began going up in the apartment windows.

I woke up in the middle of September unable to move with exhaustion and nausea, and I knew. I had never tied the bottom of my mask securely enough. By the time Mother came down with it, I figured it was too late for a mask and had put it on only to please her and Papa. I started going to bed before the shift at the mill was out. Papa was on his own with us; nobody would come in regularly to nurse the sick anymore. But Papa seemed to have more energy than ever. He liked being the one to take care of us, and he hummed the old songs as he moved from room to room, bringing us hot lemon water to drink and mustard compresses for our chests. I had never known Papa like this, and I saw how Mother watched him every minute, too weak to get up but strung tight inside, waiting for signs of his "Poughkeepsie Trouble" as she called it, to tip the balance.

I wasn't coughing, and even though I couldn't keep any-

thing down, there was no fever, so I was able to get out of
bed and make food for us in the afternoons, though all I
could bear to cook were potatoes. When the doctor came,
he looked at my throat along with everything else, then
told me that he was too busy and that I should get out
of bed, keep my mask over my mouth, and take care of
Mother. I was expecting a baby, he said, and not to bother
him again until I was ready to bring it into the world.

I hadn't even told Winslow I was sick.

The baby bled out of me six days before Winslow and I
were married in a brief ceremony attended by Ham Curtis,
Alice, and my parents. Winslow had insisted on getting
married even after I lost the baby, though I told him we
didn't have to. We were in the tack room again, the only
place I felt safe.

"I wanted to marry you anyway, Frankie. This just
makes it a little sooner." Winslow leaned his head against
his arm and stared at the ceiling. We were lying warm
under the good blanket that he kept hidden behind the
regular tack.

"Your father thinks we're only getting married because
I'm—I was."

"My father doesn't think you marry girls just because
they get pregnant, Frankie."

I pushed both hands against my belly, hating its betrayal.

"Frankie, please. I've been asking you since January.
Since before all this happened."

"People will think."

"Yes, they will. But now—"

"Now there's no baby, so there's going to be nothing for them to think."

"I wanted the baby, Frankie."

"You don't have to marry me, anymore."

"I want to marry you, Frankie. We'll have another one."

"What will your father say? What about Alice? Did you tell them what the doctor said? About losing the baby?"

"I told them."

"And?"

"And I told them that the wedding is still on and they are invited if they choose to attend."

"They won't like you getting married like this. Your father's never liked me. It's not what they expected."

"Nothing's regular anymore, Frankie."

"No." I turned my face in to his shoulder, and he pulled my hands up, pressing them tight between his broad palms.

"What about Joe?" He would be home soon.

"Joe?" Winslow sat up. "He always knew I wanted to marry you."

"He did?"

"Sure. He would've asked you himself but he knew you couldn't marry a Pawtugee."

He lay back down so that I had to look him in the eye.

"Do you, Frankie? I mean, do you still want to marry me?"

It was very grand and cold in the church, and Mother's labored breathing echoed after each word that was spoken.

Everyone including the minister wore a gauze mask for the occasion. Winslow lifted first my veil and then the gauze as we became husband and wife. He had asked me to keep my eyes open when I kissed him, and when I did I found that I was happy. We were married on the twenty-first of October, and I don't believe anyone cried at the ceremony, though it was the only wedding performed that fall in St. Paul's Church.

On the thirtieth, Joe's boat was steaming unstoppably up the coast from New York to Fall River. Winslow and I waited at the wharf for Joe with his mother and two sisters. It had taken six months to get him home, despite Ham Curtis's efforts. The hospital in France kept him for a long time after his eye operation. Then he was moved to England, where he was put into a ward for head injuries, another in-between place with many, many soldiers. The shipping lanes were unsafe, and the hospitals were understaffed. He said later that his head was mostly fine by that time, so he learned English card games and smoked free cigarettes.

Joe finally got a boat from London to New York in the middle of October, and from there he got a booking on the Fall River Line. Winslow borrowed his father's big car so that there would be room for the Barros family, and Joe could be more comfortable going home. Winslow knew his father didn't really want a lot of Pawtugees riding in his car, but now Joe was a war hero, and we rode up to Fall River with Joe's family in a car whose upholstery seemed to rebuke us. Once we got to the wharf, we all got out, leaning into a damp wind cutting across the river. Winslow kept urging Mrs. Barros to sit, but though she smiled almost constantly when he spoke to her, she refused to get back in the car. The landing was piled high with raw cotton, and a group of Cape Verde men were hauling the bales back and forth from the boat landing to the train cars. It was like standing in the middle of a maze with constantly shifting walls. I noticed how the cotton turned red around the baling wire with the blood from the men's cracked hands. There was nothing really soft about cotton, I decided, pulling my new winter coat tighter and trying to look away from the bright pink smudges. Mrs. Barros stood very still, her eyes flicking between the dock and the river where Joe's boat would appear. Winslow talked non-stop about how the Fall River Line would have to expand farther until it reached Rock Harbor.

"It's only a matter of time. My father says that cotton prices are still on the way up, and with the war and all, we should be able to convince the line to make another landing in Rock Harbor. Save money and manpower on shipping . . ."

On and on and on.

"You sound like you want to keep the war going just so you don't have to drive to Fall River," I said.

"Frankie." Winslow's eyes went wide at me for a second. "I'm only saying that it makes sense because—"

I reached for his hand and kissed it quickly. All I wanted was for Winslow to please, please stop talking. We hadn't discussed Joe except for the details of getting him home. Winslow didn't ask about the letters, and I had no idea what to say. I couldn't tell him that my letters to Joe were how I looked at the world, if the world existed without Winslow. That for a while I had been able to invent a world without him.

131

The boat was there; then the boat was here. Winslow and the Barros women pushed me along with them to the bottom of the gangplank. They were all straining forward. I kept to the other side, apart from Winslow. I thought that I could stay back when Joe came down to us. But then he was there so quickly, looking lean and sharp and turning his head in an unfamiliar way, trying to take us all in at once. His arms held me like a brother, like a stranger, and he no longer smelled like a boy.

"Congratulations, Mr. and Mrs. Curtis," Joe said right away, taking off his brown cap with a flourish that did not quite succeed. "Sorry to have missed the wedding." There was a bandage around Joe's head, hiding the one eye, and his hand trembled as he held his mother's weight against him. Winslow touched my arm possessively as he handed me into the backseat, and Joe's two sisters never stopped talking, but I don't remember anything they said. His sisters kept reaching from the backseat to touch his hair, his shoulders, the backs of his arms. His mother sat next to him in the front, speaking in Portuguese and English, feeling his bandage without hesitation.

I couldn't stop staring at the slight hollow at the base of his skull. I wanted to touch my fingers to his scalp and feel the pulse of blood moving there. I sat in the backseat and stared at that one spot of light brown skin with the whorl of black hair just above it, praying for forgiveness.

We had picked Joe up in Fall River on a Wednesday, and a little more than a week later he was eating dinner with us at the big house on Highland Avenue. After the wedding, Winslow and I had moved into his childhood home. I could hardly believe that I had anything to do with that house, the house I had walked past so many times, the house where Joe had come out of the side yard with the money and the bicycle. I loved walking up to the front door and opening it without bothering to use the brass knocker. But all I truly felt qualified to do was to put my arms out and spin circles in the foyer when nobody was looking. I tried not to look around for somebody else when the servants called me "Mrs. Curtis." Alice moved back in as well, and she oversaw the hiring of new servants to replace the ones who had left when the house was closed up for quarantine.

"I don't think these people are very likely to go down with the ship," Alice said, after introducing me to the new cook, maid, and gardener. I was so thrilled at the idea of having other people to do the cooking and the housework that I wasn't paying much attention to the details. In Poughkeepsie, gardening was a primary subject of conversation, and nobody we knew had a full-time gardener. I suddenly wondered if my mother would approve of a gardener, though I knew that she approved of the house, the marriage, and the Curtises. Perhaps I had solved everything. It all felt like playing house, just as I had done with my cousins under the dining room table with a sheet thrown over the top for walls. We would order the dolls and stuffed animals to clean up the patty pans and real china tea set after they had finished having a party—but we always knew who really had to clear things away at the end of the game. I had been living in the Curtis house for over a week, and I was still waiting for someone to tell me that I should put away my things. I was self-conscious when left alone in the house, and each morning I wished desperately that I was still going to have a baby. Every day I counted how far along I would have been, but I never told Winslow. He wanted so badly for me to be happy, and I told him that everything was perfect. I knew I was terribly lucky to be waking up in such a room, in such a house, with such a man. Perfect.

Alice and I were alone one afternoon, after she had introduced me to the new staff. She had kicked off her shoes and stretched out on a horsehair couch that could barely contain her, her knees hooked over one end as she dangled her feet in the air. Outside, it was the kind of day that makes you finally give up on autumn, a rain that seemed to get colder as the day went on without ever managing to turn to sleet.

"No, that cook is not a stayer, I'm afraid. But the war will be over soon, and they'll be glad to have a job." Alice wore her silk stockings rolled down to shock the Rock Harbor matrons. I still wore my dresses longer than she did and never rolled my stockings down.

"They seem happy to be here." I leaned back, pretending to be at ease.

"Oh, yes. I'm sure they are happy enough." Alice looked closely at me. "The main thing with servants is not to be afraid of them, Frankie."

"Of course I'm not afraid of them!"

Alice smiled quickly. "All you really have to do is tell them how many for dinner and what you'd like them to prepare. Winslow will pay them, and when Papa comes to town, he'll have his secretary tell them what to do and who is coming." She shifted to her side. "And birthdays and Christmas, you give them money. Don't forget."

"But you'll be here too."

"Not always." She looked at me from under her long lashes. She had started wearing heavier eye makeup, and her hair was cut into a fringe that curled over her eyebrows. "I may begin to spend more time away. I told Daddy that you and Winslow were moving into Mother's old bedroom."

"But what about when he comes to stay? I mean, it's his room too. Perhaps we shouldn't—"

Alice laughed and waved her cigarette at me. "Don't be absurd. Papa always stays in his own room, the green room on the second floor. Winslow can tell you all this. He should tell you *something*."

"So, your father doesn't mind? He hasn't stayed overnight since—"

"All he wants is somebody from the family living in the house so that he can still be a resident of Rock Harbor for the next term."

She stopped talking for several minutes, which was so unusual that I waited for her to gather up the next rush of words. Out the window, the big elm swayed respectably as yellow leaves whirled off and stuck to the ground like scattered playing cards. "I don't like it here very much," Alice said quietly. "But that doesn't really matter. I hope you and Winslow will enjoy the house."

"I'm sure we will," I said. "I'm so sorry about Tom."

"There were always a lot of people here, even though I didn't like having them here most of the time. But even

if—even if everyone had come home like they were supposed to . . . Oh, Frankie, I might as well tell you. I'm
moving to New York."

"To live? Does Winslow know?"

"I'll come back and check on things, don't worry. There's
a lot going on in New York. I don't really shop there, you
know. I've decided to become an agitator."

"A what?"

"For the vote, Frankie. I can use the Curtis name to
get us publicity whether Ham likes it or not. It's much
more engaging than shopping and—" She got up briskly,
and before I knew quite what was happening, she had
slipped on her shoes and coat and was kissing me on the
cheek. "Actually, all these deaths have made me feel like I
don't have a moment to waste. And I think it's important.
Equality of the sexes, you know. I mean, equality in *all*
things. Don't look so worried, Frankie. I'm coming back
for dinner tonight. Winslow said something about Joe
Barros coming by, and I may invite a few friends as well, so
you should order the cook for six at eight."

I wandered through the house all day. I had a hope—
no, a superstition—that touching everything in the house
would transform me into the new Mrs. Curtis. I ran my
fingers over walls that were covered with wallpaper that
wasn't paper at all, but silk. A pattern of light blue land-
scapes with a girl on a swing was in the living room. Pale
yellow and white stripes covered the hallways upstairs and
downstairs, while the bedrooms had an identical floral pattern over different background colors. Those colors were
matched by monogrammed towels that hung in each bathroom. I was glad to know that the contents of Tom Curtis's

former bedroom had been respectfully packed away into labeled trunks that I would never have to open.

There were family portraits. Oil paintings of each of the children hung in the dining room at evenly spaced intervals around the long polished table and teak sideboard. Mrs. Curtis took the space above the fireplace in the living room, gray streaks in her brown hair and a touch more thickness to her neck than her daughter's. Alice wore no jewelry in her portrait, whereas Mrs. Curtis had pearls. The senator himself dominated the front entrance hall, with the seal of the Massachusetts Senate hanging midair in the upper right-hand corner, apropos of nothing in the country squire setting behind him. The same artist had been commissioned for all the portraits, and he had painted the same expression on all of their faces, altered only by the sex of the sitter. The women's lips curved slightly upward; the male members of the family were given stronger jaws and a more determined air. Every eye was blue, despite real evidence to the contrary. Winslow had been painted in his polo clothes, while Tom was wearing a school jacket and tie. The identical eyes spooked me as they followed me around the dining room through some portrait artist's trick. But more surprising than that was a slow leak of despair as I realized these paintings could never be moved or replaced.

The rugs were Oriental, and one could never feel the floor beneath them, as they were placed over thick horsehair matting. The chairs and even the sofas were shallow and taut, made for perching rather than sitting. But I didn't feel like sitting, afraid I might miss passing my fingers over something. In the living room the side tables were heavy with glass-shaded end lamps. Alice had told me they were from Tiffany, and their dense reds and blues glowed even when unlit. There was a card table with a dark green leather center and small drawers on each side that I pulled out one by one. The usual random playing pieces, dice, and shreds of loose tobacco. The mantel held a heavy glass ashtray and two crystal bowls containing painted wooden eggs. I took a cigarette from the engraved silver box that rested next to the ashtray and tried to take my time smoking it, leaning against the mantel as if I really needed a rest from something. I was posing in case one of the servants came through. But the house was very still in midafternoon, with all of the cleaning and polishing done for the day. I put the cigarette out halfway, feeling sick. What did married women do when they didn't have a baby? I wanted Winslow to come home and remind me that I was happy.

The French doors that faced Highland Avenue from the living room were covered by winter drapes of a deep yellow color that seems to exist only in velvet. I pulled one close around me, the thick cloth warm and soft against my arms and neck. I would like to have a dress made from these drapes, I thought, closing my eyes as I realized I could go to the dressmaker and order one if I chose. Who cared if I couldn't take down those portraits? I wouldn't know what to put in their place. I curled like a chrysalis inside the living room drapes. I didn't want to change a thing in this house. I simply wanted to stay here for as long as I could, feel those solid, silk-lined walls about me all day long. I made my way upstairs, trailing my fingertips along the smooth curve of the banister, and fell asleep in the guest bedroom without meaning to, perfectly aimless.

I woke when the front door banged open, well before dinnertime that night.

"Frankie! Frankie, it's over!" Winslow was yelling. I heard him ringing the door pull over and over like a little boy. I reached the top of the stairs at the same moment that the servants reached the foyer. Winslow and Joe were standing in the front hall soaking wet and looking so blown that I was sure they were drunk. We hadn't seen Joe since the day we met his boat. The door was wide open behind them, and Winslow turned around to face the street.

"The war is over!" he yelled. "Armistice declared!" I ran down the stairs into both of their arms. The servants were kissing and crying.

Joe whirled the downstairs maid right off her feet, laughing in a way that I didn't know he could anymore. He had traded his bandage for a patch across the eye and was wearing a new suit. The purple heart was pinned onto his lapel.

"Papa called the mill office," Winslow said. "They're going wild in New York right now! Fifth Avenue is all jammed up with ticker tape, bands playing. It's over, Frankie!"

"May I have leave to go, madame?" asked Allie, the new cook. "My son is over there, and my Ned, he's at the Brayton Mill."

"Should have closed the works down, Winslow," said Joe. "Let them off early today."

"Now Joe, you always think I can do things I have no authority to do."

It was the Armistice, and that seemed enough to make Winslow and Joe friends again.

"Mrs. Curtis, may we go as well?" I looked at the remaining two servants and realized with surprise that they were speaking to me.

"Of course, of course you may go."

So the house was ours, and later that night I found myself frying the steaks that Allie had left out on the marble counter, with the fat sliced off in clean white strips. Up the Flint we had never cut the fat off the meat. I wasn't sure what to do with it until Joe came in to help. Mother always did the cooking at our house, and though I had helped to prepare, I realized now that helping in the kitchen was a little like riding in the car when you don't know how to drive. Winslow and Alice were in the living room with some of her friends, and champagne had been brought up from the cellar. Nobody had eaten a thing. It was Joe who finally took charge and insisted that we find some food for everyone.

"They're getting hungry in there," Joe said as he took off his jacket and draped it over a kitchen chair.

"They're getting drunk." I watched him cut the fat into chunks and throw it into boiling water for the rice.

"We'll do the rice Portuguese style." He raised a glass of champagne. "They'll love it."

I could tell he was a little drunk too from the way he cocked his head more to the side when he looked at me. I wasn't used to his one eye, and I tried not to stare, but the champagne made me feel loose-limbed and uncaring.

"Mrs. Curtis," he said. I giggled and shook my head. It was the first time we had been alone since he came home.

"No, no. Mrs. Curtis is dead."

"But you are the new lady of the house. Even Alice says

so." Joe was speaking quietly, but his voice had turned hard. He lowered the flame under the steaks so they wouldn't burn. "The Queen is dead. Long live the Queen."

"Joe." I wasn't giggling anymore.

He wouldn't look at me and jabbed at one of the steaks until a small pool of blood showed on the top.

"They're not quite ready, Mrs. Curtis."

"We got married when I thought I was going to have a baby. But then I didn't. We lost the baby."

"Just a little longer and they'll be perfect." He picked up the lid of the rice pot and stirred the water, which was bubbling white with bits of fat floating on the top. I felt sick to my stomach.

"I'm sorry I stopped writing to you. I didn't know what to say. It was different without you here." I held on to the side of the kitchen counter.

"Stop talking." Joe turned the flame off under the rice and the steaks. "You should stop talking now."

He picked up the rice pot with a couple of kitchen towels and gestured with his head for me to follow him up the back stairs. I went, suddenly afraid of him in the narrow passageway. The pot was steaming hot. He was going to turn and pour it over me. Boiling hot water and pellets of grain as hard as bullets. No more than I deserved. He kept walking up the stairs, and I followed. When we got to the second floor he stopped, making room for me on the landing.

"Which way is your bedroom?"

"Over there. End of the hall."

He walked down the hall, and I followed. Voices floated up from downstairs. Someone had put ragtime on the Victrola, and party horns from last New Year's Eve were being blown enthusiastically out of time.

"Open the door."

Mrs. Curtis's walls were done in a dusky pink floral pattern, and there was a forbidding oil painting of a hunting scene hanging opposite the bed. Bright blood spilled from the neck of a hare. The bed had a carved wooden headboard, built to carry the weight of all the Curtis births and deaths. Winslow and I had yet to make love in this bed. The doctor had cautioned me to wait six weeks after losing the baby before we "resumed conjugal relations."

Joe grimaced a little and shoved the door closed with his back. He still gripped the rice casserole tightly in both hands, and steam escaped into the cold room with a starchy, meaty smell. I moved to the bed and held tightly to one of its tall posts, needing an anchor.

"Pull back the covers."

The maid had been up earlier in the day, and it looked as starched and new as a hotel bed. I did everything Joe told me without question.

"Pull them down farther."

I pulled the coverings to the bottom of the bed and stepped away. He leaned down and put the casserole, still wrapped in kitchen towels, in the very center of the bed, and pulled the coverings over it.

"That's how we finish the rice," he said. "In the bed. My mother always puts the rice in the bed. It's so you don't overcook it on the stove; the rice steams the last ten minutes on its own."

I said nothing. I had begun to cry very quietly. He looked at me with his good eye, and now I was the one who couldn't look back. "I'm sorry, Joe," I said. He walked over to the door and turned the little old-fashioned key. There were tiny black skeleton keys in all of the bedroom doors. I had been afraid to touch any of the keys and assumed that they were ornamental, but this one locked smoothly.

"Get undressed."

He didn't touch me as I slipped my dress over my head and pulled down my stockings. He watched every item drop to the floor, then turned his gaze back to my body. Now that the crying was over, I was shocked to feel my insides tightening with desire for the first time since the miscarriage. I didn't turn my back as I took off my slip. Something about this felt strangely right, like penance. I felt a flush beginning just above my breasts and spreading to my neck and face, but I didn't care. I wanted him to see me.

"Get in the bed," he whispered. The towels around the casserole dish were warm, and Joe reached down and moved my legs to either side as I lay on my back, so that the insides of my thighs were flush against the warm towels. It wasn't too hot, and now that I was naked I could look straight up at him, trying to stare him down. He put his hands on the outsides of my thighs and pressed them in toward the pot of rice. The steam came up from between my legs, and as Joe leaned in closer I could smell the champagne on his breath. He pressed my legs tightly, big hands gripping the backs of my thighs. I wanted him so much just then that I reached up with my arms, but he shoved me back down.

"No," he said harshly, and I understood that he was making something even between us. I threw my head

back, and putting my hand to my own sex, I forgot everything else for him, allowing him to watch until I felt
myself let go.

I brought my hand to my mouth, breathing fast and
looking into his good eye.

"I wanted to leave you waiting," he said. "So you would
know what it feels like not to get what you want."

"I know what that's like. And I know what it's like to
miss you."

Ten minutes later, Joe carried the rice dish triumphantly
into the living room as I followed with the steaks on a
platter.

"It's done!" he announced. "The first meal of peace-
time."

Everyone applauded and moved to the dining room for
a meal without servants.

"The rice is perfect," someone remarked.

"Frankie did it all," said Joe. We drank again and again
to the end of the Kaiser as Alice tried to preach to us about
the new equality of the sexes. At around nine o'clock the
telephone rang in the hall, and Winslow picked up. We
had moved back into the living room by then, and Alice
was dancing close and fast with Joe, but I had discovered
the miracle of four glasses of champagne: I didn't really
mind. I had no idea what Joe was thinking, but now I
owed him nothing. I could smile at him over the shoulder
of the man I was dancing with, one of those groomed and
talkative friends of Alice's who always seemed like the same

man again and again. Then Winslow came back and stood in the doorway with such a strange expression on his face that I stopped quite suddenly.

"Hey, what gives?" my partner began. Then looking at Winslow, "Say, old man, I hope you don't mind a little dancing."

"That was Ham," Winslow said. "They were wrong in New York. The war's still on."

"What?"

"How can they be wrong in New York?"

"What's he saying?"

"I don't know. Newspapers got it wrong." Winslow was apologetic. "I don't know how they got it wrong, but they did."

"Hell," Alice said, looking around the room. "Hell, that's a rotten trick."

"All of New York thought it was over?" Joe asked.

"Ticker tape parade and everything," Winslow said.

"Well, I guess that's gotta be the biggest fake in history." Joe began to laugh.

"Newspapers just got it wrong," Winslow repeated.

"Come to think of it," one of Alice's girlfriends remarked, "nobody else seemed to be celebrating." She started to laugh. "I hope this doesn't mean that it's time to go home?"

Joe walked toward the hallway and slapped Winslow's shoulder. "Good thing you didn't shut down the mill after all."

"Oh, come on, Joe. Everyone, stay." Alice pulled at Joe's sleeve. "Let's keep going; the war will be over soon. We're just celebrating a little early, that's all."

"It doesn't make sense," I said to Winslow. "Was he sure?"

"Yes," Winslow said. "Oh yes, Ham says we'll read all about it in the paper tomorrow. I guess some guy with the United Press has egg all over his face."

"Funny thing," Joe said from the doorway.

"Joe!" Alice grabbed her coat. "I haven't had a chance to buy you a drink since you came home."

Joe waited on the porch for Alice and her friends, but Winslow and I were in no mood to keep going. The war was still on and the party was over.

Alice came home very late and left early the next morning for New York. She was there to celebrate with her father when the real armistice was signed on the following Monday, the eleventh of November. The bells rang out from the mills and the churches, and all the owners went ahead and shut down operations. I guess that in New York they did it all over again, but Winslow and I agreed that our own first night had taken the edge off the celebration. We walked down Front Street and had a few drinks but came home early.

"It makes me feel a little funny inside, knowing the war is over. Like everything is wide open again," Winslow said. "But it's not as wild as that night when we got it wrong. I mean, even though I know this is the real thing, I don't feel like having anybody over."

"No," I said. "I'm going to pretend Thursday was the real one. The war was over on November seventh, for us."

He turned and kissed me slowly. He still treated me with a certain delicacy. We had been married for less than a month, but I wasn't sure if this was our honeymoon or not. Everything had been so much clearer with a baby.

1919

～～～

MOTHER WAS TRYING TOO HARD. SHE HELD HER rosé so tightly her fingers made sweat marks on the wineglass. Papa circled the room trying to find a place to lean against, but nothing held him for long. He had an elbow on the mantel and was overheating from the fire that was kept going all winter, even when nobody was using the room. His face was bright red, and he kept wiping his forehead with a handkerchief so large it made every other detail even more embarrassing to me.

"Have another, Allen?" Winslow asked, taking his tumbler and refilling it with whiskey from the decanter. I was sticking to wine.

"Where did you manage to get these olives, Winslow?" Mother asked again. She had asked about everything that was set out for hors d'oeuvres: the French cheese, the Italian breadsticks, and now the olives.

"Boston," Winslow said again. "My father has a man there who sends them down."

"Lovely." Mother dutifully rolled one around her mouth. Papa and I both knew she hated olives, and we avoided looking at each other. I held out my wineglass to Winslow and told myself not to drink too much before dinner.

"You're feeling well, Mrs. Ross?" Winslow asked as he refilled my glass.

"Abigail. Winslow, you must call me Abigail."

"Abigail." Winslow pulled up a footstool and sat at her feet. He was determined to make this work. "Doctor Haywood has been good?"

"He is excellent, Winslow. I feel much stronger now."

"She never coughs anymore," Papa put in too loudly. He had said no to the Curtises' doctor coming by to visit Mother every week, but Winslow had insisted.

"Only at night," she said, looking quickly at Papa. "And Allen can take care of me when I need it."

"Only at night," Papa repeated, pulling at his tie. His wool suit, a forest green plaid that made him look poor, was too hot for the room. Winslow was wearing a dark blue blazer over gray trousers that went with anything. He had said this was just a family dinner, nothing dressy, but both of my parents had worn their funeral clothes.

"Anybody home?" Ham Curtis swung open the front door, bringing in the January snow. We all stood up, and Winslow went to the foyer while Mother and I both smoothed our dresses and she pushed in all her hairpins for the tenth time. Ham walked into the living room the same way he walked onto a stage. Winslow followed a moment later with a girl about my age. She was wearing a fur collar made from a circle of three dead foxes holding each other's tails between their sharp white teeth.

"Allen, Abigail." Ham reached for their hands and then kissed my cheek paternally. "My dear." He turned back to Winslow and the girl, who hesitated in the doorway. "Glad we can all get together informally like this. May I introduce Miss Elizabeth DuBois." He reached a hand for the young woman, and she went toward him as if she had been with him for years. She had a halting gait but carried herself in such a way that one had to look again to be sure she was limping.

Papa didn't move, and I saw his eyes glancing at Winslow, then again at the girl. Mother was the only one who moved forward to shake her hand.

"How lovely to meet you," she said.

I knew that face, despite the clothes and the lipstick. "Good evening," I said to her without moving. "Please sit down."

Lizzie smiled at me as she took a seat on the couch close to Ham. She knew me; she probably knew all of us. Had Winslow known she was coming?

"Lizzie used to work at the mill with you, Allen. Perhaps you remember her?"

Papa shook his head, and I saw him sweating even more. He reached for the ridiculous handkerchief.

"No, Allen wouldn't have known me," Lizzie said in a voice that was more cultured than Alice Curtis's. "I had to stop working there several years ago. There was an accident." She turned to me as she said this last part, and I got up to take a cigarette from the box on the mantel. "It left me with this bad leg, you see." She patted her thigh; the dress was dark burgundy silk, which folded around her like a set of expensive sheets. I offered the cigarette box; Winslow was the only taker.

"I'm terribly sorry," Mother said to Lizzie. Did she really know nothing? "The mills are so dangerous. We managed to keep Frankie from that, thank the Lord."

"Yes," Lizzie said. I wanted her to stop looking at me. It was her eyes that I remembered most. "It's difficult work, but then, you must know all about that, Mr. Ross."

"I don't find it difficult," Papa said shortly. "It's a good mill."

"Good profits still coming in." Ham took the whiskey that Winslow had made for him without being asked. "Lizzie, my dear, a glass of— What is that, rosé?"

I wanted to get Winslow alone. I had never told him about Ham Curtis and that night on the boat with the fireworks. Ham was showing the same nasty streak now, bringing Lizzie DuBois to dinner with my family when he must have so many girls.

"You're in the weave room, is that right, Allen?" Ham offered Papa a cigar, but Papa shook his head.

"I'm an engraver," he said very quietly. I could feel Mother beginning to panic as she looked at Papa, but I kept my head turned away.

"Of course, of course!" Ham filled the room with a cloud of smoke, and my mother leaned back. "I knew that, Allen. My apologies. You were in the weave room, weren't you, my dear?" he asked Lizzie, placing a hand at the small of her back.

"Yes," she said steadily. "I hardly remember it now."

"Lizzie has been training to be a teacher, up in Boston," Ham said, looping his hand around her waist. "She has a lot of radical ideas about bringing education into the workplace. All for the best, I'm sure." She placed her hand over his, and they looked around at the rest of us as if we had come to see them perform. Perhaps we had.

Dinner was perfect, leg of lamb with mint jelly and new potatoes. Papa had whiskey before and after dinner, and began to talk fast and loud. Lizzie remained sober, as did Mother; it was impossible to tell with Ham and Winslow, the Curtises held their liquor so well. Papa wanted to tell Ham the story of his family back in Manchester, and Ham encouraged him to tell everything, even things I knew were untrue about the hardships of his crossing from England. Ham Curtis liked to think of himself as a "man of the people," and I wondered how he would turn this to his advantage. Papa played the perfect immigrant, and I hated the way Mother moved apologetically through the evening. I drank more than was good for me, but it helped me not to feel that I was responsible for anyone.

After they left, Ham insisted that Lizzie tune in songs on the wireless so we could dance in the living room. I was feeling reckless by now, and I encouraged it. I wanted to see Lizzie dance on her bad leg, I wanted to see the tops of her breasts once the fox fur was set aside. There was nothing wrong with her at all, it seemed. We switched partners, and Ham pulled me close against him, resting his hands on my hips as he watched me take the steps back and forth, back and forth.

Winslow and Lizzie were more subdued, and he held

her at a careful distance, allowing her to set the pace, but she moved as fast as I did.

"Give her back to me, Winslow," Ham said at the end of the song. "I want my girl just like you want yours."

He pushed me toward Winslow so hard that I had to catch myself on the wing of an armchair. But instead of grabbing Lizzie, he reached an arm around Winslow, who looked thin under his father's muscular grasp, his white shirt translucent with sweat. The blazers had been abandoned when the dancing began.

"My little girl can't make babies, though," Ham said loudly into Winslow's ear. "Something's broke inside her female parts. So I can't get caught like you did. Though something's broken with your girl too, isn't that what they told you? No little Curtis baby after all. Seems a shame."

Winslow lifted his father's arm off his shoulder and walked toward the liquor cabinet, but Ham followed right behind. I was standing next to the whiskey decanter, having switched over from wine. "Did you hear that, Frankie?" He turned to both of us, hands on hips. "It doesn't matter to me. We like our girls, don't we, Winslow?"

He walked over and kissed Lizzie on the mouth right in front of us. Winslow stayed there, watching. I left the room. Half an hour later, they were gone, back to Boston or some hotel, I didn't care which.

"Did you know he was bringing her tonight?" I was too drunk to fall asleep.

"No." Winslow was lying on his stomach, his face turned in to the pillow.

"But you knew about her. You knew it was Lizzie DuBois."

"I've heard about her."

"With him. You've heard about her with him."

"Yes, with him. Listen, Frankie. My father always has a girl around."

"But why *that* girl? When he knows, and my father was there— He can get—"

"I don't know why her, Frankie. We took care of her, you know. After the accident, and then Daddy—"

"You don't know what he did to me."

"Don't tell me."

"It was on the boat, the same night as the accident. The Fourth of July, remember?"

"Don't, Frankie . . . don't."

I waited until he was almost asleep. Then I had the kind of sex with him that leaves marks.

Now that the war was over, it seemed everyone was going on strike. Joe started traveling all the time, organizing workers, joining strike committees, and he never stopped trying to interest Winslow in union politics. He went out to Seattle for a general strike that paralyzed the city, then made his way back across the country, having struck with the railroad workers, the letter carriers, the construction workers, and even the New York cigar makers.

He got a nickname in the Rock Harbor press: "Little

Bill," for Big Bill Haywood, who was the longtime leader of the IWW and was also missing an eye. Half the time Joe and his friends were in jail, but it always seemed like Joe was flying high when we saw him. Of course, the union organizers were so serious about everything that they never seemed to be having much fun, but they were getting famous. Joe still came over for supper whenever he was in town, and we acted as if politics couldn't change a thing between us.

I didn't care about politics. All I wanted was to have a baby, and the doctor had assured me that I would be able to get pregnant again soon. I listened to the arguments about unions and suffrage and didn't say much; but after Alice or Joe visited us, it always felt as if real life was going on somewhere else. There were no strikes threatened in Rock Harbor, but people started talking about "Reds" and "Bolsheviks" bringing down the country. They said that people like Joe and the IWW were attempting to overthrow the U.S. government, just like they had in Russia, but Joe said that was just the newspapers trying to get a headline.

"Come on," he said. "The workers are the patriots. Think about it, Winslow. Who wants to stay in Rock Harbor more than the Portuguese and the Italians?"

Ham Curtis came down hard on the Reds in the press, and we were told to be careful when opening our mail. Attorney General Palmer's front porch was bombed in June, and our maid refused to accept any packages after we read about a Rhode Island girl who had her hands blown off collecting a package for a local judge. Winslow didn't mention to his father that Joe always stayed at our house when he was in town.

"I don't sleep well anywhere," Joe told me one night. "It's better with you and Winslow around."

Winslow was good at staying out of politics, and he had been moved to a new position: managing the time-tables at the mill. Despite the general perception of the Curtises, Winslow didn't have any real political clout, so he could be friends with everyone. The mills were starting to go through a slowdown, and though wage cuts were threatened, the news wasn't as bad in Rock Harbor as it was in lots of towns. The newspapers said the cost of living had gone up, but Winslow never complained about the bills.

Then came the Boston police strike. Joe had gone up there to help organize a policeman's union. He told us that there were unions for the constables in London, and the pay was shameful for our police doing the same job. I didn't pay much more attention to this strike than any other, but Boston was Ham Curtis's town, just like Rock Harbor. In early September, the policemen formed a union and walked out, and the city was left to looters. The mayor called in the state militia on Ham's advice. We got phone calls from Alice in Boston, telling us that there was shooting in the streets.

"Daddy will fix it," she said breathlessly.

Governor Coolidge overruled both the police commissioner and the mayor (who couldn't stand each other) and hired an entirely new police force, made up of out-of-work veterans. Everyone in local politics knew that this had been Ham's idea, though Governor Coolidge got the credit as order was restored. The governor refused to grant the striking policemen amnesty, and the strike was a disaster for labor. The Curtis family always claimed that Ham had come up with the statement that made Coolidge so famous: "There is no right to strike against the public safety by anybody, anywhere, any time."

It did sound like vintage Ham Curtis, and whether or not that rumor was true, Ham certainly got his way in Massachusetts politics once Coolidge became president in '23.

Two nights after the police strike ended we found both Joe and Alice on our doorstep. They kept arguing right through drinks, right through dinner, and right over the new music I wanted to play.

"Your father broke that strike," Joe was saying. "He told Coolidge to hire the scabs. He believes in nothing."

"He believes that we should have policemen on the streets, Joe," Winslow said. "Everyone does."

"At slave wages?"

"They weren't working for slave wages," Alice said. She was smoking even more than usual. Alice and Joe had both started drinking on the train from Boston, where they'd met inadvertently. The first argument had come from his refusing to ride in the first-class carriage with her.

"You're being stupid, Joe. All you care about is what your beloved union will think of you."

"I don't care what anybody thinks of me."

"Well, the first-class carriage is a public place, but here in the living room, drinking our liquor, now that's something different."

"It *is* different—" I started to say, but Joe interrupted.

"And what about you? What do you care about, Alice?"

"Joe, Alice, come on . . ." Winslow was pouring more

whiskey for everyone, but he was slurring his words, and I wondered when he had started drinking that day.

"I care about the plight of women." Alice stood up a little more quickly than she could handle. "About equality between the sexes."

Joe started laughing. "A convenient reason to be able to bed whomever you want without having to marry them. That works well, especially if they were born in the wrong place, like up the Flint."

"I didn't need an excuse with you," Alice said. "I couldn't keep you off me."

Everything went still.

"That's a lie. Or don't you remember?" Joe wasn't laughing now.

"Hey, watch it, Joe." Winslow stood up quickly, but I was two steps behind everything. When had Alice and Joe . . . ?

"I never really wanted you," Alice moved closer to Joe, face-to-face. "Who cares where you were born but you, Joe?"

"And isn't that what your 'equality' is really about? A setup so you don't have to care?"

"Have you ever been in love, Joe?" Alice asked.

"Yes—"

I couldn't breathe, but Alice kept going. "Why shouldn't women get the same thing that men have always had?"

"Of course women should have the vote, but what do you really care about, Alice?" Joe took a step away from her. "Not the Pawtugees who built this house."

"Actually, this house was built by the Irish," Alice said, following him around the room.

"Everyone's had too much to drink," Winslow said loudly. "I think—"

Alice took another step toward Joe and he looked her up and down. "You want to know what they say about you? Legs like butter. Spreads easy. That's why I didn't want you that night—even if it was almost the Armistice, even if I *was* just back from the war."

"You're filthy—filthy Red." Alice slapped him hard across the face. He didn't see it coming and staggered slightly, bringing his hand to his cheek. He was drunk, she was drunk. I had never seen Winslow so drunk, and I had been high for hours now; it felt like the whole world was tilting. A slow smile spread across Joe's face, and I felt very, very cold.

"Get out." I heard Winslow's voice as if from a long way off.

"It's my house too!" Alice was standing in the center of the room, a pink rash spreading across her chest.

"Not you," Winslow said to his sister. He grabbed Joe. "Joe Barros, get out of my house!"

"Winslow—" I had hold of Joe's other arm by now. We were standing in a tight circle as the room spun around us.

"Get out, you Pawtugee son of a bitch!"

Joe was gone down the street and Winslow was still yelling when I pulled him back inside and slammed the door.

Then there was silence except for Winslow's hard breathing as we lurched into the living room. I could hear the servants listening, the whole neighborhood listening. I stood close to Winslow, feeling more like a Curtis than ever before.

"Well," said Alice, tipping her drink back and smiling like a fox in the old fairy tales. "That was fun."

Winslow looked over at his sister as if he weren't quite sure who she was, and slowly sat down on the couch. That was the moment I burst into tears.

1921

IT WAS A TERRIBLE BIRTH. THE CURTISES' HIGH-PRICED doctor couldn't say why I had finally conceived again after two years of trying. I was twenty, and healthy enough, but perhaps not meant to bear children. I'm too small; my pelvic bones are so close together that the baby couldn't get through. Later they told me that my labor lasted for three days. I was rocking back and forth on my bed, riding an ocean of tendons, ripped membranes, and blood. I knew that it would end in the child's death or mine, and I begged them—God, anyone—to free my body of this thing that was cracking me apart from the inside. My legs and buttocks were spread wide in the attempt, but nothing moved through them except blood. I didn't care how they did it, but I wanted to be the one who lived.

It was Doctor Haywood who decided to cut the baby out. That way the baby would live. I was very unlikely to survive having my abdomen cut open from sternum to pubis. I received last rites in a sort of blur and great secrecy, because I wasn't really supposed to be a Catholic anymore, since I'd married Winslow. I didn't want a priest in the room, but Mother didn't want me going to hell for being a Protestant, and what could I do about anything? Mother stayed in the room with me through it all. I remember that clearly, she stayed. The ether Doctor Haywood used at last came like a gift. Cold and sweet. I went to a winter morning in Poughkeepsie; there were the cousins with their sleds, and I had one too. I was riding down the big hill in front of Aunt Celia's house, lying on my stomach and steering with my hands like a boy. The snow was falling, and everything was slightly out of focus. I saw the big maple at the bottom of the hill, and instead of going around I went right through it. Straight through the thorny bark unscathed while all the cousins called: "Look at Frankie! Look at her go!" I was so far up, and there was perfect snow all around me. I wanted to stay there forever.

I woke up in terrible pain and asked for ether but got morphine instead. They told me I had a son, but I didn't see him anywhere, and then when I stopped seeing the priest in the room, I asked Mother if I was going to live. She told me that I was, and I fell back asleep, feeling almost nothing at this information.

The doctor removed my uterus when he was getting the baby out, on the off chance that I would survive, and I'm grateful for that. I had wanted a baby so much but I knew I wouldn't make it through another birth. The morphine kept coming for several weeks, and I shocked everyone by healing without any major infection, just the usual fevers.

Geoffrey surprised everyone too. He was blue and silent when they pulled him out, and his head was dented from trying to push past my bones. Mother told me later that when she first saw him she thought he must be damaged. But the doctor lifted him by his mucus-covered heels and gave him the sharp slap that knocks babies from that world into this one. Geoffrey started crying, and he continued to cry for the next three months.

He was colicky, and what little sleeping he did was in Mother's bed in the guest room while I bedded down with my morphine at the other end of the hall. I slept almost all the time, while Geoffrey hardly slept at all. By the time I was well enough to hold my son for more than a few minutes, he was nearly a month old and Mother's boy.

My milk dried up during my long recovery, and he would cry for Mother when he was placed in my arms, which embarrassed both of us. He would soon be back with her, happily sucking at a bottle as she gazed down at him with a look I didn't want to think about as much as I did. I was certain this was a look she had held back for him alone, never for me. I was bone-sad and ashamed. I loved the powdery scent that lingered at the back of his neck, but there was Mother waiting for him to be handed back to her, and I was frightened of them both. She was so sure of herself with an infant. I felt nervous whenever I was alone with Geoffrey, as if I were getting away with something by having him just to myself. It was my private wound that I felt almost nothing for Geoffrey at first. I couldn't eat, and the doctor put it down to the morphine, but even as they weaned me from that cold pillow of addiction, I had no drive to feed my own body. It became harder and harder to sleep, and I kept asking for another drug until I realized that their pity for me had worn away to something much less kind.

Winslow came to see me every day, and I dreaded the moment when the nurse wheeled in the baby tucked inside his bassinet, leaving the three of us alone. It was as if I were gazing at a picture of parenthood in a ladies' magazine. I could not inhabit my own life, and if Geoffrey woke up I had nothing to offer him but slack breasts and failure. I couldn't admit this to anyone, but I was sure the baby knew it. He pushed his head from side to side when I tried to hold him, kicking his feet against the blankets and never wanting to just lie still. It was as if he knew where the scar was along my belly, and that was where he kicked the hardest, making me gasp with pain. Then I held him tighter than ever, afraid that if I loosened my grip I would hurl him to the floor. I was the only one who knew my baby wasn't safe with me.

Papa came to visit one morning while Mother took Geoffrey on a walk in his pram. I had not yet left the house, though the doctor insisted that there was no reason for me not to begin taking exercise. It would help build my appetite, he said, something that everyone but me seemed concerned about. I wasn't nursing a baby, so why did it matter? Papa pulled a chair near the bed and sat for a while without saying anything. He looked thinner, and I wondered how he was managing with Mother spending so much time with Geoffrey. He tapped his knees nervously with the heels of his hands, and kept looking around as if he expected to see something in the room that wasn't already there.

"It's good, then, now you're feeling better?" he said at last.

I nodded, curling my wrists under the blankets. I didn't want him to talk about my weight. All anyone talked about was the baby and my weight.

"Baby's fine, then?"

"He's fine."

Papa looked at the painting of the dead hare across from the bed. "Nice thing to wake up to every day."

"Not really."

"No. I wouldn't think so."

I couldn't smile. I felt so tired.

"It's a change, almost dying." Papa was still looking at the painting.

"The priest was here," I said. "Did you know?"

"I was downstairs with Winslow most of the time." He got up to pace to the window and back again. "I still think about it, Frankie. I think about it all the time. When you know your death is right there. It can be hard to wait for it to come on its own time. Don't worry. I'm talking, that's all. Something I can pass on to you. If I can pass on anything good—"

"Papa, you—"

"Something to live for is key." He had his back to me now, looking out at the perfect lawn. "And if you can't find enough reason—"

"My child is enough," I said, making him turn and look at me with the force of my lie. "My child is enough for me."

He stared at me with eyes as wide as I remembered them from our nights in Poughkeepsie. Those wet eyes grasping

165

mine in the middle of the night while I tried so hard not to look at his bandaged wrists.

"Then that's fine," he said, cocking his head to one side without taking his eyes from my face. "That'll be fine. How it should be."

I got out of bed that afternoon.

I was nothing like Papa.

"So you've produced an heir," Alice said when she came to view the baby. "Are you allowed to have a drink?"

Yes, I was allowed to have a drink. We had a baby nurse and later a nanny, and nobody encouraged me to do anything other than what I was doing. I was to stay focused on Winslow and regaining my pre-pregnancy weight, while the baby nurse and my mother spent their days with Geoffrey. Mother went back home to sleep at night, but between her familiarity with the servants and Allie running the daily operations as cook and head housekeeper, I felt like a guest. I saw Geoffrey every afternoon, between his nap and early supper. Winslow and I began to go to parties again, and I liked to sleep late; some days I didn't come downstairs until it was Geoffrey's bedtime. But the baby seemed happy, Mother was happy, and Winslow was happy. When people asked me how I was feeling, there was only room for one reply. Yes, I was allowed to have a drink.

Having money changed everything. I liked the big house and the servants and being able to buy short dresses and long strings of beads, silk stockings that rolled down to my ankles. There was a comforting solidity to the rooms

I lived in now, and I wasn't sure if I could do without that anymore. There was a desk where you found pale blue writing paper as if by magic, and the bedsheets were soft and smelled of lavender even in the winter. I spent money on anything I wanted, and nobody I knew talked about people being out of work, or on strike.

I read everything I could find in the papers about "Little Bill" (Joe's nickname had stuck), and the more I read, the more certain I was that Joe would hate me now.

Winslow just wanted me to be happy.

After women finally got the vote, Alice lost interest in politics, and I don't think either of us remembered to vote in the election of 1920. We were too busy. I threw myself into dancing as a religion. We had to dance every night.

Somehow the money kept coming, even though someone finally ran against Ham Curtis for office, and he had to spend serious money campaigning. The mills were letting hundreds of workers go, and the mill owners forced through a 20 percent wage cut even with the rising cost of living, but they still didn't strike in Rock Harbor. Nobody wanted to worry me, and I began the new decade determined not to worry either.

We took the boat from Fall River to New York every weekend, with the idea that Winslow should be in Rock Harbor during the week for his job, but in fact most of the week was spent deciding what to do for the weekend. We tried out every ship on the Fall River Line, but our favorite was the *Priscilla*. She was outfitted with a ballroom and a band that played out-of-date music, but we didn't care. We danced to any kind of music. I loved feeling the floor shift under our feet as we danced through Narragansett

Bay and around Point Judith. Everyone danced wherever
there was a square of open space. When I was dancing, I
knew exactly what to do.

After the band quit playing, Winslow and I would go
to our stateroom, where the sheets had been turned down,
and we both stripped naked, still damp with sweat. Winslow rubbed my feet with peppermint oil each night before
he climbed in next to me to make love or just sleep with
the curve of my instep nestled high between his warm
thighs. The smell of peppermint mingled with salt from
the open porthole as we slept. The mills felt very far away.

In the morning we held tight to our breakfast china
as we passed through the currents at Hell Gate, and by
the time we reached the wharf, we were dressed and ready.
Winslow held a hatbox and a valise in one hand, while I
gripped the other. Every time we arrived in New York felt
like the first time to me. I loved staying in hotels, I loved
letting Alice dress me to go to a charity ball or a vaudeville
show. I didn't care as long as we were in the city.

Alice was teaching us how to be modern. She always
knew where to go, and she knew the rules.

"Don't tell people you're married," she whispered to
me one night as we entered a speakeasy filled with smoke
and people who looked a lot like Alice. Nobody ever
quite told you what it was in the glass they were pressing
into your hand, but it usually tasted fine if you mixed it
with something fizzy. There was too much talking and no
dancing that night, so a pale young man drove us uptown
to a party, and I pressed close against Winslow, wishing
we were alone at the hotel with a bottle of something to
share.

"Why wasn't I supposed to say I was married?" I asked from the backseat.

"She wasn't?" Winslow turned toward me. "Who didn't you tell?"

"Nobody." I kissed him hard on the mouth.

"Of course, I won't ever marry," Alice said. Our driver smiled and moved his manicured hand under the hem of her dress as he handled the wheel with his other hand. "Perhaps a companionate marriage, but nothing more."

"What's that? And how do you spell it?" Winslow asked.

"It's a practical approach to male and female relations." Alice moved her date's hand back down to her knee. "Men and women simply live together long enough to decide whether they can cohabit as mates."

"You mean, they have to see if the sex is good." The young man handed his flask to Alice.

Alice took a long drink before passing it back to us. "And to see if they are intellectually compatible as well. One doesn't always find both." She was being tart, but it sounded to me like she was making an effort.

"I know which one I would settle for," the young man said cheerfully.

Alice's hand moved over to the thigh of his gray striped trousers.

"It's this idea of possession that's so outdated, don't you think, Frankie?" she said, reaching to take the flask again.

"I suppose."

"Winslow may love you, but he doesn't possess you. That would make you no better than a table, or a lamp."

Winslow started laughing and cupped his hands to light a cigarette; all the windows were open.

"I'm serious, Winslow." Alice turned back to both of us. She looked so pretty just then, with her hair shorn close to her head and tiny black curls that somehow remained plastered against her cheeks. "Possession has nothing to do with love."

"Shall we give it up, then?" Winslow asked me.

"What?"

"Marriage."

"Sure." I leaned my head into his shoulder. "As long as we don't have to get divorced."

"But you see what I mean, don't you?" Alice glanced at her young man to be sure that he agreed with her. "Monogamy is outmoded. Scientifically speaking, it's unnatural. It's completely unheard of in the animal kingdom."

"What about swans?" I asked, but everyone ignored me.

"You sound a bit like that boy I heard about," the young man said to Alice, taking the flask from her lap. "You know the one who threw himself a suicide party? They said that he killed himself just to see what being dead was like."

"I'm talking about marriage, not suicide."

"I thought you were talking about boredom," I said from the backseat, and Alice laughed hard at that.

"Maybe I was," she said. "Maybe I was."

"So if you're bored, you'll try anything?" the young man said to Alice. "I like a girl who is ready to try anything."

"I dare you to find something that I haven't already tried," she answered, smiling triumphantly into the rearview mirror for our benefit.

We ended up at a town house that had a ballroom with high ceilings, somewhere near Gramercy Park. Alice didn't seem to mind when her young man took me upstairs for some frenzied kissing, and I wanted to be a girl who would try anything. He pushed his tongue roughly between my teeth, and I held my breath the whole time, hating it.

"Feeling better?" Alice whispered into my ear as she pulled him back onto the dance floor with her after we returned from the second floor. Winslow had disappeared for quite a while at that point, and I wondered where he was as I danced from partner to partner. I was much older than I had been ten minutes earlier.

"Did you see me kissing Alice's young man last night?"

We were in the stateroom bed, but Winslow wasn't rubbing my feet. We never had it in us to dance on the way home from New York.

"No."

"Well, I did. And it was very nice. It was fine."

He reached for the oil and started massaging my toes.

"Now, look here, Frankie, should we tell each other everything?"

"Yes, complete honesty."

"You're sure?"

"Yes. I love you, but I don't own you. I think that's true, don't you?"

"I kissed that girl from Newport last night, and once before, at the Cabot party."

I tucked my feet underneath me, and he reached back for them.

"I don't know why, Frankie. It didn't mean anything—"

"I know it didn't."

I let him have my feet, but I didn't want to look at him anymore.

"I love you, Frankie."

"I love you too. It's only natural, after all."

"Yes."

I smiled as hard as I could.

"Then, we'll be all right? You're all right, Frankie?"

"Of course I am."

"You can have—well—kissing with someone and not feel too much of anything, can't you, Winslow?" I asked him sometime near dawn.

"Absolutely." He was half asleep. "Happens all the time."

And so we were modern.

1927

~

WE ALL GOT TIRED. SOME PEOPLE GOT MARRIED, SOME people went broke, and most of them simply disappeared. Not Lizzie DuBois. She was no longer Ham's mistress, but she had never really gone away. Once she got her teacher's certificate, she approached Winslow about schooling for the mill children. Winslow convinced his father that it would be good publicity; it would offset the layoffs and wage cuts. Winslow and Lizzie were put in charge of creating the mill school, and when Ham and Alice next came through town, Winslow invited the family for a tour. The classroom was inside the Flint Mill, a converted dye shed that still smelled of chemicals, but the walls were whitewashed, and rows of benches were set up with a desk and a blackboard at the front of the room. Brass hooks lined the walls for the children's coats and work aprons.

Lizzie was so stylish that I wondered where her clothes

were coming from now. She shook Ham Curtis's hand and greeted Alice and me too familiarly, but Ham seemed happy to see her in charge. I wondered how long it had been since they were in bed together.

"This is it," Lizzie said, gesturing to the small room. "This is what we've been able to do, thanks to you, Senator Curtis." She smiled unself-consciously.

There were so many rows of benches for the students that we had to stand too close together. Lizzie's perfume mixed with Alice's and the lingering vinegar smell of the dye vats. I sat down on the front bench with Alice, but it was built for the smallest children, and our knees pressed up awkwardly. I felt as if I were in detention. Lizzie remained standing as she described the program: "We have students of all ages. The workers who are over sixteen can continue their studies past the required three months, to train for more highly skilled positions."

"There will be a class in personal hygiene," said Winslow. "Lizzie is bringing in a nurse from Mount Hope Hospital to talk to the children."

"That was *your* idea." Lizzie was pretending to be modest, and I wondered if the men were falling for it, and why I cared. "It will help keep the next generation healthy."

"And then they can be more productive," Winslow said. He looked eagerly from Lizzie to his father. Ham nodded at Winslow and tried to walk around the desk, but his way was blocked by a stack of books. He was far too large for this room.

"This was an excellent idea. I'm going to have a photographer come down and take some pictures of you with Lizzie. I want this to be a model school, understand? An example the whole state can look to." Ham picked up one of the books and flipped it open. "U.S. history. Just leave the union stuff out, will you?"

Everybody laughed, and Lizzie slid between Ham and the desk; her skirt brushed against the front of his trousers, and I admired how careless she appeared of having been his lover. She took her place in the teacher's chair.

"Doesn't she look wonderful, there?" Winslow said to Ham. "Just the kind of teacher anybody would like to have."

Lizzie blushed and started to get up, but Ham waved her back into her seat.

"No, stay there. That's the picture for the papers."

I could tell that Alice was bored, but Winslow was lit up in a way I hadn't seen in a long time. Ham talked nonstop about what the school could bring to the public image of the newly formed mill owners' consortium: the Manufacturers' Association. "This is a great thing you've started," he said to Winslow. "Modern approaches to learning and"— here he gave a quick look over at Lizzie—"for those who have suffered injuries in the mill, training for new skills."

The senator had an arm around Winslow's shoulders as we left the building. Ham, Winslow, and Lizzie walked ahead of me and Alice, who lit a cigarette as soon as we got outside.

"Well, at least she's made something of Winslow," Alice said. "Maybe this will stick."

"What do you mean?"

"Come on, Frankie. Winslow's not exactly cut out for politics or textile management, you know that." She exhaled and turned back to look at the little dye shed.

"This will work out for him, I think. He can be the idea man with Lizzie there to figure out the details."

"That's good then," I said. "She seems fine."

"She seems smart." Alice started walking again. "She knows how to work the room."

"But, she and Winslow are doing something good, something important, don't you think?"

"Of course they are. And Winslow does so much better when he has something concrete to accomplish."

"I think we all do better that way."

Alice stopped and looked at me. "What are you going to do, Frankie?"

"Me?"

"Well, anyway you have Geoffrey. So it doesn't matter as much for you."

Winslow and his father gestured excitedly, though the hum of the mill made it impossible to hear them. They were almost identical from behind, and I realized that even Winslow was now approaching middle age.

"Yes, Lizzie's quite something," Alice said after a beat. "That mill accident may have been the best thing that ever happened to her. Funny."

"Funny."

Alice surprised everyone by doing something as profoundly conventional as marrying an older, unattractive man, and the last truly grand party was Alice's June wedding to Thurston Whitehead. He was in steel, and the family came from Pittsburgh but kept a summer cottage in Newport. It was a mansion of pink granite that almost managed to dwarf the view from the lawn, which stretched in close-cut perfection to the cliff. There was the grass-green edge and the ocean turning black at the horizon. Alice's wedding was on a day when even the clouds seemed designed for pleasure. Lindbergh had just landed in Paris, and Lucky Lindy was about the same age we were, so maybe everyone was lucky now. Coolidge's second term had been a foregone conclusion, and Ham Curtis was talking about retiring to Washington. Thurston was crazy about Alice, despite her telling everyone that she finally agreed to marry him because she thought that, if things didn't work out, it would be more interesting to be a divorcée than an old maid. It was a very traditional wedding, with Alice looking shockingly virginal in Belgian lace and seed pearls. At the reception she clung to Thurston's side and kept turning to look at him with an expression that I had never seen before. She looked as if she loved him.

The marriage lasted seven months. During a party at the house in Pittsburgh, after they had returned from their honeymoon in France and Italy, where they had celebrated New Year's in style, Alice took a rifle from the gun room and shot herself through the back of the mouth. Nobody heard the sound of the shot over the band, and it was more than an hour before anyone noticed that she was missing.

The press reported it as an accident.

Winslow had gotten the news by cable, and now it was nearly dawn. We had stayed up all night together. Ham Curtis, Thurston Whitehead, and what was now called "the body" would be arriving soon.

"Maybe she didn't love him," Winslow said. Neither of us seemed able to get drunk that night.

"That doesn't seem like enough of a reason."

"Tell me what enough of a reason is."

Hadn't Alice always seen a way out of everything she didn't like to do? I didn't know how to stop thinking all the same things over and over again. I wanted Alice back. She wasn't kind, but she was funny, and she had taken me in despite thinking that Winslow could have done much better. She had brought me into the private world of girls without boys and, later, women without men. Now that she was gone, I had no women friends. But my solitude couldn't approach Winslow's; he was never meant to be the last of the Curtis siblings. He never quite got over becoming the eldest when he had always been the youngest.

Winslow's aunt Beverly descended upon us like a great mourning bird. She handled the funeral and the food and the wreath on the door. Protestants didn't seem to mind suicide as much as Catholics did, and Alice was buried next to Tom and her mother. Ham moved back into his old room for the funeral. After Aunt Beverly returned to the North Shore, Winslow, Geoffrey, Ham, and I began a muffled life. I wasn't sure where Winslow went at night, but I was determined not to ask any questions. It was hard enough for him to get dressed and walk out the door. Geoffrey was seven now and had never really known his aunt Alice except from a distance, but he took in everything, including his father's absences.

Geoffrey spent most of his time at my parents' house up the Flint. Ham spoke little, demanded nothing, and ate what was put in front of him. It was as if someone had reached inside and turned the key off on that big engine. I wondered how long he would stay.

"Hey, Ma, will you take me to the library?" Geoffrey had recently graduated himself from "Mother" to "Ma," and I liked it, though I didn't tell him so. The funny papers were spread out on the living room floor, and because it was raining he hadn't gone over to my parents' house. I didn't want to tell him that I didn't know exactly where the library was.

"Is that what you want to do? I can take you to Grandma and Grandpa's house instead."

He gave me a look.

"What do you want to do?" I asked again. His skinny legs crossed each other tightly, and the newspaper was crumpled underneath them. He made two fists against the floor and pressed his face hard into them. He was just barely taller than the newspapers spread lengthwise, and with his arms flexed, I could see three mosquito bites stand out red against the backs of them.

"Let's go to the library," I said.

He held my hand as we walked down the hill to Main Street. I had an umbrella in my other hand, and the rain fell in a hard, clean circle around us. He was being careful to avoid the puddles and kept talking the whole way. This seven-year-old boy who knew everything about everything. My son, I kept reminding myself, knowing there must be something very wrong with me if I had to tell myself this.

Before this mourning period began, I had never spent much time with Geoffrey. Winslow and I hardly saw my parents; I didn't know how to be their daughter when I was in the Curtis house. But Geoffrey saw them every week, sometimes every day. Mother liked to pick him up after school for a plate of cookies at home, or to go to the drugstore counter for a treat. She always brought him back to the Highlands in time for supper. Was it easier for her because he was a boy? Or because she was older and didn't have her sisters to distract her? I had thought about it for seven years now but understood only enough to know when I was not wanted.

The librarian greeted Geoffrey by name and smiled at both of us as I shook the umbrella into the stand by the front door. The building was a brick Carnegie library, high-ceilinged and open on the first floor, with a wide stairway leading to the second-floor balcony. Geoffrey pulled me up the stairs to the children's section. He knew exactly where to go.

"What do you want to read, Ma?" He sounded self-conscious.

"Whatever you want." I'm no good at this, I kept thinking. He knows I'm no good at this.

"Ma, you gotta be quiet." He looked around, but there was nobody else on the second floor. "We're in the library."

"Sorry," I whispered.

"It's okay." He smiled as if we had gotten away with something.

"I like this one." He pulled down *Robin Hood*. "It's got the best cover." He pointed to the name of the illustrator, N. C. Wyeth. "I read all the books by him." He pushed his hair out of his eyes with a gesture so exactly like Winslow's it stopped my breath. "They're not really *by* him." Geoffrey looked up at me, worried. "I mean, he does all the pictures."

"Show me."

"But then you'll know how it ends."

"Have you read it already?"

"Yes, but I don't mind."

"I don't mind either. Show me the pictures, sweetheart." Sweetheart. I stumbled on the word, but we both pretended not to notice. He was being so careful, and I wanted more than anything not to be a fraud.

We flipped through the pages, stopping at all the illustrations. "See, this is when he goes to Nottingham with his mother. Here's Little John."

"Who do you like best?"

"Robin."

Then he read aloud to me, in his high, intent voice.

I was falling in love. It had been a long time.

I began giving the nanny the night off and reading to Geoffrey myself before bed. Actually, he was reading to me. We both liked it better that way. When we came to the picture of Robin shooting his last arrow, I stayed in Geoffrey's bed all night. In the morning, I felt a little guilty to be waking up in his room, and I wondered if Winslow minded. Then Geoffrey brought me a breakfast tray with weak tea and too much sugar that he had made himself, and I gave him the day off from school. We lay in bed talking about how we both wished that Maid Marian had stayed out of the story.

I missed my husband less and less, and thought that we

could go on like this for a while; maybe this was what a family could be.

When I walked into my parents' house two weeks later, Geoffrey and Papa were practicing their knots. Geoffrey had been given a knot book for his birthday, and he and Papa were going through them one by one. Square knot. Bowline. Hangman's noose.

"Look, Ma!" Geoffrey ran up to me with the cord in his hand. "My first bowline. Want to see?"

I hugged him hard.

He undid the knot and stood in front of me so that I could learn how to do it myself. He made a small loop and then took the other end of the rope in his hand. "This end is the rabbit," he said and licked the frayed end so that it would pass through the hole more easily. "See? The rabbit goes through the hole, around the tree, and into the hole again." He pulled it tight triumphantly. A perfect oval that held. "That's the bowline. Want to try?"

"Later." I kissed the top of his head, and he jumped back onto the couch next to Papa.

"Let me see," Papa said, and Geoffrey passed it over for inspection. Mother was in the kitchen and hadn't come to say hello.

"Mother?"

"Mmm?"

She offered her cheek without taking her eyes off the dishes. I waited to be asked, then sat at the kitchen table.

"Papa says you're going up to Poughkeepsie?"

"Boat leaves tomorrow." She was strenuously cheerful.

"How long will you be gone?"

"Two weeks. Maybe longer. I'll have Easter there and then decide."

"Give everyone my best."

She had finished the dishes, and now she was working on the countertops. There seemed to be no reason for her to turn around.

"I've left some food for your father, but I expect you will keep an eye on everything."

"Yes, of course."

"And Geoffrey." She paused at the end of the counter and flipped the dishcloth over her shoulder. "I don't believe he will be any trouble for you."

I walked to the sink to fill a glass of water from the hand pump. It was one of the things Geoffrey loved most about this house. I couldn't get the water to come up right away; I had never been able to. Mother took the glass away from me and pumped it hard; the water gushed.

"Your father," she said, handing me the glass, "is very involved with the Textile Council now."

"He told me he's been to the meetings."

"He goes to meetings every night."

The Textile Council was the alternative to the IWW, and a union only for skilled workers like himself. Papa had told me he wanted to help broker deals between craftsmen and management. At last Mother looked at me, no longer pretending to be cheerful. She had always asked him to stay clear of unions after Poughkeepsie went so wrong. I waited, and she went over to the back door to look at the garden. Geoffrey and Papa had moved from the parlor to the front porch.

"I'll ask him to dinner over at our house while you're gone," I said. Mother didn't turn around, and I got up to stand next to her. She had been angry for weeks now, ever since Geoffrey began to read aloud to me. We had gotten through *Kidnapped,* and now we were on *David Balfour.*

"I've told your father he shouldn't go to so many meetings." We stared out the screen door. "He gets very excited, and he hasn't been sleeping."

"I'll be sure to have him over."

"I've got to get the tomatoes planted when I get back," she said. "The almanac says it will be a rainy summer, so I'm thinking of only doing cherry tomatoes this year."

"You'll see what they're doing in Poughkeepsie."

"That's right."

I couldn't stand another second and turned to leave the room, but she stopped me with her hand on my shoulder.

"Thank you, Frankie."

"For what?" I waited, trying not to hope that she could make it all better between us.

She said nothing.

"Everything will be fine here," I said.

"I know. I know it will."

Kiss. Kiss. Cheek. Cheek.

1928

⁘

B Y Easter, Winslow and I had spent far too much
time in church. The mill school was thriving, and
Alice had been right, Winslow had found a job that he
could do. He managed to stay out late and still be in church
every morning to pray for Alice. I couldn't help wondering
what she would have thought about it all, and I went along
with the routine for quite a while. But on Easter Sunday, I
changed out of mourning, and after services I decided that
Winslow could do as he pleased, once a week was as much
church as was required for Geoffrey and me. It had been
two months since Alice carefully placed that gun inside her
mouth. But everything changed in Rock Harbor on that
Monday after Easter 1928, and Winslow forgot all about
going to church.

A notice went up at the mills Monday morning announcing another 10 percent cut in wages, but this time the owners hadn't bothered to discuss it with the craftsmen in the

Textile Council. There was an immediate walkout at all the mills where the wage cut had been posted. This had never happened before, and the mayor came over first thing to have a hurried coffee with Ham Curtis. Ham announced after breakfast that he wasn't returning to Boston as soon as he had expected and went upstairs to get changed.

People were in and out of the house all day, and we never had a proper meal. I had Allie keep sandwiches and coffee coming, glad to see Winslow included in the talks, though they kept the door firmly shut against me. Geoffrey and I walked down to the Flint Mill after school let out. He had announced that he was going to be an engraver like his grandpa Ross when he grew up, but Ham had told him he was better off staying in school.

"You'll please both of your grandpas better when you're a Harvard man," Ham had said, and Geoffrey had gotten sulky when all of the adults at the table agreed. I had laughed at Geoffrey along with Ham and Winslow. Of course he should go to Harvard. I had gotten used to being Mrs. Winslow Curtis. Now, what I remembered most about my wedding was being pregnant, then not being pregnant, and worrying about what Joe would say when he found out we had gotten married.

It was a warm day for early April, and the street in front of the mill was filled with workers. I pulled Geoffrey closer to me. I was wearing my gray silk dress and a stupidly small hat. Geoffrey had on knickers and a matching jacket that would have been Sunday best for any of the mill rats. I looked for Papa, but there was nobody familiar. More and more people poured out of the main gate, and a boy threw his cap in the air as if it were the Fourth of July, shouting, "Strike! Strike!"

Everyone around him started in. "Strike! Strike!"

Geoffrey threw his cap and started yelling along with the others.

"Stop it," I said. "You look like Little Lord Fauntleroy." I pulled him even closer, fighting the sudden rigidity of his body. People were smiling as they shouted to the others coming out of the mill gates, and I heard someone say that the Nashawena Mill was shut down, and the Printworks, Acushnet, Morse, and Wamsutta mills.

Then I saw Joe. He was standing on a couple of crates waving a piece of paper in the air.

"Is he a pirate?" Geoffrey asked.

Nobody else looked anything like Joe, with his lean, hungry body and a patch over his bad eye. Joe might not even know that Geoffrey had been born. I suddenly felt as if we had been separated by more than the years. As if he didn't know me at all anymore.

"That's Joe." I was so casual. "Joe Barros."

"You know him, Ma?"

"We grew up together."

I always thought that I would somehow sense it when Joe was in Rock Harbor. But I didn't, hadn't felt a thing until right then—when it all came back just looking at him.

"The council wants to have a backroom vote!" Joe's voice was already hoarse. "What do the workers want with a backroom vote? Whose vote is it? Is it the bosses' vote?"

"NO!"

"The engravers and the carders! The fixers and the pickers! We don't need a Textile Council telling us what to do, we want One Big Union! What's your vote?"

"STRIKE!"

"The council will do an honest count!" yelled a man with a thick Manchester accent like Papa's. "The craft union members have voted, and the council will—"

"Who cares about the council!"

"Take care of themselves, the English."

I pulled Geoffrey's arm for him to keep quiet. We were surrounded by French Canadians and Portuguese, and I could only understand the conversation in bits and pieces. There were some police at the gate to the mill, but they were outnumbered. Where was Papa?

"Have the council tally up the votes in front of all of us," called Joe. "So we know you have nothing to hide."

My stomach twisted hard. I yanked on Geoffrey's hand to make him follow. My whole body was sweating, and I was forgetting the boy who reluctantly held my hand, forgetting everything as my blood rushed toward Joe. Not Joe, I thought. Not now.

"I like that man," Geoffrey said on the way home. "Can I meet him? He looks like Douglas Fairbanks with an eye patch."

"Yes, yes he does."

"But he's a Pawtugee."

"Portuguese."

"What's a strike?"

"Hmm?"

"What is it?"

A strike, I kept repeating inside my head. A strike.

"Ma?"

"A strike is when the workers refuse to work."

"But how do they make money if they refuse to work?"

"I don't know. Something to do with the unions, I guess."

"Grandpa is in the Textile Council, Grandma said." Geoffrey grinned. "Can I go where they count the votes? With Grandpa? Can I?"

In all, fifty-eight mills went out on strike, which meant about 27,000 workers on the picket lines. Father Mendalos, the most powerful priest in the Portuguese congregation, had plenty to talk about in his sermon when it came to the Resurrection and the Life. Rock Harbor was wide awake.

Nobody thought the strike would last long. For the first few days I went down to the Flint Mill again and again, hoping to see Joe. The papers said Little Bill was starting a new union now that the IWW had been abandoned or flattened, depending on whom you asked. Joe was starting a new union right here in Rock Harbor called the Textile Mill Committee, the TMC. It was to include everyone, no matter what their job was. The Textile Council hated the TMC, and the manufacturers were just as glad that the two unions were fighting each other.

I changed into some of the dresses I had worn years ago, nothing fashionable, and I traded my hat for a scarf. But now it was the strikers who dressed in their Sunday best for the picket line. There was singing and union picnics, and nobody minded a little holiday. Geoffrey begged to go down to the picket line after school. He told everyone that his grandpa was Allen Ross, engraver and member of the council—no mention of his other grandfather. I left it alone.

People were kinder to each other on the picket line than they were on the street or in the grocery store. Even in my old clothes I wasn't taken for a mill hand, but Geoffrey helped me come across like just another mother to them. I didn't march in the pickets, but I asked questions and always, always looked for Joe. Geoffrey learned the songs, and we sang them furtively at bath time:

> On the line, on the line,
> On the picket, picket line
> Boys and girls together
> In all kinds of weather,
> Singing on the picket, picket line.

Ham Curtis left Rock Harbor in the middle of April. He was confident that the strike would be broken within a few weeks. The strike had brought back his old energy; he snapped at me about everything, and I couldn't wait for him to be gone. But even after his father left town, Winslow's evenings out didn't change, and now his days were much longer. Our conversations were at the breakfast table and political. It was the safest way I knew; not asking what he was doing at night, not asking what he was thinking, since that could mean I would have to tell him what I was thinking or whom I was looking for every day. I tried not to think about Joe, and if thirty minutes went by without him in my head it was a relief. I met Geoffrey after school, and we would go to the library or up the Flint, take a look at the picket lines, and stop by the council office to make sure that Papa was eating. Mother had decided to extend her stay in Poughkeepsie, and I got the sense from Papa that she might even stay through part of the summer this time. But he didn't seem disturbed by her being gone; all of his time was taken up by the union.

Winslow and Lizzie moved the mill school to a storefront on Water Street and turned it into a soup kitchen. They followed the guidelines of an English workers' club that fed the children of striking workers every day. The children called it the "Bread and Lollipops" strike. Winslow liked to boast that, even though it was an English club, it fed Portuguese, French-Canadian, Polish, and Italian children as well. Lizzie planned the menu and gave away pamphlets about staying healthy. I served food there two or three times a week, and Geoffrey helped give out candy. Lizzie knew everyone's names, and if I was dressing down for the strike, she was dressing up. She smiled when she saw me and always thanked me when I left.

In that first month of the strike, the whole city acted as if it were on holiday. It was spring. I was surprised when Winslow wanted to make love to me for the first time since Alice died, and it was very late when he came in and woke me up with an urgency that pulled me back to him despite it all. Sex with Winslow always made me think that everything would turn out fine.

I kept thinking about what Alice had said that day at the mill with Lizzie and Winslow. Yes, I had Geoffrey now, but what *was* I going to do? I walked all over the city trying to talk it out with Alice in my head. Flippant Alice, who never read a bedtime story to a child in her life; Geoffrey would have fallen madly in love with her. I told her what I knew: I could run the house, if Ham stayed out of my way. I could bring up Geoffrey. I knew now how much I loved my boy, and I was pretty sure that I loved Winslow. But Alice hadn't asked me about any of that, she had asked me what I was going to do. I kept walking. When I came across a rally, I stood at the back and listened, and I started to understand why this pay cut had been the last one the city could stand after ten years of wage loss and layoffs. But what I was really doing, all day, every day, was staying invisible and looking for Joe. I couldn't even talk to Alice about that, because it's a lie that the dead don't talk back.

One morning I stopped by the council office without Geoffrey.

"Is Mr. Allen Ross here?" I sounded too nervous. I never spoke to anyone on my walks around the city.

"He's always here." The woman at the front desk jerked her head without looking up. "You know where to find him."

Papa was sitting at a small table covered with so many papers you could hardly see the map of Rock Harbor spread out beneath them.

"Frankie!" He pushed the chair aside. "Is everything all right at home?"

"Yes, yes, everything's fine."

The room was hardly large enough for Papa, his table and desk chair. The window was open and the sky was holding back rain, and nothing stirred.

"Tea?" A kettle near the windowsill had steam coming from the spout. He moved a stack of papers to clear the chair for me. I smiled at Papa and suddenly felt as if I were home.

"Tea would be good."

"There's lots to do, Frankie. Lots to do." He was talking very quickly as he poured. "I've worked harder since the strike began than I ever have before."

"What are you doing?"

"All these notes." He sounded urgent. "Notes from the meetings of the council. My job is to take notes, type them up, hand them off every day. I put in my hours. More hours now your mother's out of town."

He couldn't sit down. "I type whenever I can. Every day. I do a bit." He closed and opened the window, slamming it up hard and shoving in a piece of wood to hold it open. "They say it will rain and I don't want the papers to be ruined, but I can't stand it when it's so close in here."

"Have they given you a typewriter, Papa?"

"Oh, yes. There she is." He pointed under my chair, and I saw a typewriter pushed back against the wall. "The engraving of the letters on the keys is very fine indeed."

I stood up so that he could pull it out. He held the Smith-Corona in both hands, a bit away from his body, as if he were afraid it could shatter. I cleared a spot for it on the desk, and he gently pressed each key to show me the workmanship. He showed me the lever to switch from lower case to upper case and the gleaming return bar.

193

He smiled when the bell rang at the return, and then he had to do it one more time. The ribbon was still wound tightly on the left-hand spool. "She's a beauty, isn't she?" He traced the keys with his thick fingertip but didn't press down.

"I can type, Papa."

"Oh, no. I'm fine. I'm just fine."

"I know you are, Papa. But why don't I give you a hand?"

He stared at me, and I thought he might begin to shout. Why had I said anything? I should have only admired, as Mother always did. I thought of the woman at her desk down the hall, and I started speaking faster. "Papa, I'm free until Geoffrey gets out at three-fifteen. I'll just help out a little today. You can read me the important parts, and I'll type."

"They're all important—"

"—Just like a secretary. I did get up to thirty-five words a minute in typing school—"

"—I can do it." His eyes, which matched mine, narrowed.

"Please, Papa. I need to do something as well."

"What about the soup kitchen? Geoffrey?"

"The soup kitchen is Winslow's, Winslow's and Lizzie DuBois's. I help out there, so does Geoffrey."

"Well, then."

"Well, then?"

The first week was only typing, and I could tell it made Papa happy to have me there. We had our sandwiches at lunch, our tea in the afternoon. He was tender in his quiet way, when we were alone, and he showed me off when the other union men were around. When Papa was told to go around to the landlords and the grocery stores and ask them to extend credit, or lower the rents temporarily for the strikers, I came along.

The stores were mostly cooperative about extending credit. "It won't be long," Papa told them. "Just to tide us over."

The churches were preaching against the wage cut, and the newspapers agreed, but they were all behind the council; they attacked the TMC and called Joe a Communist. Papa was surprised that I knew as much as I did about the strike.

"You haven't seen Barros, though?"

"No."

"The council's always been able to make a compromise with management, just by talking it over. People want to be reasonable. But listen, Frankie, what happened to Joe? He used to be a good kid."

We were walking from store to store, and the wind from the harbor smacked hard.

"He's not a Red. Not according to him."

"He left town for a long time, didn't he? And then to come back like this."

"I haven't seen him since he came back."

"Don't know why he ever got involved with those anarchists. Maybe it was the war."

I didn't say anything, and Papa pulled his coat closer around him. "Lord knows he can speak well, though," he said. "People love him. Not our kind of people, I mean the people who haven't even been in this country long enough to know any better. Not their fault."

195

"Joe's not a Red."

"When was the last time you spoke with him, Frankie?" We were walking downhill again and were nearly at the river.

I didn't answer. Didn't want to put the years to it.

Flocks of birds swooped around the mills, darting in and out of the empty chimneys as if it were a dare. It was still a shock to see the skyline without smoke; everything appeared to be lifted a few feet off the ground.

"He's out of touch with Rock Harbor now. You have to take care of your own first. We've done all right here because we've mostly produced the fine-weave cloth. Down south it's a whole different market; they do the coarse weave. We're not in direct competition with the South, and the owners are not unreasonable people. Profits are actually rising for the fine-weave. Ask your father-in-law."

"Ham always tells me that he's in the business of politics, not running a mill."

"It's the same thing, Frankie." Papa started laughing. "Exactly the same thing."

Summer came full on by July, hot and humid, and the strike kept going. I heard that Joe was getting funds from the Communist Party for workers' relief, that he was going to turn everyone who joined the TMC into a member of the Party. But despite all the rumors, there were still big picket lines every day, and the TMC meetings kept moving from place to place, backyards and abandoned lots, so the police had a hard time finding them.

"How do people know where the meetings are when they keep changing the location?" I asked Winslow.

"They pass the word on the picket line. It seems so haphazard." He looked at my father, who was eating at our house again that night. Winslow had come home for dinner, though he would be leaving again after the meal. "But you know, Allen, whatever they're doing is working."

"They're better organized than they seem," Papa said. "But they're still a bunch of Reds."

After he left that night, I went into the kitchen and asked Allie where the next TMC meeting was going to be held.

"And how would I know that?"

I picked up the cloth for the silver and rubbed a fork that was lying on the counter. "My father has a message for Joe Barros, and I told him I'd be sure to deliver it in person. I've known Joe since we were at Borden."

"I remember him coming around when Miss Alice— He was arrested, I heard."

"Arrested?"

"He's always getting arrested, ma'am. More than anyone else, I imagine."

"Is he really a Communist?" I rubbed harder at the imaginary tarnish.

"I don't know what people say at those meetings, ma'am."

"Where's the meeting?" She looked away. Allie and I usually got along; she knew where I was from. "You haven't told me anything, Allie," I said, trying a smile.

"The Reds aren't so funny, ma'am."

"No, of course not," I said. "But you're not one and I'm not one, so let's not worry about them."

"Very well, ma'am."
I was being asked to leave the kitchen.

When Allie left that night, I grabbed my coat and followed. Winslow and Papa had gone out after dinner, and
Geoffrey was in bed, but the maid would be downstairs.
The humidity had never really broken, and the lawns lay
heavy and damp. Thick branches of trees split the sky into
puzzle pieces that went from navy blue to black overhead. I
trailed Allie down the hill toward the mills and Corky Row.
People were sitting out on their front porches drinking and
talking. Even the babies were outside in their prams, everyone trying for a breath of air. I hurried past like a stranger
in my own town.

Mother would be sitting on a screened-in porch with
her sisters right now, their three fans whirring like caught
dragonflies, talking about everything but politics. Most of
my cousins had children of their own, and the grandchil-
dren would be playing ringolevio for hours in the twilight
of the Hudson Valley. I wasn't sure what the Poughkeepsie cousins thought of me now. They probably assumed
the worst, since I had married into money. I thought of
that English garden in front of my aunt's house, and I was
afraid to go back and see the summerhouse grown smaller
than it was in memory. Rock Harbor was home. I turned a
corner into the shadow of the Acushnet Mill and smiled in
the dark, wondering what people must think of me following Allie's quick steps like a thief, my scarf and plain cotton
coat hiding where I slept at night.

Allie took another turn, then went through a side door into a warehouse. I waited outside with my head turned away; I didn't want Allie to know what I had done to her. Once enough of a crowd had filed past me, I slipped inside. Bales of raw cotton lined the walls and filled most of the room. It was hotter inside than out, and the smell of dust and sweat mixed with something else: a dense, yeasty smell that I realized was the cotton itself. People were sitting on it and leaning against it, and children were asleep on top of the highest bales, out of the way. There were dents where people had been sitting, and as I tried to find a place near the door, I slipped into a spot that felt as worn as a church pew. Of course, I thought, the cotton has been here since Easter. I didn't quite fit in and got some curious looks, but I was tolerated. There was a nearly constant coming and going, and the people who hadn't managed to get to the front leaned forward to listen. The bales closest to the center were broken open, spilling their gray insides over the baling wire onto the floor, and a space had been cleared by a young girl who kept sweeping it back.

Joe was standing right there, one leg up on the chair, too full of energy to sit. Geoffrey was right, he did look like a pirate.

"They say that we're trying to take this industry away." His voice was soft but carried all the way to the door, and everyone was trying to sit still and listen. "The carders, the ring twisters, the sweepers, the doffers—but we're shut out of the weaving room. Who pushes *us* away?"

"The English," somebody said, and there came a

woman's voice: "The council." Her accent emphasized the wrong syllable, coun*cil*. "The coun*cil* keeps us out."

"That's what the manufacturers want you to think." Joe's voice became even softer. "The council is only made up of mill hands, just like us. So, they're English, Scottish—"

"The French!" somebody called out. "The Canucks are with the council now, Joe, and the papers say you're a Red."

"And who do you think is behind those papers? But they don't own the Portuguese papers, do they? They don't own the Polish papers."

Joe said something in Portuguese, the soft *th*s and *sh*s blending together as his voice rose and everyone strained toward him, his body rocking back and forth on the chair. I saw the Joe who would jump from the Tiverton bridge with Winslow, that summer when they taught me to swim and showed off for me every day. I tried to pull back, but I was surrounded by people leaning closer and closer.

He broke back into English. "More than these wage cuts," he said, and there was another surge forward.

"We demand a twenty percent wage *increase*—"he said, and here the crowd began to shout.

"A forty-hour workweek." He turned in a circle on the top of his chair so that everyone could see him. People were standing on the cotton bales against the walls.

"No more speedups, no more discrimination against union members. No more children in the mills. First in Rock Harbor, then in Massachusetts and the whole country."

They began to chant something in Portuguese and

stamp their feet. The room was hot; there was no chance of sitting down.

"When you wake up tomorrow, don't picket the mill where you worked. Picket the mill closest to you," Joe called over the noise. "It doesn't matter if you've ever worked there or not. We'll keep the mills shut down!"

Everyone crammed toward the center of the room. It was only the sweeper girl who kept any kind of circle cleared around Joe.

"Tomorrow morning. The women and the children, the dyers and the carders—go to the mill closest to your house! Women and children with the men. If they're old enough to work, they're old enough to strike." He got down from the chair; the meeting was over.

Somebody started singing as everyone moved out into the yard. I pushed sideways through the crowd so that I could lean against the building. Up between the corner of this warehouse and the next was an odd yellow moon that looked too heavy to hoist itself over the roofs. They were still singing:

> *A ramboia, a ramboia*
> *Ande sempre a ramboiar.*
> *Quem casar com a papo-seco*
> *Não precisa de trambalhar.*

Then Joe was right next to me, holding my arm to keep me from pulling away as he continued the song.

A menina do papo-seco, o ai!
O ai!
A woman who loves to dance,

he continued in English,

is always dreaming.
Whoever marries a dandy
Does not need to work.

He smiled and leaned closer. His breath was sharp with tobacco. "Isn't that right, Frankie?"

"Stop."

I pushed him away, and he didn't resist; letting go of my arm, he leaned against the wall and pulled out a cigarette. I realized this was the first time he had seen me in nine years. I wasn't yet thirty, but how old I must have become to him. I told myself not to care.

"Why did you come down here?" He offered me a cigarette, and when he held the match his hand was shaking. There were so many quick answers. I thought of all of them later, but nothing came out of my mouth.

"I heard Winslow's become a humanitarian, running that free lunch place with Lizzie DuBois."

"Winslow doesn't know what to do since Alice died."

He paused, but I figured he must have known already. It was written up in all the papers when it happened: WEALTHY NEWLYWED IN TRAGIC GUN ACCIDENT.

"Too much money, the luxury of unhappiness." His voice was hoarse, but it wasn't any gentler.

"Alice didn't die because she was rich."

"Why, then?"

"How do I know what she was thinking?"

There were voices inside the warehouse, and I glanced toward the open door, but Joe ignored them. "So Winslow doesn't know what to do with himself?" He drew hard on his cigarette and paced in front of me.

"You're good, Joe."

"What?"

"At speaking. They listen."

"Listen to the Red. We'll see for how long."

"Are you a Red, Joe?"

"You and Winslow better stay away from me. That would never fly in the Highlands, where they're not quite sure how to spend their days when they wake up in the morning."

"Winslow can't help where he was born."

"How about you?"

"What?"

"Do you know what to do when you wake up in the morning?"

"No. Is that what you want to hear? I don't know what to do in the morning. I came down here because you never came over after that stupid fight with Alice—"

"That's not why I stopped coming over."

"Everyone was drunk that night, including you."

"You're married to Winslow."

"You know why I got married."

"And?"

"And then Alice died and you never said a word to him—to us."

"I was in Passaic the year after the strike. Or do you even know about Passaic?"

"Why don't you just talk to me, Joe?"

"Why don't you leave me alone?"

I was half a block away before I heard him running behind me.

"Frankie." He moved lightly in front of me, still the basketball star. "Please. Are you all right?"

"Fine."

"Frankie?" He held both of my shoulders so that I had to stop and look directly in his face. That one eye with a web of lines around it now, and that jaw, that mouth.

"I'm not crying," I said, though he could see I was lying. "And I know my way home."

He touched one cheek and then the other with the tip of his finger, callused and smelling of tobacco. I didn't move as he put his finger into his mouth, catching the taste from my eyes.

I moved around him and kept walking. Not crying as hard as I could.

"There, look at that." Ham Curtis slammed the newspaper down on the breakfast table. He had been back from Boston for a week. "Judge Anderson threw the Barros kid in jail again. Listen to this: 'An anarchist, outsider, and well-known agitator is responsible for disturbing the law-abiding tactics of our Rock Harbor labor leaders.'"

"Joe's no outsider." Winslow reached for the paper.

"He put himself outside." Ham grabbed the front page back from Winslow to read aloud: "'The parade that the TMC has scheduled for today does not have a city permit, and residents are discouraged from attending or participating in any way.'"

There had been daily meetings at the breakfast table. The senator was definitely back in charge, and though I hated having to live with his backhanded acknowledgment of me, I wondered if his return meant that the mill owners were getting worried after all.

It was two weeks since I had gone down to the TMC meeting, and Joe's strategy was working. The picket lines were bigger every day, despite the fact that more and more people were being arrested for disturbing the peace.

"Frankie," Winslow said. "Geoffrey wants to know if he can go to the beach with the Morrow boy. He told me to ask you."

I realized that Geoffrey's handball had stopped banging against the side of the house. I walked over to the long windows that were open to the yard and looked down, first glancing at Winslow, who smiled at me, and then his father.

"You can go," I said quietly, surprising Geoffrey, who jumped red-faced and dirty out of the flower bed.

"How did you know where I was?"

Ham and Winslow started laughing, and Ham walked over to the window. "Of course you should go to the beach," he said, leaning over the low sill. "I don't want my only grandchild to be spending his summer on the picket line like those pinko kids."

"I like going down to the pickets with Grandpa Ross."

"The council kids don't picket," Winslow said.

"Am I a council kid?" Geoffrey asked.

"You'd better scoot or the Morrows will leave without you," I said.

Ham Curtis reached into his pocket, and a coin glinted through the air. Geoffrey tried to catch it, missed, then grubbed it triumphantly out of the dirt. Geoffrey had a famous grandfather with pressed linen suits and pockets full of change. "A nickel for ice cream, Geoff; you can treat the Morrow kid. And remember: Buy it for a nickel"—he paused, giving Geoffrey a breath to join in so that they chanted together—"sell it for a dime."

"Thanks, Grandpa!" Geoffrey took off almost in time to miss my kiss on the top of his head, the salty taste of summer. As I turned back into the room, Winslow caught my eye. Before Ham returned, it had begun to feel more like our house. Now Winslow and I were back to hardly seeing each other. I worked more and more hours with Papa at the council. I missed Geoffrey, but I was determined to work Joe out of my system, and it was easier when I was too tired to think.

Ham poured himself a third cup of coffee. "So." He pulled his chair in closer. "The Barros kid's gang found itself a new place to meet, since McNally shut down TMC headquarters?"

An officer named Timothy McNally had been promoted to police chief. He was from Corky Row, and he used to work privately for Ham. Between the stepped-up arrests, Judge Anderson's sentencing, and the English, Scottish, and French Canadians who dominated the juries, the jails were always full. Except for the singing, the picket lines didn't look like a holiday anymore.

"They've got DeRoche's lot at the north end," Winslow said. "It's fenced off, and they're within their rights to meet on private property. I don't think McNally's going to be able to get around it. They've got some lawyers up from New York. Guys that were involved in the Passaic strike. I heard they already got Joe out so that he can lead the march today."

"Damnit to hell." Ham got up from the table. "Anderson was supposed to keep Barros locked up." He spread his large, soft hands out on the table. "We want only the council in this march." According to the paper, the council was a group of "seasoned workers," while the TMC was made up of "radical elements intent on destroying a way of life." Ham loved reading those bits aloud.

"Of course, you have to tolerate the council pickets," I said. "The more the council and the TMC fight each other, the better it is for the mill owners. Do I have that right?"

"You do have that right. Better for you too, my dear, and Geoffrey." Ham Curtis took a satisfied sip of coffee, and I smiled right back at him.

"But that's not what this is about," Winslow said.

"No," said Ham. "Once these Reds are out of the way, we can work together again. Labor *and* management, like we have for twenty years. Now, about this march—"

"Parade," said Winslow.

"We're calling it a march, and so is the newspaper, Winslow. You can make sure of that by stopping by the office of the *Tribune* after breakfast."

Winslow nodded.

"It might rain," I said. "But they're expecting a big gathering." I thought for a minute. "It's a lousy beach day, actually."

"The Morrows have their place down there," said Winslow. "If it rains." He turned back to Ham. "The council is showing some division. There's council members who don't think it's right that the TMC folks can't get city relief like the council families. People have been driving all over: Taunton, Fall River, New Bedford, picking up vegetables for TMC kitchens."

"What do you want, Winslow? You want everybody to like you?" Ham grabbed another slice of toast and moved his heavy jaw mechanically.

"It could be bad publicity," Winslow said quietly.

"They've got a couple of ovens set up in an abandoned lot to bake bread," I said. "People are saying—"

"Good for them. Bread being baked in a lot? The Pawtugees are resourceful people." Ham pushed back from the table. "It's not that bad out there. I saw twenty men fishing for bluefish yesterday. As long as the blues are running, nobody will go hungry."

"It's going to be a big gathering," Winslow repeated.

"Worst summer in ten years, always raining. Rotten weather for pickets." Ham walked to the window and held his hand out over the flower bed where Geoffrey had been hiding. As if he had commanded it, the first fat drops began to fall. Ham turned back to the room. He stared down at the wet marks on his hand. "Sometimes things just work themselves out."

We got up to leave the table, and Winslow kissed me on the mouth, surprising me; then he pulled back and gave me a look I couldn't quite interpret. He said that he would be home as early as he could, but he said this every morning, without the kiss. We both knew that meant after the bars had closed, with martini breath and an urge for sex that I usually went along with. That part always worked, though outside of the bedroom there was a new formality between us that came with the understanding that it would not be in one's own interest to ask questions. I was sure Winslow would never divorce me, but I wasn't quite modern enough not to care that he didn't come home at night. I watched him walk steadily off to the newspaper office for his father and realized that I had no idea what he thought about our marriage. *If* he thought about our marriage.

Maybe this was how it was for everyone, and people just didn't talk about it.

The rain broke all at once, and I went to close the windows. I met Papa an hour later to go to the North End with marchers from the council. It was the same drenching rain that had poured over the pickets all summer. It got you wet but didn't cool you off. There were hundreds of black umbrellas jostling each other down the side streets to join the march.

"All this without a permit," Papa said. We never even got close to DeRoche's lot. The march was coming, and we were pulled into the stream along with everyone else. Hundreds of children were carrying signs bigger than their bodies, singing:

> *Strawberry shortcake, huckleberry pie,*
> *Who gave the bosses a punch in the eye?*
> *We did. We did. And who are we?*
> *We are the members of the TMC!*

Joe and Father Mendalos were walking arm in arm at the front. A greengrocer who recognized Papa yelled: "Is the council marching then, Mr. Ross?"

"It's not a march, it's a parade," Papa called back, and people linked arms under their umbrellas. Just behind us were the Cape Verdean women in traditional dress, still bright in the rain. Ten or twenty people were holding the edges of an oversize American flag spread horizontally above the ground, like an enormous quilt moving magically along the street. I could hear drums and a marching band. It started raining harder, and when people in front of us began to slow down, I thought it was because of the streams coming from the side streets in tiny waterfalls. Then I saw the police wagons and trucks blocking the street. In front of these were soldiers in uniform, holding rifles with bayonets. Joe and Father Mendalos held up their hands, and we tried to slow down, but the people in back kept pushing us forward.

"Nobody said anything about the National Guard," Papa said.

"Guarda Nacional." I heard it repeated in Portuguese. Papa pushed me to the side. "Get out of the crowd, Frankie," he said. "Go over to the sidewalk."

But I wasn't going to leave Papa, and none of us could get out of the way, we were packed too tightly together. Joe approached the line of soldiers, who were pushing back against the crowd with their rifles in the air. Chief McNally was there too, and two of the Cape Verdean women linked arms with me, calling over their shoulders in Portuguese. I could hear only pieces of what Joe was saying. That's when I noticed the size of the black clubs McNally and the other Rock Harbor policemen had at their waists—bigger than regular billy clubs, even I knew that much. Then McNally's club came down on the backs of Joe's knees, there was the snap of a rifle, and Joe's voice was cut off in the middle. Everyone heard him stop. Father Mendalos reached out as Joe crumpled below the surface of heads and arms. Papa yelled and tried to push somebody out of the way. I saw Papa stagger, then I couldn't see anything but shoulders and backs pushing against me. I held tight to Papa's arm and felt one of the women grab me by the elbow and pull hard. We fell or were pushed to the ground, and there was a soldier holding his rifle above his head.

"Hold your fire! My sister's on strike!" he yelled, and I wondered why he looked so young. There was a sudden clearing to the side of us as a gang of policemen walked in formation, using their clubs. One woman bit a policeman's bare arm as he pulled her from the ground, and he dropped her back down, grabbing at the blood that streamed toward his wrist in the rain. I heard something else smashing but couldn't see what, and a child started crying very loud. Five mounted police rode into the crowd, the metal-shod hooves right next to our bare heads and hands. The horses slipped sideways against the rainy cobblestones, but it worked. The street cleared out around them, and I was pushed against the side of a building. I put my hands over my face as more soldiers ran past; then I felt a hand pulling my arm.

"Frances." It was Father Mendalos. Rain and dirt were dripping down his face and smearing his glasses so that his eyes looked like holes. "Your father's been arrested." I had let go of Papa. How had I let go of Papa? The priest pushed me up a side street, and I began to run. I didn't run up to the Highlands or over to the police station, I

ran up the Flint. Everyone on the street was either heading into the march or running away from it. I was holding up my skirt as I ran, and I reached our front porch
almost before I knew where I was going. I started to turn
the door handle to let myself in, then stopped. When was
Mother coming back from Poughkeepsie? She had been
gone so long I'd lost track. I knocked, and the beveled
glass rattled. I knocked again. Rain was pouring out of a
side gutter and landing with a splatter on the pan lid my
mother used for a birdbath. The ringing sound echoed
around the yard as I looked above the sill for the key they
kept hidden there.

It was so spotless inside that it looked uninhabited.

I walked into the kitchen and took a look at myself in
Papa's black-framed shaving mirror over the sink. My face
was red, and my hair had fallen into limp, heavy strands. I
closed my eyes and worked the iron pump to splash water
on my face. I got it to work, for once. The water was cold,
and I cupped my hands to drink, wondering automatically
if Papa still kept his liquor in the bathroom. That's when I
noticed Geoffrey's pictures. Colored drawings from when
he was a little boy covered the lower cabinets of the kitchen,
and following the row of them, I saw that they went into
the pantry as well. Chaotic lines and figures were tacked
up to the highest cabinet doors and dominated the neatly
arranged Mason jars of pickled tomatoes, cucumbers, and
cranberry jelly. Most of the pictures were of houses that I
slowly realized were all this house. Flowers that were her
flowers, the Poughkeepsie roses filling an entire sheet of
paper with red crayon, round and sloppy, but I recognized
them. A picture that must have been Mother: a huge, red,

smiling mouth for her face, and the tiny, fully formed boy on her lap was Geoffrey. Another with the two of them holding hands, the red flowers pushing up around their legs and almost covering the sky with blossoms. He had rubbed the sky-blue crayon hard between the crimson petals, turning the paper a patchy purple when he covered a flower with sky by mistake. Determined yellow circles showed a sunny day for Geoffrey at his grandmother's house.

She had put all these up before she left for Poughkeepsie; it must have been after that day with Geoffrey practicing knots, or I would have noticed. Some of them looked so old. How long had she saved these pictures? And who was this woman he had convinced to mother him? I looked at each of the drawings, tracing his image of her with my fingers. Then I found Papa's whiskey and drank two glasses very fast. I rinsed my glass carefully to rid it of any residual smell and put it back exactly where it had been. I needed to find Winslow. I wanted to know what he had meant by that look this morning before I went off to the march. Had he known about the Guard? I didn't even know where Winslow was right now, and I had to get Papa out of jail.

But it wasn't me or Winslow who got Papa out of jail, it was the TMC. Both of the labor unions posted bail for their members, but the TMC was better organized than the council—they were used to being arrested. When I finally got down to the jail after circling back to the empty house in the Highlands, there was somebody calling names out to the crowd gathered in front of the building.

"Allen Ross?" I pushed my way up. The man raised his eyes from his clipboard. "Across the street."

Joe and my father were sitting together on a covered stoop across the street from the jail, staying out of the rain. They didn't even notice me until I was standing right in front of them, the rain beating against my umbrella.

"Frankie!" Joe looked up first. He jumped down the steps and held me by the shoulders. "You're all right. I sent one of my guys—"

"Father Mendalos got me out right away." I suddenly felt like crying and wanted Joe to stop touching me immediately. "Papa?" I hugged him hard. "I went home, to our house I mean, to look for Mother—"

"She's still in Poughkeepsie." He winked at me, and that scared me. Papa never winked. "I'm doing fine for an old guy."

"Some old guy." Joe took the umbrella from me so that I could sit down where he had been.

"Joe made sure I got out," Papa said. "Not sure the council would have bothered with my bail for a while."

Joe stepped back under the overhang to get out of the rain, and I saw him stumble slightly.

"Banged up my knees pretty good," Joe said. "Nothing that won't heal."

"Was anybody shot?"

"The soldiers mostly kept their heads. They fired into the air."

"Those clubs," I said. "And the horses."

"The soldiers should not have been there." Papa looked out at the street and wiped his hand across his mouth. He had a bad scrape on his cheek, but I knew better than to fuss over him in front of Joe. "The mayor ordered the National Guard in last night. Ham never told the council. They never told anyone."

"Allen, I have something I'd like you to see," Joe said. "I know you've got to get home and rest up after this—"

"Rest up!" Papa's accent thickened. "The council is not resting, Joe, no matter what you think of us."

"Papa." I held on to his arm. "Joe's right. Let's go home."

"No. The council always thinks there's somebody better than me to see what's what." Papa pulled away from me, his voice rising. "Let Allen take the notes. Well, I've had enough of it now. I'm not their secretary."

"I know you're not, Papa. But you should rest, now."

"Leave me be." He walked down the steps into the rain. "What is it you wanted to show me?" he said to Joe.

I knew Joe was looking at me, but I kept my eyes on my hands, those hands that always seemed to lose hold.

"If you've got half an hour, then," Joe said. "I got a tip, and if it's true, the council should know about it."

Papa nodded and looked hard at Joe, not bothering to wipe the rain from his face.

We walked down toward the water without talking. I knew Papa didn't want me there, and I pretended not to notice how heavily he was leaning to one side. He wouldn't let me touch him now. Joe's blind eye was to me, so I could take my time looking at him. There was a cut on the back of his head, matted with blood, turning his hair even darker. We went slowly down the steep cobblestones that

215

followed the Wampanoag River to the harbor. Warehouses loomed on either side of us, and everything began to look familiar.

"Isn't this where you had your meeting?" I asked Joe.

He nodded briefly. "One of our meetings."

Papa looked over at us without saying anything. The side door was closed, but Joe took out a penknife and slid it next to the doorframe until the lock popped.

We stepped into the warehouse, and I heard skittering sounds as the gray light from the doorway made a rectangle on the floor.

"Let me get the light," said Joe. "Frankie, shut your eyes for a minute."

"Why?"

"Give the rats a chance to get used to us."

I closed my eyes, and Joe switched on the lights.

"All right," he said after a moment. "They know we're here now."

I looked around. There was still some scratching, but I didn't see any rats. "That's an old mill hand trick," Joe said. "Just give them a minute to get out of the way."

"Live and let live, Joe?" Papa stepped into the big empty room.

Joe limped ahead of him, then turned to Papa with his arms spread wide and his face shut tight. His good eye roamed furiously around the walls.

"There's nothing here, Allen. Just like they told me."

"What are you talking about, who told you?"

"One of my guys. Frankie—" His voice echoed. "Remember all the bales that were here?"

"Everyone was sitting on them."

"Sitting, standing, people could barely fit in here with all that cotton."

"Yes, that's right."

"That was a little over two weeks ago. It's all gone." He spun around to the back of the warehouse so quickly that he nearly lost his balance with his hurt legs. "The cotton's gone."

There was a long pause.

"The bastards," Papa said at last. I turned. Papa almost never swore. Now he was looking around the room just like Joe.

"It's the same with all the warehouses along here," Joe said. "All the cotton's gone."

"So what?" I had to get Papa home. Couldn't Joe tell it was too much? "So what if the cotton's gone? It's not supposed to stay here all the time, is it? It gets sold, shipped out—" I stopped. "You mean the cotton's been sold off when they said it wouldn't be?"

"They never said anything." Joe limped past us so that he could lean against the wall. "They never said anything except there's a twenty percent wage cut."

"They sold off the inventory," Papa said. "That's why they're ready to open the mills now. That's why they haven't been fighting the strike until today. The strike is just what they wanted." He was speaking much too fast, his Manchester accent hardening every word. "They had too much raw cotton, too much of the wrong kind of cloth for the market, something, I don't know. So they announced the wage cut just to give themselves time to sell it off."

I wanted him to stop and breathe, but there was no chance.

"And to see if we would stand for it," Joe said.

"So the strike took care of the inventory for them?" I was still two steps behind.

"Ham Curtis and the rest have been making money off this strike since the beginning," Joe said. "Now they're ready to go back to work, so they bring in the National Guard—"

"And open the mills?" I asked.

"And try to open the mills." Papa looked at Joe. "They're going to try to open with scabs. You know that."

"What are you going to tell your people?"

"I don't know." Papa looked blown apart. "What *can* I tell them? They don't listen to me. We thought the owners were going to be fair. No—but as fair as could be expected. This is what they think in the council. It's how it's always been. I thought that Ham Curtis—"

"You can tell the council about *this*," Joe said. "Tell them what the owners have done with the inventory, and why. Then, when they try to reopen tomorrow, nobody gets past the pickets. No scabs."

Papa moved heavily toward the street door. "They don't listen to me, Joe. There it is. But I'll tell them tonight. I'm glad you brought me here." He reached the doorway. The rain was darkening the daylight, and the wet flooring was littered with cotton lint and baling wire. "I'm going down to the council meeting; they'll be expecting me to take notes, and I will do my very best," Papa said. "Frankie?"

I couldn't see Joe's face in this light. He was standing very still. I looked and looked, but he said nothing.

"You coming, Frankie?"

Joe still said nothing, so I walked with my father back

up the hill through the rain. Papa and I didn't have to speak. He gave me his arm, and I held on tight. I could tell he understood about me and Joe.

I got home late that night. By the time Papa and I arrived at the council meeting, everyone was talking about the news from the Manufacturers' Association. Ham Curtis had just been made president of the association, and he had already held a press conference defending the use of the National Guard in response to the Communist threat posed by the TMC. He scheduled a meeting with the head of the council for the next morning to discuss ending the strike. Down at the council office, everything was back on track. Craftsmen and mill owners would talk it through as they always had. I watched Papa jotting notes and waited for him to speak up. At the break for coffee and cigarettes, he got his coat and started for the door.

"Papa?"

"I'm going home now, Frankie. It's late."

"But aren't you going to tell them about the inventory?"

"I'm tired." He held a hand out to see if there was still any rain. "Been a big day."

"Come to our house, Papa. I need to clean up those cuts."

"I'll be fine."

"What about supper?"

"Frankie. I have plenty to eat at home. Your mother's coming back tomorrow, and there are some things to clean up around the house."

I knew how clean it was at home, I had just been there.

We were standing on the street in front of the council office. The rain had nearly stopped, and the men were standing in excited clumps, talking about tomorrow's negotiations.

"I can stay for the rest and finish the notes," I said.

"It can wait."

"Papa, please come home with me. Geoffrey's missed you."

He paused a moment. "Can't do it, Frankie girl. Not tonight."

I couldn't think of anything else to convince him. He pulled his collar up around his ears. "Don't stay, the meeting will go on with or without the notes," he said. "Geoffrey might still be up."

Papa was too old for this. I wanted to put ice on his knee and remember what Mother would have done to make him go to sleep. Whiskey with warm sugar water. He walked away. I wasn't invited. I went back inside and stayed to the end, taking his notes; it was all I could think of to help him.

I went home to a quiet house. There was stew left out by Allie, and I was glad to sit alone in the kitchen, my dress drying by the stove. I would take a hot bath tonight. Bring a glass of whiskey upstairs.

Geoffrey wasn't in his room.

I looked in my bed. No. I opened every bedroom door. No. I woke Cinda, the downstairs maid, who slept on the top floor. She had put Geoffrey to bed at the regular time and heard nothing unusual. Her face went gray, and I shook her hard by the shoulders.

"Where did he go?"

She began to cry, and I loosened my grip.

I ran back up to Geoffrey's room as if I could have missed him. I started yelling for him on every floor while Cinda followed behind, useless.

Down to the Massasoit Club, where Winslow was alone at the bar. I didn't have a coat on, and he knew right away it was Geoffrey.

I couldn't speak properly, and he kept interrupting.

"I don't know" was all I could say. "I don't know."

There was Main Street and the Old Boston Post Road, both leading away from Rock Harbor. There were men standing around homemade fires in oil drums down on Corky Row. There was a fast river and a harbor with no boats working at the docks. It was raining again.

Winslow got some men from the bar to check the ferry dock and along the river. He tried to make me go back to the house. "But he's not there," I said.

"He might come right home."

"Then you go back."

We went outside as if that would help us know what to do. Winslow held me close. "Think, think," he whispered hard. "Where does he go?"

"The library."

"Library's closed."

"Doesn't matter."

We started pulling each other down the hill to Front Street. Maybe he had gone to Pitcairn's Island, maybe he had gone to Sherwood. But the library was dark, and nobody was sitting on the steps, nobody was walking on Front Street. I was having trouble breathing.

"Up the Flint." I looked at Winslow. "Papa."

He took my hand, and we ran as fast as I could, which was slower than I could bear. Straight uphill. Stopping to lean against the walls of buildings. I told Winslow to go ahead without me, but he wouldn't. It took longer to get up the Flint than it would take a boy to drown or get hit by a car.

The door was open at the house, and the lights were on. The rain had been coming in for a while, and I slipped on the floor as I went inside. The back door was swinging wide, and I couldn't see anything in the sudden dark of the porch. But Winslow got there first, standing under Geoffrey, who was under Papa, who was hanging from the metal pole we used to dry the clothes that Mother didn't want the neighbors to see. Winslow got Geoffrey out of the way and pushed up against Papa himself.

"Push him up, push him!" said Geoffrey in a hoarse voice. I grabbed for Geoffrey, but he didn't respond. Winslow told me to get him a chair. I couldn't let go of Geoffrey, but he wrenched away to get his father a chair from the kitchen. Shoulder under Papa's hip, Winslow climbed onto the chair and struggled in the dark. I could hear Winslow breathing hard while Geoffrey held the chair steady. Then a car pulled up, and suddenly Joe was there with us, helping Winslow push, trying to get Papa's head free, the two of them.

"I've got a knife," Joe said. There was a snapping sound, and Papa toppled forward, the chair fell down, and Joe was taking Papa by the arms while Winslow took his legs.

"Close the door," Joe ordered, and Geoffrey ran to the front, slamming the glass door against the rain.

"Water," said Winslow as they laid Papa on the rug. I saw Joe moving Papa's chin back to where a thick red line sheared sharp on his skin. He was breathing, wasn't he?

Wasn't he?

I had the glass of water, but I was shaking so much it mostly spilled down his shirtfront. Winslow supported his back, and I didn't know how hard I was crying until I saw the steam from Papa's breath against the glass. He opened his eyes and swallowed, then looked right at me.

"Don't cry," he rasped.

Geoffrey came in holding a piece of rope. "He used the wrong knot," he said. "It's a bowline, not a hangman's noose."

We all looked.

"How long were you holding him there?" Winslow asked Geoffrey.

"I wasn't tall enough."

I stayed in bed with Geoffrey for a long time after he fell asleep. I had to watch him breathe. Winslow and Joe were still drinking when I came downstairs.

"He's all right?" Winslow asked.

"They're both asleep." I had insisted that we bring Papa back to the Highlands, not the hospital. Hospitals were where people went to die. Winslow poured me a whiskey, neat.

"Geoff was going up to leave a present there for Mother. She's coming back tomorrow," I said. "He told me he couldn't sleep, so he snuck out to do it."

Joe looked down, and I took a long sip.

"What was it?" Winslow asked.

"What?"

"The present."

"He bought her a bracelet at Simmon's."

Winslow passed around the cigarette box.

"Joe?" I asked. "How did you get there? I mean—"

"My boys ran into the men at the wharf looking for Geoffrey. I was down there watching the docks for scabs, and I thought . . . maybe . . ."

"Good thing you did," said Winslow. "Not sure I could have managed."

"What did he say, Frankie?" asked Joe. "When you got him settled."

"He said he had a sore throat."

We all looked at each other and started to laugh.

Mother came home and wanted to know why it happened, but I couldn't tell her why we weren't enough for him to want to stay here with us. She blamed herself for being away so long, though I told her over and over that he had seemed just fine, busier than ever after the strike began. Maybe it was the council men ignoring him that brought on the old anguish, or maybe that choice had never been far away for Papa ever since that time in Poughkeepsie, no matter how hard we both tried to keep him close. Maybe nobody can keep anyone safe and it's just a question of the wrong knot or the right gun.

By October, a lot of people were simply getting hungry. The council voted on the proposal by the Manufacturers'

Association: the owners had changed their offer to a 5 percent wage cut, along with a speedup. The TMC leadership wasn't included in the negotiations, and their membership wasn't allowed to vote. As a concession, the head of the mule spinners' contingent, who was secretary for the TMC, was allowed to count the votes. The vote was rigged from the get-go, but everyone went to the Labor Temple to wait for the results while the TMC picketed outside, protesting the process they had been locked out of. There were thirty thousand workers on strike in Rock Harbor; the two thousand who were council members were allowed to vote.

I drank cup after cup of stale coffee as we waited around long wooden tables on the ground floor of the Labor Temple, newspapers spread out under coffee cups and ashtrays. All the council leaders were there, and Winslow had come over too. Papa had stayed away from the council meetings ever since Mother came home. He never put up a fight with her anymore. I kept going, taking his notes. I explained that Papa wasn't well, but nobody in the council seemed to pay much attention. Outside the Labor Temple, hundreds of people were waiting for the results. Ham was at the Massasoit Club with the Manufacturers' Association.

"Joe Barros is here," somebody said.

"Joe?" Winslow looked up quickly.

Joe was in the doorway, needing a shave but otherwise not looking much like a man who spent most nights in jail. Judge Anderson had kept Joe locked up as much as possible during the negotiations. He smiled at Winslow and me, nodded his head to the rest. "Out on bail," he announced to the room. "Just in time."

He shook Winslow's hand and pulled up a chair.

"Winslow, this vote is wrong." Joe spoke to Winslow but included everyone in earshot. "You can't stand by these results when most of the workers are not being represented. You know that."

"We have to find a solution."

"But it's wrong, Winslow—"

Winslow got up from the table. "It's your man up there counting the ballots. Isn't that enough? Maybe they'll vote it down."

"Maybe they will." Joe tipped his chair back, looking relaxed. Winslow smiled at him in a way that infuriated me. They suddenly seemed so much younger than they really were, both dressed for the occasion in suits and ties.

"How's jail been, Red?" Winslow asked Joe.

"Good night's rest. Good meal. Ready to fight the good fight." Joe tapped his fingers on the table. "How's the relief work with Lizzie DuBois?"

I almost didn't see the falter in Winslow's smile. "The relief work is fine. Helping out a lot of your people too, Joe. Where's the TMC relief money going?"

Joe tipped back and forth. "Maybe you should ask your father where all the money goes in this town."

"Maybe you should ask your own party."

"Which party is that?"

Winslow's smile lingered. "It's not the Republican party."

"Well, it's not the Communist Party either," said Joe lightly.

There was a quick pounding of feet on the stairs from the room where they were counting the votes. The TMC mule spinner stood there red-faced. "No," he said. "The vote is no to the proposal."

"No!" Joe leaped up. "The vote is *no!*" Joe shouted out the window. "No to the bosses! No sellout!" The street exploded with clapping, whistling, and hooting. It was a TMC victory even though it wasn't their vote.

Winslow looked at me. "I thought it was going to be over." His voice was strangely flat under the din.

"Me too."

I wanted to hear what Joe was saying to the crowd and started to get up.

"I shouldn't talk politics with Joe," Winslow said, reaching for my hand and holding it tightly.

"Let's never talk politics again."

After the vote, Winslow drifted away from the Labor Temple. I couldn't even remember him saying good-bye. The neighborhoods near the mills were out celebrating, while the houses in the Highlands were lit up and silent. Cars were coming and going in front of our house all night long, but I hid upstairs with a cold pitcher of gin and water after putting Geoffrey to bed. I simply wanted to be with my boy and have Ham go back to Boston. Tucked close to Geoffrey's sleeping back, I pressed my hand gently along his forehead, feeling his pulse beat solemnly at his temples. He had changed. After Mother came home, he spent more and more time up the Flint. I wanted so much for him not to have to be a watcher, but it was too late. There were the three of us watching Papa now: Mother, Geoffrey, and

me. Five if you counted Winslow and Joe, and when had I
not counted them? Mother didn't seem to hold me responsible for what had happened. She must have seen that I
didn't need any help carrying the blame, and I decided to
be grateful. I let her have Geoffrey until suppertime and
overnight on the weekends. I knew that Geoffrey would
always come back to me now, with his bright hair and tan,
confident Curtis body. He had just begun the third grade.

Geoffrey's bedroom was over the porch, and I woke up
to voices out front. I was afraid that Winslow had gotten
too drunk and needed to be brought upstairs, but when
I opened the door, Joe and Winslow were both sitting on
the front steps.

"Hello, my love," Winslow said. He was drunk, but not
too drunk to walk. "Look who's here."

"Did we wake you?" Joe was propping his head up with
his hand, elbow against his knee.

"No." I pulled my wrap closer and took a step out of
the porch light, figuring I must look awful with my hair all
rumpled. "Yes. What are you doing?"

"Is it late?" Winslow asked.

I walked past them and sat down on the porch swing,
kicking off with my bare feet.

"Did you know that the winter stars are the clear-
est ones?" Winslow pointed up. "Now it's fall, so they're
clearer than they were in summer."

"That's because there's no mill smoke," Joe said.

"Oh, right." Winslow hummed a tune to himself. I recognized it as a picket song from outside the Labor Temple that afternoon; there was something relentlessly cheerful about it. Joe started whistling along, and then he broke off, laughing softly. "One Big Union, right, Curtis?"

"Just don't tell my father."

They both laughed. I kept swinging back and forth.

"We ran into each other at a little celebration down at the Black and White," Joe said, running his hand through his hair.

I nodded. It wasn't such a bad idea for Joe to walk Winslow home. There had been stories about Corky Row in the papers lately. The Row was mostly council members, craft union families, but I remembered reading something about food being cooked right out on the street as people were evicted. I wondered how Winslow had ended up in that part of town, nowhere near the Massasoit Club, but then it was a strange, high night all over the city. A night for serious drinking.

"Joe, listen." Winslow leaned over confidentially. "About my father." I stopped the swing with my toes against the cold wood of the porch. "He's not going to stop at this vote. I guess there's a lot going on." He started to cough, out of nervousness or too many cigarettes. Joe sat quietly, not looking at either one of us. "He's been meeting with the newspaper editors tonight, and down at the Massasoit Club this afternoon. They're going to go after another vote. They'll say this one wasn't fair because the balloting closed too early or something, I don't really get it. But the priests—the church is going to back them up this time. I thought maybe you should know. They're going to get another vote."

Of course he had said too much.

"I know," Joe said. "I know all that, Winslow. But thanks."

We stared out at the lawns where no leaves were allowed.

"The important thing to understand, Winslow, is that it's over for Rock Harbor. The senator knows this better than anyone. The strike just helped them get the most profit they could out of the body."

"What do you mean?" Winslow asked. "What's over? The strike?"

"Not the strike. Not yet." Joe went down the steps to the lawn. I balanced myself on the edge of the porch swing, ready to do almost anything to stop him from leaving. His shoes made white footprints in the frosted grass. "The whole thing. Boom Town. Spindle City. New Bedford, Fall River, Lawrence. The mills down south have upgraded their equipment. In the last six months, no, in the last six years, while the mills up here were pretending it was all business as usual. Make it and spend it and never buy anything new if you can help it. Yankee thrift, right?"

"What do you mean?" I didn't know what he was talking about, drunk or not.

"New England was where you got your cotton done, right? Sure, they did the coarser weaves down south, denims and canvas, but we were big business. Now the southern mills can do printing and fine-weave better than us, faster and cheaper. No unions, or hardly any. Some of our mills are even trying to sell off their company names since nobody wants our equipment. The carding machines, the spinning frames, even the looms; takes too many people to run them. In the end, it's only a story about machinery."

"So, none of this really matters anymore?" I leaned forward. "The TMC, the council?"

"Everybody's getting out. Getting as much cash as they can before it all goes to the Carolinas." Joe kicked the ground.

Winslow started shaking. Joe and I both looked at him, but Joe got there first. He put an arm loosely around Winslow's shoulders. "Want to tell me what's so funny?"

"It's just like the old Curtises." Winslow slowed his breathing enough to speak. "Remember what we used to say at Borden: The sperm that built New Bedford? Got that street named after Captain Curtis, remember?"

"A few streets up here too."

"Right." Winslow wiped his eyes and took some deep breaths. "The Noble Forebears were smart enough to get out of whaling."

"Winslow," I said, moving over to sit on the other side of him. I put my arm around Winslow's waist, and my hand brushed against Joe's arm, still warm in the cold air. "Winslow, let's go inside."

Winslow looked from one to the other. We were huddled so close together that his quickened breath felt as if we were all breathing too high in the chest.

"But you can't get out of everything, can you?" Winslow spoke faster and faster. Every exhale was half laughter, half words. "Tom didn't get out of the war. Maybe Alice got out. She's not here anymore, that's for sure. But no— that's not right—maybe she didn't get out of anything. I got out of the war. Got out of politics. I'm so lucky, I get out of everything, don't I?" Joe and I crushed him close between us, my head bent close and Joe's long arm around both of us.

"I'm sorry." Winslow was rocking back and forth now. "The war. The strike. I'm so sorry, Joe."

Joe pulled back abruptly.

"You're sorry?" Joe pulled Winslow by his shoulders so they were facing each other. Winslow tried to cover his face with his hands, but Joe started peeling Winslow's fingers back hard. Winslow didn't have a chance, and Joe's voice broke loud over the sleeping houses. "You've got it all, Winslow."

He threw Winslow back against me and walked away. I couldn't take my eyes off him. Lights flicked on inside the house, and a dog began to bark. Joe's back was swept up by the shadow of an elm, and Winslow came into my arms. We held on to each other for a long time, terrified to be so alone.

Winslow was right about the strike. The newspapers pressured hard for another vote, claiming that the balloting had been irregular, and five days later the council announced that there would be a second vote on Saturday morning. The police surrounded the polling places to make sure that no TMC members were able to get in. Joe and the other leaders were kept locked up for "loitering and idleness." The same seven craft unions voted again, and this time they accepted the wage cut. At the start of the morning shift, thousands of workers walked right past the remaining TMC pickets and back through the gates.

Some arrests were made. A few rocks were thrown. The strike was over.

Ham threw a party that night at the house. Of course, nobody called it a party, not with elections in November. Ham said it was a dinner for close friends, but it was a real Yankee meal, more alcohol than I had seen in over a year and nothing to eat but olives, nuts, and oyster crackers. People were drinking gin out of china teacups, and Ham had a woman friend down from Boston choosing music programs on the wireless. Everyone was dressed and polished. Mayor Chapman was there with his wife and son, and Chief McNally made a brief appearance. Ham was resigning as president of the Manufacturers' Association and going back to Boston to do what he could for the Hoover campaign.

"I love to resign," he said. "Nothing frees a man up like being out of work." Everyone laughed, the faces of the mill owners' wives taut with enthusiasm.

Winslow propped himself against the mantel and drank many cups of "tea." He was wearing his gray flannels, and he looked as if that night on the front porch with me and Joe had never happened. I had on a dark blue silk dress with a pearl necklace and matching earrings that had belonged to Alice. I had chosen the outfit thinking of her, and how she would dress to intimidate. Tonight I had dressed to stop conversations rather than begin them. Geoffrey darted in and out of the room, sneaking handfuls of sugared almonds. I watched Winslow leaning toward a mill owner's daughter who flushed with a modesty she looked too old for. I refilled my teacup and drifted toward the front windows.

"Somebody ought to tell the senator," a man was saying.

"Takes nerve for him to come here tonight."

It was Joe at the end of the walk. He was standing in full view of the party, and more people inside began to notice and talk, wondering what Ham would do. I didn't look at Winslow as I walked out the door without my coat.

Joe watched me come as if he had been expecting me, and we turned down the street together, away from the house and the lights. As soon as we were around the corner, I put my arms around him so tightly he almost lost his balance.

"I thought I wasn't going to see you again," I said into his chest. "I mean, not for a while. They've been talking about more arrests. McNally was calling it a 'clean sweep.' He's in the house right now and—"

"Sssh." He pulled me behind the shadow of a tall hedge. We couldn't stop kissing, though his mouth wasn't nearly enough for me. It was so dark and he was so close that I had a hard time seeing him clearly. I ran my hands over his face, and when I reached his mouth, he began kissing my fingers. I felt his hands reaching up under my dress, and I was glad, I was ready to do anything. But Joe pulled his hands back.

I didn't want to stop.

"No, not like this," he said.

"I don't care."

"You will." He pulled back slightly. "I jumped bail."

"What?"

"Judge Anderson can do whatever he wants now that the strike's over. Deportations for being a Communist, not being a citizen—"

"But you were born here and you're not a Communist."

234

"My papi brought us over here when I was two years old. Nobody ever seemed to care. The army didn't care. There are things I haven't told you—"

"Joe, please—"

"There's Party business just as bad as the Curtises. That's why, when Winslow was apologizing—I couldn't listen. I've got more reasons than the strike, I guess, to not want to hear about how sorry he is." He took a deep breath and began speaking more quickly. "There's been more money for strike relief than the people back in New York were willing to hand over. The Portuguese, the Poles, everyone was cut out, and then our own people lied to us. I didn't know. Didn't see it. Stupid goddamn Pawtugee, right?"

I kissed the center of his palm.

"I jumped bail because Anderson would love to deport me even though I got the purple heart. I don't want to go to Russia or Poland or any other Communist country. So, I came here to see—it's a lousy offer, but . . . you wouldn't want to come with me?"

"Yes."

"You don't even know where I'm going."

"Yes."

"I'm going up the coast. Canada, or near Canada for a while. I've been offered a job that could be pretty lucrative as long as Smith doesn't get elected in November."

"Something with the unions?" I didn't really care.

"No." He pulled his hand away. "That whole system— it's all make-believe."

"Then why does the November election matter?"

"Because Smith is wet. Hoover is dry. And this particular job is only going to last as long as Prohibition does."

235

"Joe, you're already in trouble—"

"President Hoover sounds like a good bet to me, and I know the coast pretty well."

"Not all the way to Maine you don't."

"I can learn. Technically, I'm a fugitive."

"You're going to be on a boat?"

Don't drown.

"Just the first few days. There's some kind of central drop-off point from Canada. I'll start making money soon. Real money. We could maybe . . . have a place somewhere. I'll be gone a couple weeks a month. No, one week, just one week a month. And it won't be forever, Frankie. I'll just make enough money to get out. Go out west, maybe." He let go of me.

"Out west?"

I'll go anywhere.

He was looking at the ground, the trees, everywhere but me. "When I was over in France. Those letters, they were like nothing I'd ever said to anybody. I thought I was most likely not coming back. Most of us 'went west.' When you said that in the army, it meant that you had snuffed it. You went west. That's what we used to say before the big ones: Going west in the morning. So I figured, who cares what I say now? But then I came back despite a bullet in my head and you were married to Winslow. And happy."

I started to speak, but he kept going. "Maybe you never read those letters, and I can't really remember them anymore. I don't remember exactly what I said."

I pulled his mouth shut against mine. Open and shut. Open again.

"Winslow will hate me," he said after a bit. "And there's Geoffrey."

He looked in the direction of the Curtis house. Muted dance music came down the street. I had no idea how long Joe and I had been out there.

"I'm going to be on a fishing boat down at Draper wharf in the morning," he said. "The boat's called the *Theresa Marie,* and she's out of Gloucester."

I nodded. "You need to go home." He looked around as if he could fit it all into his good eye.

"Everyone's too drunk to notice where I am."

"I wouldn't have asked if I was sure you were happy. When I first came back, you seemed so content."

"I was happy that you came back."

"But you *were* happier then, you and Winslow, weren't you?"

"I don't remember."

"I do."

There were more cars pulling in front of the house, and the party had gotten louder.

"I'll be there," I said. "At the *Theresa Marie.*"

I started toward him again. It was the only way I could think of to get him to believe me.

"Don't," he said. "Don't kiss me again, please."

I kept having to watch him go. But Joe was wrong. I was leaving with him in the morning. I pulled that secret tight inside of me as I walked back into the party, not caring who saw me come or go.

"Ma!" Geoffrey called out as soon as I came through the front door.

"Geoffrey, I thought you were in bed. It's late."

"Ma, don't." His hair was plastered close to his scalp with sweat. "Dance with me, Mama. Come and dance."

He pulled me into the foyer and put his hand seriously on my waist. He had begun dancing lessons this year. The top of his head now reached the bodice of my dress. The floor was polished, and we moved easily to the sound of the wireless. I felt a little above the earth, dancing with my son and watching myself dance with my son. I remembered to let him lead.

"You're a good dancer, Mama."

"Thank you." We speeded up a little with the next song. "It's easy with the right partner."

"I know. Daddy said you were the best." His dark green eyes were filled with light. Winslow's eyes, those same eyes that had looked so lost that night on the porch.

Everything tumbled away from me.

I stopped, tripped, and Geoffrey caught my balance for me.

I wasn't going to be up all night. I didn't need to pack because I wasn't going down to the wharf in the morning. My boy's eyes were looking right into mine.

"You all right, Ma?"

I held him tighter.

"Perfect."

Eleven days later what had been apparent to everyone else finally became apparent to me. My life was suddenly laughable, and even though I recognized the comedy as it was unfolding, I couldn't laugh just yet. Perhaps the problem was that the characters weren't as clearly defined as they should have been. I was cast as the beautiful and loyal mother, blind to her husband's flagrant infidelity. Winslow was the cad who had been leading a double life but not quite keeping things secret enough, so that he shamed his wife publicly as well as privately. It was Lizzie DuBois, of course, who took on the role of the Other Woman. The girl at the office, the poor girl whose tragic accident had brought about an illicit connection between herself and the boss's son.

I was certainly blind if not exactly loyal. And if Winslow had only been a cad, it would have been simpler. But this was not a drunken moment on a pile of coats at one of the big houses down in Little Compton. Lizzie had a certain kind of power over Winslow. Yes, she was smart. Yes, she was pretty. But there was that hold she had on him. I suppose it must have been sex. Sex with Winslow had been better than ever the night before I found them together. I remember how he pulled me out of my warm sleep. He was so tight with desire that I doubted he would be able to hold himself back long enough to wait for me. When he did hold back, I took it as a gift. I was grabbing everything good I could find. Joe was gone. I had decided to stay.

There were certain absurdities I kept trying to forget:

The song that was playing so happily from the wireless while I looked from one to the other. I had shut the door as quickly as I could, terribly embarrassed.

I had almost brought Geoffrey. Papa was the one who stopped me, and later I began to see how well known Winslow's affair must have been. Geoffrey had been let out early that day, back from a class trip to see the naval academy in Newport. Papa came with me to pick him up from school, and when I suggested going by to meet Winslow at the mill school's old storefront, Papa insisted on taking Geoffrey directly to the drugstore and meeting us there for a lime rickey.

When Lizzie walked out, I was the one who looked away, ashamed. I stood there feeling as if I should stay and wait for my husband.

"Shall we go home?" Winslow asked when he appeared a moment after Lizzie had closed the street door behind her. Only later did I realize that I had been given a choice, whether to allow him to return home with me or not. Lizzie was the only one who played her role with any panache.

Portuguese gardeners were raking and burning piles of leaves on the front lawns during our silent walk up the hill to the Highlands. The smell reminded me of our old house in Poughkeepsie; Papa always let me jump into the leaf pile with my cousins before he set it on fire. We went upstairs quietly, and Winslow asked permission to follow me into the bedroom.

"It's not my bedroom," I said, surprised.

The day was sunny, and squares of light came through the window, patterning the Oriental rug as they did every afternoon. Everything was just the same. I sat down on the chair opposite the bed and asked Winslow quite formally if he was in love with her. He paused.

Maybe I should have felt relieved. Maybe I should have felt free to go to Joe, to take Geoffrey, to move to New York City, to get out. A divorcée with some money is no bad thing, Alice would have said.

Everything trembled violently and fell apart.

There was so much drinking and too much talk. That I still loved Winslow was embarassingly apparent. I told him everything about Joe; I was so unsophisticated. He had brought Lizzie around Geoffrey, but he was sure that our son knew nothing. Winslow had brought Lizzie to the Massasoit Club with his father. He had brought her to polo matches at Newport. It had been going on since before Alice died, before the strike. Why hadn't he kept her more out of sight?

Lizzie hadn't liked that. He did what Lizzie liked.

Again and again. Cheap and cheapening.

Irony returned first to the bedroom. When we had sex, I was trying not to think about Lizzie, and Winslow must have been trying not to think about Joe.

I went to Father Mendalos, but he had no idea how to reach Joe. I told him everything in a rush, including that I didn't believe in God.

"We're not in the confessional," he remarked. "We're only in my office."

He gave me a cigarette and asked if I loved Winslow.

"I didn't do this," I said. "I didn't do this to Geoffrey."

"What does that matter?" He watched me smoke. "All that matters is what you do next."

I didn't say anything.

"Were you close?" he asked. "Were you and Joe close to doing this to Winslow? To Geoffrey?"

"Yes."

"And Joe didn't tell you about Winslow and this girl, even though he knew?"

"Joe wanted me to come with him."

"Perhaps you could keep doing the right thing," Father Mendalos said, almost to himself.

"It doesn't make any difference."

"You could do it anyway."

On the twenty-seventh of October, 1928, the telephone downstairs rang before dawn. There was only one telephone in the house, and it didn't ring that often since the strike was over. Winslow and I both woke in a panic, staring at each other as the phone rang again and again. I always jolted abruptly from sleep to consciousness; panic was at skin level all the time now. Winslow grabbed his nightshirt, but I didn't move. I thought it might be Joe. I always hoped that it might be Joe. I would explain everything, and he would tell me what to do. Winslow got up, and I must have fallen back asleep despite myself, because the next thing I knew was the terrifying feeling that somebody was in the room watching me. Winslow was on the window seat with his feet curled up underneath him like a child. Shots of red light leaked across the pale autumn sky.

"My father is dead," Winslow said to my opened eyes. "The senator died last night."

Our house became very public very quickly, from that morning to the morning three weeks later when the house was sold or, rather, foreclosed.

STRICKEN IN HIS SLEEP, the headlines proclaimed. But of course Ham Curtis hadn't really been asleep. He had been rutting some girl in Boston when his heart and his urge gave out simultaneously. Perhaps not quite simultaneously, but who would ever know? The senator had died in his sleep. President Coolidge came to the funeral in Rock Harbor. He was the second president Ham Curtis brought to Rock Harbor, but this time the president didn't spend the night. All the Boston politicians came, well-dressed men from Providence came, and it was quite a show. A horse-drawn wagon draped in black. The mill owners walking solemnly in their top hats behind the carriage. It was the first event to shut down Front Street since the strike had ended.

Geoffrey and I dressed and behaved well. Winslow looked handsome and quite senatorial himself in top hat and tails. The only thing missing was Ham Curtis taking advantage of the opportunity to get more votes. The crowds turned out to pay their respects and of course to get a look at Coolidge. All day long I wondered what part of the coast Joe was motoring past, and if he had heard the news.

The lawyers informed us that there was no money. Really, really no money except for the debt that Ham had built up financing his campaigns and the houses in Rock Harbor and Boston. Winslow and I nodded like adults, but we had no idea what they were talking about. No idea what one did when all one inherited was debt. It turned out you sold everything, and after that you declared bankruptcy.

We moved up the Flint into the apartment upstairs from my parents. Winslow got a job cataloging inventory at the Flint Mill as production began to drop citywide, but there was no job there or anywhere for me. Geoffrey took the room that was a floor above my old one. He knew the house already, and we had kept his collection of N. C. Wyeth books and toy soldiers from the estate auction.

Maybe Geoffrey guessed at more than he said about his father and me. After Ham's death, my list of tasks kept me from making any big decisions, and I didn't mind moving mechanically from one thing to another. Things were changing for everyone. Pay cuts started again at 10 percent and went to 15 percent along with the speedups. A lot of the mills were shutting down for good, or moving operations down south. Most people began leaving town, but Papa held on to his engraver's job. He read the history books coming out about the Great War and didn't ask any questions about my marriage.

Winslow and I returned to the Massasoit Club and drank as much as we could afford. Winslow didn't complain. Life had simplified, and he must have been grateful that something had come along that was bigger than his affair with Lizzie. Like everybody else, we got by. Mother and Geoffrey were inseparable after school now, and he was what we could talk about. It was easier for her to add three more plates to the table than to teach me how to cook. It was easier for her to put him to bed than to wait for me to come home at night. I almost believed Winslow when he told me he loved me. I almost believed him when he said he wasn't seeing Lizzie anymore. I went back to church, but I wasn't sure what forgiveness was made of other than the longing for it.

A year later, Joe came by driving a Packard and quietly loaned Winslow some money. Winslow told me about it later, and I never even saw Joe. I wanted him to miss me as much as I missed him, but I never heard a word. I told myself he no longer loved me, but it made no difference. I tried to accustom myself to the exhaustion of thinking about him every day, certain this was exactly how the rest of my life would be. Winslow's declaration of bankruptcy came eight months before Black Friday and two years before Rock Harbor became the first city in New England to declare bankruptcy, giving over all municipal finances to the state. Eighteen mills were liquidated in 1929, and nine more shut down in 1930. The mills had always been taxed by the city according to the number of spindles they had, and by the end of 1930 the number of spindles in the city had dropped to two and a half million, compared to four million in 1915. Only half of the corporations and individuals had been able to pay their taxes at all. The state began to erase Rock Harbor, cutting more and more services every year. The whole country was in a depression, though nobody called it that yet, but Rock Harbor may have been the first out of the gate.

One night in February, after we had been living above my parents for just over a year, a fire started at the Acushnet Mill. They had been clearing out the last of the machinery, and someone lit a fire in a barrel to keep warm. Once the oil-soaked floor of the mill started burning, the fire spread through the oldest part of downtown. Four banks, the King Philip Hotel, the library, and St. Paul's Church were among the twenty-one buildings burned that night. The temperature hit a record low, and the fire department's hoses froze solid. Fire engines came from as far away as

Providence, the National Guard and naval reservists came into the city, but in the end they couldn't do anything but keep the crowds back as windows burst from the heat and granite walls leaned too far, then fell. We watched the fire from the hill in front of Borden, trying to stay warm under the quilt Mother grabbed as we ran out the door. Geoffrey pressed close against his grandfather's legs.

"It's like watching a ship burning at sea," Winslow said.

1934

I KNEW PAPA WAS DEAD THE MINUTE MY MOTHER CALLED me Frances.

"Frances!" she whispered when the telegram arrived. It was more of a sudden exhale than a whisper, a gasp in reverse, and it carried all the way from the front parlor to the kitchen.

He had gotten on the train for South Carolina two weeks earlier. I drove him to the station in Providence myself. Papa gave me a quick kiss on the cheek, grabbed his suitcase from the backseat, and left. I know that I watched him stop and buy a paper before driving off, but I wasn't really thinking about him anymore. I was already on to the next thing. So how was I supposed to believe that he wasn't going to be living in this house anymore? For days Father Mendalos kept talking about time. In Time. With Faith. I didn't think I had much of either.

The last person to see him said that Papa caught a ride

with a mill hand back to the boardinghouse where he was staying. He was riding in the rumble seat, and the southern evening air would have been warm in a way he had never known in New England. Fragile smell of magnolias and jasmine mixed with car exhaust, almost tropical. He must have been feeling pretty good. He had already gotten a job at one of those southern mills we'd been hearing so much about, and we were all going to join him there. Sixty-six isn't too old to start over, he'd told my mother on the telephone the night before.

Father Mendalos said it was the shock of the accident that made me feel like I didn't know what happened to Papa despite a list of facts. The speed of the car. How far he was thrown. His broken spine. The body coming back north by train. People repeated these things to each other over and over again, as if this information could create a holding place for the plain fact of it becoming *the* body instead of *his* body. I wanted to say to Father Mendalos that I didn't know how anything ever happened. But that wasn't true either. I was thirty-three years old, and my papa had loved me in a way I thought I'd never find again. Papa was the first one to call me Frankie.

In Rock Harbor they love a wake, and nobody ever goes home until Jimmy Talbot locks the door. It got up to ninety-eight the day of Papa's wake, even hotter inside Talbot and Sons, the best funeral home Rock Harbor has to offer. Winslow's aunt Beverly paid for it even though Mother was Catholic. Beverly knew we couldn't afford anything more than what the union money would cover, and she wanted it at Talbot's so the rest of Rock Harbor could see that in the end the Curtises took care of their own. Papa was Winslow's father-in-law, after all. I didn't like the idea of an open casket, but Mother seemed to want it, and I couldn't take on her, Father Mendalos, and Aunt Beverly on my own. Winslow would put up with almost anything in order to avoid discussing the bill.

I didn't have the willpower *not* to look at Papa, so now I have that face forever.

"Grandpa's got powder on his face," said Geoffrey, who couldn't get enough of staring.

"That's because they dress up dead people here," I said, loud enough for Jimmy Talbot to catch—the overhead fan was humming, so he pretended not to hear me. Jimmy had gone to Borden with us; then he took over his father's mortuary business and made a decent living burying the Curtises and anyone else who wanted something tonier.

"How come they do that, Ma?" Geoffrey asked. He was thirteen years old now and wouldn't give anything up.

Mother patted her lap, and Geoffrey leaned against her, looking handsome and lost in his new suit, which we had put on layaway down at Lamont's. I tried to drink my way through the afternoon but remained disappointingly clear. Jimmy told us not to leave the door open because of the heat, and he didn't allow smoking inside the funeral parlor. Perhaps the smell of embalming fluid and tobacco didn't mix well enough for the fee he charged to keep a dead body in plain sight. So Winslow and I hung about the doorway, ducking in and out of the dull August sun. Winslow wouldn't sit down on the front steps of the funeral home out of respect for the occasion and the creases in his trousers, which Mother had ironed the night before. I had told him he should wear his linen suit, considering it was high summer, but he just shook his big head at me. Maybe he was right; the slack, bluish bags under his eyes seemed darker than usual when he wore black, and it gave him an air of suffering. He *had* loved Papa, but the suit showed it more.

I was shaking hands all day: "Thank you." Shake. "Thank you." Shake. I hated it so much. I hated it.

I wished I could be more like Winslow, who had been shaking hands since he could walk. Winslow, who was not yet forty and looked thirty. I stood next to him in that condolence line and thought: Maybe there's still time for something to take hold. Papa had looked old at forty because of the mills, but he had a skill. Winslow and I were devoid of skills, though no one expected much of me. Winslow could still play polo with deceptive ease when he got an invitation, and I didn't want to believe that I was aging either. Thirty-three didn't feel old until Papa died.

I knew that Joe would come down from Waltham to Papa's wake. I dressed for him as much as for Papa that morning. My good black dress, of course, but instead of covering the neckline with a shawl, I chose the amber necklace I had kept back from the estate sale. I wanted a color other than black and white, as if that would change things.

But Joe didn't come all day.

Mother finally took Geoffrey home, and Winslow and I decided to go down to the bar at Sakonnet Point after

Jimmy locked the door. Winslow and I always went to the Point when we wanted to drink alone. There was a fishermen's bar we liked, with local boats moored between the marshes and the breakwater. It was pretty much lobstering year round, with cod and swordfishing all the way out to Georges Bank. In a good season the harbor was almost empty, though the boats looked too small to go so far out. There was a chart behind the bar that showed how far away and to the north the fishing grounds were, with a pencil line marking the fastest way out and back. Sometimes we walked to the lighthouse, where the Sakonnet River emptied into Rhode Island Sound. The light was not so much to keep boats off the rocks as to welcome the fishermen home. If they didn't know the waters by the time they were that close, they never should have gotten on the boat, Andy Farrow said, and he was the bartender, so he knew.

The bar was in a separate room from the restaurant, with orange fishing nets spread across the ceiling and a tank of live lobsters bubbling quietly around the corner on the restaurant side. Before we were married, Winslow took me to Sakonnet Point on a date and dumped his martini into the lobster tank to make me laugh. We didn't have lobsters in Poughkeepsie, and I was disgusted by those black eyeballs suspended on rubbery antennae. They looked like big underwater insects to me, and there is still something slightly obscene about a bright red, freshly cooked lobster; though I have learned to adjust.

I drank two martinis very fast, and since I'd escaped the wake without eating anything, they had an effect. Winslow ordered some fried clams at the bar, and I watched as he ate with great delicacy, dipping them into the white tartar sauce with a wooden toothpick, since this bar didn't provide any of the tiny silver forks he was brought up using. I loved this about Winslow: he had very good manners at table but wasn't afraid to be coarse in bed. He'd had me against walls and on the sand and on the bathroom sink of one of the big summerhouses in Newport. It was that great hunger of his that always made me want him right back, as much as anything else. I still wanted him that way, even though I loved Joe Barros.

After two drinks I mentioned Joe, how I was surprised he didn't come down to the wake.

"I spoke to him."

"Really, when?"

We were being competitively offhand.

"Today. He called the house this morning, while you were out with Geoffrey."

"And?"

"He's coming tomorrow afternoon. He hoped it wouldn't be too late, but I assured him, you know. He has a lot of business to take care of on Saturday morning."

"Today."

Winslow glanced at the clock behind the bar. It was five minutes to twelve, or ten past midnight, bar time. "And Friday is almost yesterday."

He offered me a clam. If Joe came down tomorrow afternoon, that meant he wouldn't be leaving Waltham tonight. Joe paid rent on an office and claimed to keep regular business hours, but nobody was really sure what he did these days. I had telephoned once or twice, and the phone just rang and rang.

"Joe loved your father."

Winslow plucked the speared olive out of my martini and ate it. He knew that I only liked the look of olives. Andy set down two more drinks without being asked, and I had a rush of appreciation, too much for such a simple thing. But maybe he remembered Papa, or Winslow bringing me down here sixteen years ago, when he got the lobsters drunk. Maybe it was just the gin.

The bar at Sakonnet Point closed at one, and we were the last ones out. I leaned my head against Winslow's shoulder as he helped me down the wide wooden stairs to the parking lot.

"I'm finally drunk," I said. "I've been trying to get drunk all day."

"It's been a rough day." His voice was a little thick, but I knew he could drive. Winslow could always drive drunk.

"Papa died today." I stopped before getting into the car. Winslow was holding the door open for me.

"He died on Monday," Winslow said. "The wake was today."

"The first day of the wake," I said. "Tomorrow we get to do it all over again."

I didn't feel like going home. Home was quiet and filled with sleep, and there was a black wreath from the union on the door.

"Let's go to the beach, Winslow. Just drive by the beach on the way home."

He swung the car out of the lot and headed away from Rock Harbor. I didn't have to tell him which beach. There was only one beach that meant anything to both of us, or all three of us, if you counted Joe. We drove through Tiverton and took the twisting back roads, which were empty at that time of night. We were driving Papa's big Chevrolet, and I liked the sound of the car rushing softly around the curves. I rolled down the window and rested my chin on the edge of the glass. The salt air tasted good after all those cigarettes in the bar.

Winslow laughed. "You look like Roxie with your head out the window like that." Roxie was the dog Winslow had when he was in high school. He spoiled her, of course, and she used to hang her black head out of Winslow's Model T when we took her to the beach, her tongue lapping up the wind. I was glad that Winslow didn't tell me to pull my head in or roll up the window.

The hedges and stone walls of Little Compton lined the roads, summerhouses of the rich standing confidently in the night. They looked so peaceful at this hour that I wanted to roll up one of those long gravel driveways and just lean on the horn. Wake everybody up.

"Those houses should be burned," I said to Winslow, who was so surprised he took his eyes off the road.

"We had a good time in some of those houses, Frankie."

"So what? There's a depression on, don't they know that?"

"Just like they knew about Prohibition."

"Thank God that's over."

Winslow smiled and paid attention to his driving. "People had more parties then."

"We did go to some big parties. That was after Joe came back from the war, wasn't it?" Why did I ask things when I already knew the answer?

"Mostly. Most of those parties were after the war, I guess."

I leaned back against the seat and cranked the window closed. Everything got quieter.

"Are you too sleepy to go to the beach?" Winslow asked after a time.

I looked out the window and saw the big white mansion on Draper Road at the crest of the hill. "We're almost there."

I wasn't too drunk to know everything I loved was still there. The dunes with their crooked wooden fences, low enough for a child to step over. The pond where the swans circled self-consciously, muddy water that went only as high as your waist no matter how far out you walked. Children waded out to the high square rock in the middle of the pond, which they called an island because it had patches of grass growing on top.

They were all grand houses along the beach. Big porches that turned one corner and kept right on going to the next one. There were gables, turrets, and more than one widow's walk crowning houses that were built by sea captains, whaling out of New Bedford. Some of these families had been hit hard by the crash, but with the grace bestowed upon people accustomed to privilege, most of them seemed unchanged in their habits, though a few kept their beach houses closed for the first time. Tonight, the shutters were fastened tight, and the big houses slept carelessly through the night, maybe through the whole Depression.

We passed a house built in the Italian style, stone steps leading from the porch right down to the water. At high tide the ocean crashed against the stone parapet, and since the owners knew Winslow's family, we had invited ourselves into this house, into every house along the beach for cocktails by the time I was twenty. I remember standing at the seawall when a big wave came over and soaked my dress. The hostess couldn't understand why I didn't want to change out of it. Why I always wanted to stand too close.

Winslow pulled the car into the parking lot across the street from a few wooden bathhouses, and we were home. What the summer folk called a beach club was really no more than a dozen simple changing cabanas that were so frail they had to be rebuilt every year after the winter storms.

"Do you want to get out?" Winslow asked. "Or just sit tight?"

"Let's get out."

The wind off the beach was warm. We walked across the tar road and clambered over the dunes toward the water. The sky was overcast, and I couldn't make out anything but the dull glow of sand slipping under my feet and black water in the distance. The surf was a thin white line somewhere in front of us. I took off my heels and carried them. Winslow rolled up his pant legs and left his shoes on the steps of the old Curtis cabana out of habit. The mothers and nannies had all of the beach equipment safely locked away for the night. Tomorrow the beach would be packed with children, but now everything was empty and the surf was quiet. The waves never got too big here unless there was a real storm. This bottom edge of Massachusetts faced the Atlantic, but the surf didn't have the feel of open ocean like off Martha's Vineyard and Nantucket. In the hurricane season, locals bodysurfed the tidal surge while families kept their children out of the water and competed for a handyman to board up the windows.

I dropped my shoes and walked down to the water, wading up to my knees. The ocean was cold and sucked at my heels as I stood resisting the pull, wanting to keep going.

"Your stockings are getting ruined."

"Take them off."

Winslow knelt next to me, up to his thighs in water, and reached under my dress to unhook them from my garters and peel them down. His fingers never fumbled in the dark, and I raised one foot and then the other, resting my hand on the top of his head for balance. There were small piles of wet sand gathered at the bottom of each stocking, and he offered them to me silently. I shook my head, and he threw them far out in the water, where they hovered for a moment before sinking. Silk stockings were expensive. I didn't care. We both had this terrible habit of acting as though we still had money to spare. His mouth was warm on my thighs, moving slightly with the back and forth pull of the water. I leaned against him with both hands as he raised the hem of my slip and pulled my panties out of the way. He was no longer delicate, and I pulled that rough head closer and held him there. He was my balance, and I let him have what we both wanted.

The sound of Geoffrey playing peggyball in the alley below my window woke me on Saturday morning. I heard a sharp *whack* as a broomstick hit the wooden ball. It sounded like they were playing right next to my pillow.

"Twenty! You can't do it in less than twenty!" Geoffrey

called out. I waited, hearing his friend's feet slap the pavement as he took giant steps to measure how far Geoff had hit the ball.

"I did it in seventeen, Geoff. I'm up." It was Eddie Morrow. He lived in the Highlands, but we had the best alley for peggyball because it was almost perfectly flat; unusual for Rock Harbor, built on seven hills.

"Like Rome," the senator used to say in his speeches. But Winslow laughed hardest when Joe told us what they called Rock Harbor up in Boston: the city of hills, mills, and unpaid bills. *Smack!* went the peggyball again, wood on wood and right through the back of my head. I heard Geoffrey laughing and leaned up on one arm to watch him through the window. He wasn't as big as Eddie, but he was quick like Winslow. I watched him brush his hair back from his face, concentrating on the game. I loved to look at him being thirteen years old. I could have spent all day. But peggyball had never made sense to me. The boys balanced a wooden ball on a broken shingle with a notch cut out of the top, like a homemade golf tee. Then they hit the ball as far as they could and bet on how many strides it would take to get to where the ball landed. The ones who weren't batting had to reach the spot in fewer strides than the batter said they could. Older boys working at the mill bet money on peggyball. I'd watched hours of it when I first arrived up the Flint, but I still didn't know how they figured out who won.

"Those were leaps, not steps, Morrow," Geoffrey said, admitting it was over. "Your turn."

I looked at the clock, nearly nine-thirty. Winslow was long out of bed, and I was naked. The night before he had told me to put my arms over my head like a child while he slipped off my dress. He liked us both to sleep naked, but I always got cold and wore a nightgown, even in summer. The sky was just going transparent when we got into bed, and he had said something about the color.

"Red sky at morning, sailors take warning."

"But it's always a red sky at morning." I was still sitting up, completely undressed except for my shoes. Winslow noticed the sky every day; he said it came from being a mariner, a word he used whenever he could.

My tongue felt glued to the roof of my mouth, and I didn't need to look outside to know it was going to be another hot day. We slept right above my parents' room in the fancy brass bed we'd brought from the house on Highland Avenue. We still had good furniture because even the nicer stuff didn't sell for much, and it was all Winslow had left for Geoffrey from the Curtises. It had been six years since the money disappeared, and it really didn't matter much to me anymore. We had our habits, Winslow and me, and Geoffrey was growing up; perhaps we had gotten through the worst of it.

Then I thought it for the first time that day: Papa was dead.

That was why everything was different this morning. I could die anytime; even with Geoff out playing in the alley and Winslow downstairs in my mother's kitchen. The next thing I was certain of, as if it had been waiting for me to see it all along, was that I couldn't stay here forever. I had no idea where else I would go, and it made no sense, but it was true.

The summer curtains were hanging perfectly still in the

open window, the same curtains Mother had hung for us when we first moved into this apartment. I thought about how many times I had washed those curtains, packed them away when the weather got cold enough for the winter drapes, and taken them out again in spring. Maybe Papa had been the one to carve that faux Dutch pattern of windmills and ducks into metal plates; they were certainly bought on the cheap from the mill store.

Papa was dead.

But I wouldn't be buried by Jimmy Talbot; I wasn't going to die in Rock Harbor.

I didn't do so well on four hours of sleep, but Winslow was actually whistling downstairs. He was probably making johnnycakes for breakfast. He fried them in bacon grease until they were crisp on the outside and soft batter in the middle. Mother and I wouldn't eat them, but Papa had liked them, and Winslow and Geoffrey could eat them every day. Winslow has a strong body; chances are he'll outlive me. The thought of johnnycakes made me put my head back down on the pillow. It was the second day of Papa's wake. Joe would be coming to Rock Harbor this afternoon. Maybe he would spend the night.

There was a new sound coming up the street. The click of heels with just the slightest drag against pavement. There was a scuffle to that step which was almost indiscernible if you weren't listening for it. I knew who it was before I heard her voice.

"Geoffrey! Geoffrey Curtis! You want a Chiclet?"

I heard the boys stop. "Yes, ma'am. Thank you, Miss DuBois."

"Geoffrey!" I called out the window. "Geoffrey, come inside. Breakfast is ready."

"I already had breakfast, Ma!"

I raised myself off the pillow and leaned out onto the sill, no longer caring if Eddie Morrow saw me with only a sheet wrapped around me. "Geoffrey! Right now!"

Geoffrey turned and looked up at me, shifting his eyes away in embarrassment. I must have looked like an angry ghost, bare-shouldered and uncombed. Eddie kicked the ground and mumbled something I couldn't hear. Lizzie didn't move; not even walking up the hill in that heat wilted her. She put the package of gum back into her small beaded purse, and I watched Geoffrey start to chew as he looked at me resentfully. I wanted to run down and pull it out of his mouth, like the poisoned apple from the fairy tale. But instead of falling down dead, Geoffrey kept chewing and balanced from one foot to the other, debating whether or not to talk back to his mother.

"Good morning, Frances." Lizzie had her hair cut short, but not so short that it didn't soften her face with dark brown curls. She looked younger than me. Close up, you forgot about the limp right away because all you could look at was her eyes.

"I was sorry to hear about your father."

"Thank you, Lizzie. It was a shock." I felt hollow and pulled the sheet closer to my body. Did she ever drink too much and sleep late in the morning? Did she ever wish she wasn't teaching fifth and sixth grade since the mill school shut down? Did she think about me naked with Winslow at night?

"I'm going to the wake. I'm on my way there now."

"The family's not there yet." That was stupid. *We* were the family. None of Papa's relatives came all the way over from England.

"No, the family's here, right, Geoffrey?" She was speaking to my son but looking at me.

"Geoffrey, please come inside," I said.

He scuffed his feet but obeyed. Eddie retreated a little, staying on the sidewalk to watch.

Lizzie smiled again. "Sorry to have disturbed you, Frances."

I could have told her that she never disturbed me, or told her not to come around my son and to stay away from my father's wake. Instead, I let the curtains fall back into place. I listened to her start back up the hill, humming something vaguely familiar and patriotic.

I had to get out of bed. Winslow thought I liked to sleep late, but that wasn't it. I didn't sleep that late, I mostly lay awake. I still like to stay in bed in the morning; it often feels like the safest place to be. But that day was no longer deniable. I got dressed thinking of what Joe liked, what I knew I looked good in. It had to be black, of course. But tight black. The problem with tight black, once I zipped up my skirt, was that it made me look heavy. I patted my stomach and twisted around to peer at my behind. Fatter, lower. If it hadn't been so long since I last saw Joe, he might not notice my getting older.

"Johnnycakes!" Winslow announced in triumph as I walked into the kitchen and poured a cup of coffee.

"Later." I smiled even though I didn't feel like it, and it probably showed. Geoffrey looked at me warily as he spooned sugar and butter on top of his johnnycakes. I stepped onto the back porch to smoke.

"We can come home for lunch," Mother said. "There's chipped beef."

All those dishes the neighbors had brought over. Feed the living or something. Problem was that the living had lost their appetite. When Geoffrey followed me out the back door and gave me a hug, I was surprised by my tears and let my hair fall over my eyes.

"Morning, Ma," he said.

"Morning, sweet boy. Sorry about the gum. I'll buy you your own Chiclets later."

I hated being hard on him, and he was usually the one to make it right. I didn't know how he turned out so well, but he was the best-loved boy in the world, and maybe that was the secret.

"You'd better go get changed," I told him, and he rolled his eyes to make me smile.

"I know," I said. "Grandpa didn't like suits either."

"You look pretty," he said.

"Not without my makeup on."

"Uh-huh."

"Well, you have to look handsome all day, so you better get going."

He climbed the stairs two at a time, not because he

wanted to change clothes but because that was how Geoffrey did everything. Fast. An hour later, I was wishing I could walk faster up the long hill to the funeral home in my black skirt and heels. It was close enough to walk, but I wished we were driving. Mother was slow, and Winslow matched her stride. Geoffrey spread his arms out so that his suit coat became wings. Mother made a clicking noise in the back of her throat when she saw this—she thought we should do something about him, but neither of us said a thing. Geoffrey swooped around a lamppost and ran back toward us. He was sailing.

"Look, Dad!" he called out. "She's running downwind!" The back of his jacket puffed out as the wind caught the cloth. "That means I have to tack!" Geoffrey circled us and began to zigzag toward the crest of our street again, his arms flipping from side to side each time he changed direction. Winslow gave him lessons at the club even though we didn't have a boat. I wished I could run alongside him. Flying from lamppost to lamppost is still flying. I worried about the tightness of my skirt across my stomach, the tightness of the skin around my eyes.

Borden was on our left, implacable and grand. Geoffrey would go there, and I would see my old classmates at school events. We'd look each other over competitively. Everyone would be tallying how things have not turned out as expected, and they would be happy that I no longer lived in the Highlands. It would almost make up for my having had only one child and not gained enough weight. I have to get out, I thought again. I have to leave.

I was relieved to see Jimmy Talbot opening the funeral home as we arrived. It meant that Lizzie had come and gone. I knew she'd be back, but I wasn't ready for her yet. I knelt in front of the open casket trying not to think about Papa's face; it was impossible to pray. I heard the door open but didn't get up. I knew that today was going to be a big day because it was the weekend, though I hadn't realized how many mill hands were already out of work until I'd seen them here yesterday.

"Uncle Joe!"

And it was Joe, and he was looking right at me while he steadied himself from Geoffrey's leap into his arms. Geoffrey's hair was shoved up against Joe's face, and his long legs and arms were wrapped around Joe like those of a three-year-old. Joe looked back over Geoffrey's head and turned three-quarters toward me because he thought the glass eye was ugly, but it was simply surprising. The brown glass was such a deceptively neutral part of his face, his lovely, liquid face.

Joe put Geoffrey down and steadied him. He pulled on Geoffrey's jacket, skewed by the leap. "Nice suit."

"I hate it," Geoffrey said in a whisper we could all hear.

"That's your job," Joe whispered back just as loudly. "Hate the suit."

"Joe." Winslow stepped forward. Joe clasped his hand over Winslow's and went to Mother.

"Mrs. Ross," he said. "Don't get up. I am so sorry about Allen."

"It was a shock," she said quietly. "Thank you for coming, Joe."

Joe kissed her lightly on the cheek. I was standing next to him by then. He hugged me no longer than he should have, but I held on tight.

"He loved you, Joe." It was the closest I could come to the truth.

It turned out that crying was the best thing that I could have done, because it gave everyone something to do. Winslow got me a chair, Geoffrey brought a glass of water, and Mother loaned me her second handkerchief. I don't cry easily in front of others, so it made an impression. Geoffrey still cried hard whenever he got hurt; blood scared him, and he couldn't bear the pain of a skinned knee or a bad splinter. I didn't blame him for crying, and I always told him it didn't matter that he was a boy.

"But you don't cry when you get hurt," he always said. "You never cry."

Being a mother had made me such a good liar.

While everyone was fussing around me, Joe stepped over to the coffin and paid his respects. His mother had died years ago, and I wondered if it was easier for him to pray than it was for me. What I really wanted was a cigarette, and after Joe got up from his knees, the three of us went outside. The heat slapped up from the sidewalk, and I closed my eyes. It was noon. I could smell water on hot concrete; somebody must have been washing their car.

"So, Allen was heading down to South Carolina when it happened?" Joe asked Winslow, who was folding his coat up as a cushion for me to sit on the steps.

"He'd been there a few days, already gotten a job at one of the new mills. The plan was to join him there, all of us; then this happened."

"Pay's not much good down south, I heard," Joe said, pulling on his cigarette.

"No?" Winslow tapped another cigarette out of his pack and lit it for me. "Well, things are slowing down, all right. You heard about the printworks?"

"Of course he did," I said, more abruptly than I meant to.

Winslow looked apologetically at Joe. "Of course you heard."

"No," Joe said. "No, I didn't. I've been away. They're shutting down?"

"Announced two weeks ago." Winslow was trying not to show how much he liked the fact that I was wrong. We saw right through each other. All three of us.

"That's what made Papa decide to go south," I said.

"I can get about six months' work out of the print-works' closing," Winslow said. "Selling off the old parts, liquidating . . ."

"Maybe I can help you there. Buy some equipment."

"What do you mean, buddy?" I knew something was coming, but Winslow was still acting casual. "Are you moving into liquidation now?"

"I'm going to Lima." Joe looked at me quickly. "I've just come back from there. Closing the office in Waltham."

"Lima? Peru?" I tried to scramble up, but it was hard in my skirt, and my heels slipped under me. Joe reached for my arm.

"Hang on, Frankie. He's not leaving today." Winslow was sweating and pushed his hat forward to keep the sun off his face.

"When are you leaving?" I asked.

"I've been back and forth once already. Leaving again next week. There are cotton mills in Peru, Winslow. They need our expertise. Big cotton exporters, and they're mostly centered in Lima. Nice city. I'm going to try settling down there long-term, I think."

"Well, well. Lima, huh?" Winslow stubbed out his cigarette halfway through and squinted at Joe. "And we thought the Carolinas were pretty far south."

"South America." The words rolled around in my mouth. Another continent, an upside-down triangle, colored pink on the scrolled maps of the world they used to pull down like window shades in our classrooms at Borden. Where exactly was Peru?

"It's cotton, cattle, and coca—cocaine." Joe smiled. "Those are their three biggest resources. So I figure I can sell cotton, eat steak, and sniff cocaine when I'm bored. Want to come?"

"Yes," I said quietly. He heard me and continued talking to Winslow as if I didn't really say it.

"Sure, you could all come down. Give it a try, Winslow."

"No. I'm the undertaker of the mills; my work starts when the patient is dead. Might bring you bad luck." He wasn't laughing enough to convince either of us that it was all that funny. "Besides, there's Frankie, Geoffrey, and Mother Ross."

"I'd like to go," I said.

"It's pretty rough down there." Joe was still talking only to Winslow. "Like a frontier town. Can't see Mrs. R. taking to it at all."

"I want to go!" I said louder. The trembling in my body got stronger, and so did my voice. They both turned to me, and I realized that I couldn't stop shaking.

Winslow didn't move, so Joe put his arms around me. I

wasn't crying, but I couldn't stop repeating myself: I want to go. I want to go.

The door of the funeral parlor opened.

"Dad?"

The sound of Geoffrey's voice stopped mine.

"Nerves. Heat," Winslow said. "Joe, take her for a drink. I'll tell Mother Ross. Meet you there."

Joe's car was even hotter than the street, and he handed me a flask, though my shaking had gone back to a quiver. Sweat was pouring down the back of Joe's neck. The whiskey tasted good, warm.

Joe turned the car onto French Street. He reached across me to crank down the window all the way.

"Doing better?" he asked.

"Thanks."

"Where are we going?"

"The Massasoit Club. But let's not go right there, Joe. I need to drive a bit."

Joe turned a corner that led away from the water, and I knew he would take the loop around the Highlands and the cemeteries before bringing us downtown.

"You and Winslow still go to the club, huh?"

I didn't say anything and handed him back the flask. He screwed the top on tight and stowed it beneath the driver's seat.

"Been rough, Frankie?"

He reached across the front seat and held my hand. His skin was hot, and the air rushing through the open windows wasn't drying the sweat off either of us. I curled my hand into a ball inside his hand, those long fingers completely covering my fist.

"Put me in your pocket, Joe."

He laughed a little unsteadily.

I looked over at him. "I can do it now, though. I really can."

He didn't say anything.

"It's not like before. Everything's changed since Papa. I can go with you."

"Why? Because of Allen?"

I looked away. It wasn't only grief, but I didn't know how to speak this part aloud. "It's not because of Papa, it's me. But this does . . . bring it all so close. My death, your death. I don't think— I don't really have much time anymore."

"Sure you do."

I looked at him until he had to take his eyes from the road. "No, I don't. *We* don't have that time. Can't you see it?"

He didn't answer. He drove on, and I knew it was a lousy explanation, but I couldn't say it any better.

"What about Geoffrey and . . . all?"

"Do you love me?"

He brought my hand up to his mouth and peeled it open without taking his eyes off the road. He kissed the salty center of my palm.

"Maybe it's now," I said. "I think it's now for us. I love you," I said, and he held my hand tighter against his lips. "I don't want to get old in this town."

"So, I'm a better option than South Carolina?" He put my hand back on the front seat and squinted through the windshield.

"Please. Please don't be mean to me."

He turned away from the road so that I could see his good eye and what he really meant. Nothing there was cruel. What he said was "You're not getting old."

The car stopped at the club, where Winslow's car was already parked in front.

I held on to the Tom Collins at the Massasoit Club as if it were the most solid thing in the room. Maybe it was. They mixed the drinks strong there to make up for the bad food. I felt steadier than I did in the car, but objects were still swimming at the edge of my vision, giving me the sense that everything around me was moving just out of reach. I wanted something to give me the impression of safety, and the glass between my fingers was not enough. I looked from Winslow to Joe, then back to the menu, wondering if Joe had heard any of what I said to him in the car. I knew I'd said it to him once before, but this time it was true. I took a sip of my drink and wondered if the cocktail would make me feel more sober.

"I'll take a lobster roll," Winslow said to the waiter, who looked new to me, younger, but then we hadn't been there much this summer. The maître d' had known Winslow since he was a boy, and he always greeted us with a certain deference that I used to find laughable, but that afternoon it was comforting. Winslow pretended he could remain a member of the club without paying dues. No one had stopped us from coming in so far, but I held my breath for a second every time we walked through the door.

"I'll take one too." Joe looked at the waiter, and for the first time I noticed that the boy was Portuguese. "Does it come with potato salad?"

"I think so." We were the only lunch customers, and I wondered if the waiter had mixed the drinks himself.

"Frankie?"

"No, I'm fine."

"Come on, honey." Winslow put his hand over mine, and I fought the urge to pull away. "Have a cup of chowder. Good for you."

I felt as if the room just got hotter. I looked to see if the windows were open, but the wooden shutters were closed against the sun. A fan spun ghostly over the dining room, and I breathed hard, trying to ignore the claustrophobia that made me want to push back from the table, to push everything out and away.

Winslow turned to the waiter. "When did they make the chowder?" he asked. "This morning?"

"Last night, sir."

"I mean quahog chowder, not clam chowder, you know."

"We've only got quahog chowder, sir."

"She'll have a bowl."

"A cup." My voice sounded louder than usual. I had to slow down my breathing. The cigarette I was smoking helped with that: slow inhale, hold, exhale.

"A cup," Winslow said, and he dismissed the waiter as if he had just ordered a bucket of ice for my champagne. I gently removed my hand from under Winslow's and pretended to smooth back my hair, unable to read Joe's expression.

"It's so hot," I said, embarrassed by my marriage.

"Too hot, too hot." Winslow reached to take a handkerchief out of his suit pocket to wipe his forehead, then stopped. "Damn. Forgot my handkerchief this morning. I missed it at Talbot's too."

Joe started to reach for his own handkerchief, but Winslow stopped him. "No, I'm fine."

"What difference does it make? Go ahead." Joe's handkerchief was a dark blue patterned silk, which pooled against the white tablecloth as he set it down carelessly.

Winslow's forehead was as moist as the glass sweating between my palms. "Thanks, old man," he murmured.

"Good thing the funeral is tomorrow," Joe said quickly. "I mean, with the heat and all."

"Sooner the better." I took an ice cube in my mouth and sucked the taste of gin.

"Some people may stay away because of the heat, but . . ." Winslow trailed off.

"Your father had a lot of friends."

"Not really." I smiled at both of them and put out my cigarette. My hand was shaking, but the breathing was better. "Anyway, it will end this 'viewing of the body' stuff. That has no more to do with Papa than this tablecloth."

"The wake?" Joe looked sharply at me. He was still so Catholic beneath it all, I always forgot.

"The body itself. That body never had anything to do with my father."

"Well, he'll be buried tomorrow, and we can get on with it," Winslow said.

"Get on with it?" A quivering began to rise up inside my throat, and I was afraid of the taste of bile. "Get on with what? Geoffrey doesn't even have to go to school on Monday."

"Maybe I'll take him to the beach," Winslow said mildly.

"Tell me—tell us about Lima," I asked Joe. He and Winslow seemed unaware of how hard it was for me to keep sitting at the table. Or maybe they were just ignoring it. If I ignored it too, would it go away?

"I have an idea," Joe said, leaning forward on the table and looking quickly between us. "You know how you've been selling off the mill parts around here for junk?"

"It seems like a strange job for me, doesn't it?" Winslow said.

"Not really, no." Joe lowered his voice. "You remember I wanted to stake you to some business a few years ago—"

"Joe, I've never been good at that kind of business. People see right through me. You know I can't pull off anything funny—"

"This isn't that kind of business, and you were right. It wasn't the business for you." Joe's forehead gleamed beneath the side of his palm as he pushed his hair back. "Old machinery doesn't pay peanuts when you junk it, Winslow. And what happens when the mills are all liquidated?"

"Did you know that the Quechechan Mill could start up tomorrow if there was business?" Winslow leaned back with his gin and tonic. "If we only had the demand. Even after ten years of shutdown, that building is solid. No leaks, no loose mortar. A few panes of glass is all, where some boys—"

"They built them to last. Nobody was looking very far down the road," Joe said.

"Not in Rock Harbor."

"Not anywhere. Listen, Winslow, you know just about every mill family in New England. Now, think of all the mills between here and New York. Boston to Portland, then over to Troy and Albany. Every single town has a mill shutting down, selling parts, or with the machines still locked inside because nobody wants to buy them."

"Hard to find anybody to buy, the machines are so old. Henry Ford was buying machines off the floor in New Bedford for his museum, that was the—"

"Grinnell," Joe interrupted.

"Right, the Grinnell Mill. That's why I can get rid of the stuff now. They missed their chance with Henry Ford, and so all of the spinners, the looms, the jack frames— they're still sitting there."

"But then you have to hire some greenhorns to move the equipment, and on top of that hire a truck, so you barely break even." Joe lit another cigarette.

"I get by," Winslow said, looking down at the hands he had learned to manicure himself.

"Lunch," I said a little too brightly. The waiter was standing next to the table, nervously shifting his tray back and forth.

"It's fine," I told the waiter. "They'll stop talking for food."

"And we'll take another round." Joe held up his empty glass.

I squeezed in spoonfuls of salty chowder between puffs on my cigarette.

"How's the chowder?" Winslow didn't look up from his lobster roll.

"Good. Lobster roll?" I asked automatically.

"Good." Winslow loved lobster.

"A little heavy on the mayo." Joe opened his roll to show Winslow.

"They never used to skimp on the lobster meat."

"No, no, they didn't."

"Still, I guess you won't be getting any lobster rolls in Lima." Winslow wiped his mouth, careful to leave no residue of food on his mustache.

"I'd better get it while I can."

"I can make them better than this." I was pretending so hard to relax, and all I could think about was Joe's mouth against my hand.

"Frankie could throw you a cocktail party like they've never seen down there in Lima," Winslow said. "Lobster rolls and all."

"You should both come visit," Joe said. "Bring Geoffrey." He put down his fork. "Listen, Winslow. Here's what I'm thinking. I stake you some start-up cash—"

"No," Winslow said so sharply that Joe and I looked at each other directly for the first time. "No cash from you, Joe. I mean it."

The waiter froze over by the bus tray.

Joe leaned in. "Winslow, you have to think this through. Just let me finish."

Winslow lowered his voice. "No cash."

"You know I'm a greedy Pawtugee, Winslow, so don't worry so much. Listen, the machines are outdated, but they're still working fine, right?"

"Mostly. But they're slower than the new ones, and they need more workers than the machines down south."

"Okay, you start a liquidation company that controls most of New England. You have the cheapest rates and the most storage, because we move it right onto the boat to Lima. It takes some time to get there, but then the machinery outfits a new mill for me. I pay up front for the machinery, you take a paycheck, and the profits go to buy more equipment for the next time."

"You're going to own a mill in Lima?" Winslow asked slowly.

"I already do. Once we outfit my mill, I can sell the equipment off to other manufacturers." Joe took a long sip of ice water. "Labor's cheap enough down there to make it work. Cotton's cheap, and labor's cheaper. So it doesn't matter about the old machinery. A legitimate business, Winslow. None of the funny stuff."

"No unions?" I had to ask.

"No." Joe finished what was left of his drink. "I don't think the Wobblies ever made it to Lima."

"Except for you." I raised my glass to him, and Winslow laughed.

"Except for me," Joe agreed.

Winslow ordered another round. As if this was going on our tab.

"Listen, I never minded the funny stuff, Joe." Winslow twisted a fist absently inside his other hand. "I'm just no good at it. The family got out of whaling in time, but we stayed in cotton too long. Never have been much good at business."

"You can be good at this, Winslow." Joe took a cigarette from my case, and it made me stupidly happy that he didn't need to ask.

"I don't want a stake." Winslow smiled gently at Joe and took his own cigarette from my case. "I'm sure you're right, Joe. But we're doing fine."

"Winslow, you talked *me* into it too, once." Joe got up from the table. He had left his suit coat over the back of his chair, and there were ovals of sweat under his arms.

"What?"

"The basketball team. I took your goddamn lunch money till we went State."

"That was a lot less money." Winslow looked at Joe and smiled.

"It was all we had at the time."

"We?"

"That's what you said: 'Forget about it being my money. It's not mine. It's for the team.'"

"I guess I did say that."

"What's the difference?"

Winslow raised his hands helplessly. He could never talk about money.

"It will help me with this Lima business. And when the mills up here give out completely, they'll be getting rid of their newer machinery down south. You can move into the southern market, and I can upgrade."

Winslow looked at me.

"Say yes, Winslow."

"You're sure?"

I wasn't. I wasn't at all sure what the three of us were agreeing to. I wanted Winslow to have real prospects; these temporary fire sales would never last. Maybe Joe was right and this could work; Winslow had always needed some-body telling him exactly what to do. All those Yankees, and nobody ever taught him how to make a profit. But none of this was really about the money. I rested my palm on top of Winslow's square, open hand, cradling him as best I could. I felt worse than ever.

"Say yes," I repeated. I was smiling at both of them, baring my teeth at the future.

"Can I really have whatever I want?" Geoffrey looked from Winslow to me, then finally at Joe.

"Of course you can," Joe said.

We'd gotten through lunch at the Massasoit Club, gone back to the wake for the afternoon shift, and now Joe was taking us to dinner at the Brayton Hotel. Mother had decided she'd rather stay home, meaning she didn't want to eat dinner with Joe, but Geoffrey was thrilled when Joe invited us out. I hadn't been farther than the bar of this hotel in six years, and we were the only guests in the dining room, but the style was unchanged. The ivory wallpaper with its tiny gold fleur-de-lis pattern still went up fourteen feet to the peeling gilt ceiling, hung with four large chandeliers. Ham's victory celebration was here in 1920, again in 1922, 1924, like clockwork every two years until the day he died. Alice's rehearsal dinner was at the Brayton, and I still have the dress I wore that night.

"Do you want to share a lobster, Ma?"

Geoffrey was used to sharing with me when we went out to eat. That way we paid for only two entrees and everyone still got plenty. We usually shared the soup, and I didn't care about dessert, so he always got that to himself. It didn't take much to fill us up.

"Have your own lobster," Winslow said grandly. "And I'll take one myself."

"Why don't we all have one?" Joe said. "Summer doesn't last forever."

Joe called the waiter, who was standing with perfect posture and a pressed suit by the entrance, looking through a reservation book. I wondered if there were any other reservations. The only nod to hard times that I could see was the fact that the waiter seemed to double as the maître d'hotel.

"Four lobsters," Joe said. "Boiled, of course."

"Yes sir."

"I'll take a chick," I said quickly. "A quarter-pounder is too big for me."

"Should I take a chick too?" Geoffrey was still worried about the money.

"No," Winslow and Joe said together and smiled.

"Have a quarter-pounder," Joe said, and Geoffrey's cheeks went pink.

"Champagne?" added Winslow, raising his eyebrows at Joe as if they were going to pay for this together. "Very cold, please." Joe never let Winslow get very far with pretending to pay, but this part was important to them. The waiter knew Winslow, of course, and he was making his own assumptions. Most people in town didn't believe that the Curtises had really lost all their money. There must have been far too much to lose.

"Champagne? What are we celebrating?" Geoffrey

tugged at his collar and tie. "Grandma said we shouldn't go out at all, that we're supposed to be mourning."

"We *are* mourning," I said. "Grandpa loved lobster. He would have wanted you to have one in his honor."

"But he didn't like champagne," Geoffrey said. "He always drank ale."

"Have you ever tried champagne?" Joe asked Geoffrey.

"I'm too young for cocktails."

"Yes, you are." Joe leaned back in his chair. His good eye was turned to Geoffrey, but I could feel him taking me in on his blind side. "But I don't think you're too young for champagne, do you, Winslow?"

"Thirteen is just the age. I started at nine."

"Really?" Geoffrey looked over at me, excited.

"Not too much," I said. "Just a taste."

"You have to learn how to drink," Winslow said. "Then you can control it like a gentleman. You know those boys we see sometimes after the game at Borden? Nobody ever taught them how to drink."

The waiter returned with the ice-filled bucket in its tall silver stand. He held the chilled bottle wrapped like a newborn in a thick white cloth.

"Who taught you how to drink, Daddy?"

"The senator."

Pop! White linen and smoke from the top of the green bottle.

Geoffrey's eyes went wide as the waiter filled Winslow's glass, then moved around to each of us. Geoffrey looked at the bubbles clinging to the side of the tall champagne flute and picked it up. He was terrified of breaking it.

He looked at me. "Who taught you to drink, Ma?"

"The first champagne I ever drank was on the senator's boat."

Winslow was holding his glass up to Geoffrey. "Never drink too fast. Small sips, that's the secret."

"To Allen," Joe said formally. "To the memory of Allen Ross."

"Allen," repeated Winslow.

"Papa."

"Grandpa."

Geoffrey took a tiny sip, then replaced the glass very carefully on the table. We were all looking at him.

"What do you think?" I asked.

"I like it." He made a swishing noise with his mouth. "It's sort of bitter . . . but then it goes pop."

"Only one glass tonight," I said.

But soon Winslow was refilling everyone for another toast.

"To Lima."

"To Lima."

"Uncle Joe, tell me about Lima, please?"

So he told about Machu Picchu, the Incas, and the conquistadors. Joe's story was for Geoffrey, about men on horseback being taken for gods, and the search for El Dorado. There was coca and cotton and gold, with Tom Swift and diamond mines getting all mixed up with Quetzalcoatl and human sacrifices. Peru was the place any boy would want to go with his brilliant uncle Joe. Any boy or any girl.

We were cracking the thin red shells of the lobsters between our hands and dipping the meat into warm butter with all the right tools. Winslow was teaching Geoffrey how to eat as well as to drink tonight. The miniature silver trident was to pull the meat out after the individual nutcracker had been used to open the claws. Fingers were allowed only to break off and hold the little legs from the underbelly, sucking out sweet slivers from inside. The tail could be attacked with knife and fork, and the roe itself was to be eaten with a small scraper the size of a salt spoon. Geoffrey was shown the salt holder made of filigreed silver and blue glass, but one never puts salt or pepper on a lobster, only butter and lemon.

"The salt is in the ocean," Joe explained. "No lobster needs any more than that."

Geoffrey was almost finished with the second claw when his head tipped forward onto the table. I had lost track of the champagne. The allotted glass was never allowed to be empty, so it was hard to tell.

The three of us looked over his head and laughed.

"He'll be all right," Winslow said. "First champagne, first quarter-pounder."

I picked up Geoffrey's head and placed my folded napkin under his cheek.

"Don't tease him tomorrow, Winslow," I said. "He had such a good time."

"I'll take him home." Winslow got up and pushed his chair back. "You stay, Frankie."

"But what about dessert? A nightcap?" Joe stood also, but not me. I didn't want to go anywhere.

"Thanks, Joe, but this has been perfect. Great for the boy, for all of us to get out. Really perfect, but I think I'll take him home."

"Why don't you take him home and come back?" said Joe. "We'll wait for you."

Winslow hesitated, and I pretended not to feel him looking at me. "No," he said. "No, I'll just take Geoffrey home. See you before you head off, old man. Thanks so much for this, really, and for coming down."

"I won't be long." I glanced up at Winslow as he hoisted Geoffrey to his shoulder. Geoffrey was so tall that his feet dangled well below Winslow's knees. Winslow and I looked at each other, and part of me wanted him to insist that I come home with him.

Winslow smiled. "Take your time."

He lumbered out with Geoffrey, and Joe sat back down, looking slightly bewildered. "Why did he go so quickly?"

"I think that's the first time that he hasn't pretended to want to pay the check."

We both laughed and looked down at our still, quiet hands. The waiter came to clear the white platters, heavy with shining lobster.

"Do you want dessert?"

"Not really, you?"

He shook his head.

"Nightcap?"

"You?"

"Not really."

The waiter circled again, and Joe paid the bill.

"What next?" he said. "Shall we go to the bar?"

"Are you afraid to be alone with me, Joe?"

He smiled using only half of his mouth. "Yes."

"But you keep coming around."

"Took a little while."

"Nine months the first time."

"I had to make some money."

"Was that it?"

"Mostly."

The waiter returned, but Joe gestured for him to keep the change from the check. Like most poor boys, he was a big tipper. The waiter backed away, and Joe looked around the empty dining room.

"It's a little spooky being the only ones here. You sure you don't want a nightcap?"

"I haven't had champagne in a long time. I think I'll leave it as it is."

"Do you want—"

"I don't want to talk anymore, Joe. Not right now."

"Frankie—"

"I just want to take off these high-heeled shoes for a while."

He didn't say anything to the man at the desk while we waited for the elevator to take us upstairs. It was a small cage with mirrors set into the walls, and the three of us barely fit inside. I held myself up very straight in front of the bellhop and pretended I was somebody else. Joe opened the door to the room, and I could smell his body as I walked past him. He had a suite. There was a living room with a bar and glass tumblers and ice buckets and even a bouquet of white lilies. I walked from the living room to the bedroom opening the windows. There were wooden shutters that swung out toward the river, more smokestacks than trees. The room faced the back side of Front Street, so there were no lit-up marquees between us and the water.

I turned back to Joe. "You always travel like this?"

"I like to get a suite when I can."

"And the lilies?"

"I asked for those."

"Just in case?"

"Just in case."

"In case you got a girl to come upstairs with you?"

We both laughed, and he moved a little closer. I stayed with my back to the window. There was no breeze, and the air was like syrup.

"Do you like them?"

"Yes."

His lips tasted sweet and sour, like champagne. His neck tasted like tobacco and aftershave. His back was wide and slick with sweat. His legs and buttocks were light and heavy and stronger than I knew. His nipples were delicate and rose brown. His belly tasted like salt, and he broke inside of me and I broke inside of him. Over and over again.

The idle on Joe's Plymouth was quiet as he pulled in front of the house, then turned off the engine.

"You're sure you don't want me to come in?"

I looked at the bare white bulb lighting the front porch. The mill had repainted all the houses last year, but they'd painted them burgundy. The union had sent the wreath for Papa in the expected color and size.

"I'll be right back."

I was out the door and up the steps without looking at him. The front door opened quietly, and there was a light on in the kitchen. I walked in, heels clacking my presence on the linoleum, but nobody was there. Rows of unfamiliar casserole dishes with matching lids kept watch over the tile counters, ivory squares rimmed with blue. I walked down the hall to the back stairs and took my heels off as I passed Mother's door. I wondered if she was awake, but I didn't stop. Upstairs, inside our bedroom, Winslow was lying on his back with one arm flung wide. I listened to his breathing as I went to the bureau to pick up a small box with my jewelry and all of Geoffrey's baby teeth. I paused and silently put my finger in my mouth and sucked at the knuckle, working my two rings over the patch of saliva. I left them in a wet circle on the bureau and turned to leave.

I was sure Winslow was awake now. I waited, listening to the change in his breathing. Light from the streetlamp flooded the bed from the window, and I could see that he had shifted position and his face was toward me now. I thought I saw his eyes flip closed, but I couldn't be absolutely sure in this light. I waited. He could stop me now if he wanted to. He could have me forever, despite it all. Even forever. Winslow breathed quietly, steadily. I waited. He was not breathing the way he did when he slept, and I walked recklessly out of the bedroom.

The door to Geoffrey's room was always left slightly open. He didn't like falling asleep in the dark. The cane chair next to his bed creaked with my weight, but he didn't move. Winslow had put him in bed with all of his clothes on, and I thought automatically about how wrinkled his new suit would be in the morning. He was on his side, limbs tossed over and under the covers. His pant legs had ridden up, and I saw the outlines of muscles under the skin, hair growing dark along his shins. He breathed heavily, growing larger in his sleep. I leaned down and touched my forehead against his temple. The smell of this boy, his breath coming quietly between those lips, was like a miracle. Like nothing at all. I could not close my eyes or I would never get up. I had made Joe a promise, and we both understood this was our last time around. I was going to get settled, then Geoffrey would come to live with me and Tom Swift in Machu Picchu.

"I'm coming back." I was speaking aloud, but maybe it didn't matter. It was a promise either way. A promise, a vow, a binding oath, as they said in the books he liked to read. "I'll come back for you, Geoffrey."

I got up and emptied my jewelry onto the seat of the chair, where he would look first when he woke up. A few rings, one necklace of good false pearls, and several long strands of hematite beads that felt more valuable than they really were. Geoffrey used to tug them around my neck when he was a baby. Five pairs of earrings. The rhinestones reflected the light from the hall like a pirate's treasure, and I wanted so much to wake him up to see everything in this light. But I stood there staring instead, holding a small wooden box with nothing but baby teeth left inside.

None of this was planned.

Walking down the hall, I was afraid to stop as I passed our bedroom again. If I stopped now, I would never, ever leave.

I picked up my shoes at the end of the hall and slipped them back on in the parlor. The house seemed strung with wakefulness, or was it just me? I didn't look back as the screen door clicked shut behind me. I walked carefully down the steps, and Joe pushed open the passenger door from the inside. I slid in next to him, and he started up the car.

Nobody said anything.

Motors rumbled. Big wide cars and boats and airplanes flew me all the way south. The soft gray ocean and the big blue sky. South, South, South America. Where the water turns green and the sky turns white.

Acknowledgments

IMUST FIRST THANK MY BRILLIANT AND DEDICATED AGENT, Irene Skolnick, who loved this book from the first read, then found the very best home for it at Scribner; her true friendship and commitment to my work continue to sustain me. The good humor, smarts, and attention to detail of Vita Engstrand, Erin Harris, and Sarah Westbrook at Skolnick Literary have made all the difference along the way. My editor, Kara Watson, has my deepest admiration and gratitude for the kind of editing that supposedly doesn't get done anymore. Kara's discerning eye and keen intelligence are evident on every page. I must also thank Nan Graham, Rex Bonomelli, Dan Cuddy, the extraordinary Susan Brown, and everyone at Scribner for their enthusiasm, support, and dedication.

Alice Mattison has been more than a teacher; she has been a mentor whose effect on the shape of this story has been profound. I thank her especially for seeing me truly, when I needed to be seen.

There have been many people whose criticism, suggestions, and encouragement have helped me in countless ways.

291

These include my family: my mother, Jean Valentine; my sisters, Sarah and Zoe Chace; and above all my daughters, Pesha and Rebecca Magid, who are more than a daily joy: they are a reason to live. I am deeply grateful to have been sustained in many ways by: Louis Begley; Lizzy Berryman; Mark Chace; Michael "The Senator" Chace (in memoriam), who let me tour his mill in Fall River; Jennifer Collins; Susan Cobb Merchant; David Conrad; Mary Derbyshire; Kate Doyle; Amy Edwards; Florence Falk; Leslie Gat; David Gates; Ann Godoff; Pesha Ona Klein; Annik LaFarge; Gwyn Lurie; Peg Peoples; Sylvie Rabineau; Hilda Speicher; Cindy Speigel; Glyn Vincent; Tim Weiner; Marisa Silver; and Jack Sherman (in memoriam), who shared his childhood stories and postcards of the Fall River Line. Thanks also to Beverly Edwards and Peter Collias for sustaining us all.

I revised this novel at the Bennington College Writing Seminars with crucial support and criticism from Sheila Kohler, Amy Hempel, Lynn Sharon Schwartz, and Sven Birkerts, in addition to Alice Mattison. Thank you to Bennington for giving me a place for my work, to the Doghouse Band for a place to play, and to Victoria Clausi for everything.

I would like also to thank the Fall River Historical Society, the excellent *Spinner* series of books on the history of southeastern Massachusetts, and the American Textile History Museum in Lowell, Massachusetts. I was given time and space to write through residencies and grants at the Hall Farm, the Ragdale Foundation, and the Santa Fe Art Institute (with extra thanks to Bob and Catfish).

This book would not exist without the stories that came from my father, James Chace, to whom this book is dedicated. I hope he would be proud.

Printed in the United States
By Bookmasters